SEAL OF MY HEART

SEAL BROTHERHOOD SERIES BOOK 7

SHARON HAMILTON

This is a work of fiction. Names, characters, places, brands, media, and incidents are either the product of the author's imagination or are used fictitiously. In many cases, liberties and intentional inaccuracies have been taken with rank, description of duties, locations and aspects of the SEAL community.

ISBN-10: 1500322768
ISBN-13: 9781500322762

AUTHOR'S NOTE

I always dedicate my SEAL Brotherhood books to the brave men and women who defend our shores and keep us safe. Without their sacrifice, and that of their families—because a warrior's fight always includes his or her family—I wouldn't have the freedom and opportunity to make a living writing these stories. They sometimes pay the ultimate price so we can debate, argue, go have coffee with friends, raise our children and see them have children of their own.

One of my favorite homages to warriors resides on many memorials, including one I saw honoring the fallen of WWII on an island in the Pacific:

"When you go home
Tell them of us, and say
For your tomorrow,
We gave our today."

These are my stories created out of my own imagination. Anything that is inaccurately portrayed is either my mistake, or done intentionally to disguise something I might have overheard over a beer or in the corner of one of the hangouts along the Coronado Strand.

Wounded Warriors is the one charity I give to on a regular basis. I encourage you to get involved and tell them thank you:

https://support.woundedwarriorproject.org

CHAPTER 1

Airports were mostly happy places for Kate. She pretended she was going on an exotic vacation, a tour of lands where everything from the smells to the language and customs of the people was foreign. In her fantasy, she'd meet a gorgeous, mysterious man and they'd spend a romantic week together exploring, indulging in glamorous restaurants and glittering casinos, and sensual delights.

And even though she was engaged to be married to the most eligible bachelor in Sonoma County, the favorite son of the favorite first family of wine, she couldn't help it. The fantasy lurked just around the corner in her psyche, waiting to wrap her in a sensual blanket and whisk her away from the reality of her humdrum future.

It worried her some that she wasn't happier about her upcoming wedding or that she was even considering escape. Why didn't she feel more like a blushing bride-to-be?

Something seemed…wrong, uncomfortable, but she forced herself not to think about it, writing the whole thing off as stress-related panic over the big day.

Her airport fantasy persisted, though, and was kicking in big time this afternoon. She felt like having an adventure, something far away from everyone she knew, perhaps something far different from what she'd ever imagined for herself and her life. And, as she examined the crowded terminal in San Francisco, she couldn't quell her quickening excitement while she boarded the plane, even though Portland was not even close to being an exotic land, and her sister was a poor substitute for a dark, handsome man who would sweep her off her feet.

It was going to be a fairly full flight and she wasn't lucky enough to have an early boarding ticket. She preferred to sit by a window, but figured it was unlikely. Scanning down the rows ahead of the slowly shuffling line of passengers, she only saw one open window spot on the left, with someone occupying the middle one. When she came upon it, a briefcase lay on the cushion at the aisle. The young man in the middle seat was fully occupied in reading a book.

He looked up, as if he'd heard her silent plea for the window position. His warm blue eyes lit on her face casually. She knew he wanted to scan her figure but stopped himself, and then he smiled.

What was it about handsome men who smiled easily? Did the smile mean he would like permission to engage? Did it mean he liked what he saw? Did it mean he was hiding something? He didn't look like the type to feel awkward, certainly not as awkward as she felt.

Her eyes darted to the open position next to him, and his glance followed hers.

"You want the window?" he asked.

She didn't say anything, stuck in place as if her feet were encased in concrete. A passenger from behind pushed into her back, reminding her she was holding up a line of travelers yet to be seated.

"It's yours if you want it," he whispered in a bedroom voice.

Damn.

These sorts of attractions to strange men weren't supposed to happen to a happily engaged young woman whose life was planned out nearly moment-by-moment. In spite of her fantasy life, which was *not* planned out and definitely *not* scripted, she decided to allow herself to get dangerously close to this stranger.

He was dangerous because he was perfect in enough ways to upset her ordered life. And he matched her fantasy man to a T.

"Thank you. That's very kind of you," she said.

Kate saw he was not only good-looking, he also revealed himself as tall, very fit, and muscular as he eased gingerly across the aisle seat and slowly uncoiled the muscle and sinews in his upper torso. And, boy, did she react…enough for him to hear her heartbeat, probably, or see the slight involuntary shaking of her knees or the quiver of her lower lip. She caught his scent with a hint of lemon from an aftershave applied earlier in the day. She loved lemon on a man.

She actually heard a low growl of approval and that made her traitorous panties go wet. It was all the right and oh-so-wrong kind of chemistry, in front of impatient strangers. Over two hundred of them.

And she didn't care.

Kate turned a shoulder, crouching to sidle in front of him, her butt grazing the tent in his pants with interesting discoveries. She didn't dare say she was sorry. Just best to pretend it never happened. She settled at the window, placing her Kindle and her slim briefcase on the seat next to her and stashing her purse on the floor. Then she watched, out of the corner of her eye, as he settled himself back into place and then connected his seatbelt with long, strong fingers.

So far, so good. No harm, no foul.

She became extremely interested in the loading of bags into the cargo hold, the position of the little vehicles servicing the plane, the weather, other planes taking off in the distance, all the while willing her breathing and her heartbeat to return to normal. When she thought sufficient time had passed, she let her eyes drop to her lap, and then she shot a furtive look at the stranger at her side without turning her head.

He was reading his book again, not paying the least bit of attention to her. She told herself it shouldn't matter what kind of book it was, but she was *dying* to know in spite of herself.

She could tell he knew she was watching him, because his eyes scanned the pages, and his lips stayed pressed together, but began to quirk up in a smile. The laugh lines at the corners of his eyes were deliciously short. His shiny, dark hair was slightly curly, a little longer than it should be, which made her think maybe he was an older college student. A retread.

She faced forward while the cabin doors closed. Then she sighed, and it did seem to let out some of the tension.

He brought out a small set of expensive ear buds and plugged them in, adjusting the pieces into his ears before resuming his reading.

Kate closed her eyes and told the fantasy in her head to chill, explaining to herself and the cast of fantasy characters who wanted argue about it that she wasn't in any danger of doing anything inappropriate, and that today's trip was going along a normal, well-worn path. She told them it was going to be a boring day.

Until he tapped her on the shoulder. He was smiling again and holding his book out to her.

"You read romance?" he asked.

"Y-yes." How hard was it to admit the truth?

"Well, I've just finished my sister's book, and she said to give it away to someone else who might like to read it, so it's yours if you want it."

Of their own volition, her fingers snatched the book. Did he notice how quickly she'd made up her mind?

Be With Me. The title was familiar. She'd read about this particular book on one of the blogs she followed. A time travel romance, by Linda Gray. It was exactly what she needed to get her mind off the handsome stranger to her left.

"Thank you." She smiled in spite of herself. Trying to play it cool.

She glanced back down at the book, and flipped open to the title page, and found a signature.

"My sister," he said, nodding at the page. "In case you were thinking I read romance as a regular thing."

"I've known some men who read romance," she lied.

"Really?" His eyebrows scrunched atop his nose. "I've never known any."

"You just said you read this book."

"That's different."

After a short pause, she asked, "You don't think they're manly?" She was enjoying this a bit too much. A fall was coming. She knew it just as surely as she knew the plane had started to move and announcements were being made over the loudspeaker.

Mr. Gorgeous had to lean in closer to her to be heard, and she found herself meeting him halfway—involuntarily, of course, just so they could hear each other over the blaring intercom.

"Kinda embarrassing about all the sex scenes," he said. "I mean reading them in public, with a cover like this." He ran his finger over the front cover and touched the back of her hand in the process. The male torso on the cover looked oddly familiar.

She looked back up at him. "That's you on the book?"

He wiggled his eyebrows. "She says she uses me as her inspiration. My sister. My sister wrote the book."

"She *writes* romance?"

"Yes. Does quite well, I guess."

This was definitely not the twist she'd expected. She examined the shirtless torso on the cover again, the ripples of muscle, the huge arms, veins that snaked out along his shoulders and forearms, and one dangerous vein that disappeared into the top of a pair of jeans hung almost low enough to—to—He was hotness personified. And as handsome as he was on the cover, all wet, dark and brooding, in the flesh he was even more impressive.

She didn't know where her next comment came from. "Your girlfriend must be jealous of all the women who fantasize—"

"Don't have a girlfriend. So, does your fiancé get jealous of you reading romance?"

Fiancé? Oh, yes…there was that huge two-carat diamond on her left hand that people practically had to wear sunglasses to admire properly. How could she have forgotten? But still, it meant he'd checked her hand out. Not like she'd waved it in his face to draw attention to it, but the thing was hard to miss, all the same.

"My fiancé—my fiancé—" That's when she realized the answer to his query. She was about to marry a man who knew nothing of her tastes in romance. As a matter of fact, she wasn't entirely sure he'd approve of her reading them. And how was that going to work? "He's never said anything. I doubt he notices."

"Really?" The guy gave a puzzled smirk. "Lets you wander around, reading about strange men and the things—" Now it was time for him to stop. He leaned back into his headrest, his eyes straight ahead as if fascinated by the texture and pattern of the fabric on the seat in front of him. He adjusted his pants discreetly. Rested his hands palm-down on his massive thighs. A circle of thorns was tattooed onto his forearm. His chest expanded with each inhale, expanding a good two inches, then his upper body relaxed back into the seat, his abdomen going concave. His jeans were loose-fitting, and she was busy figuring out they were loose for a reason when he suddenly opened his eyes and caught her examining his package.

Oh shit.

She darted a peek back out to the little window to her right and blushed in spite of herself.

"I'm sorry," she said out of the side of her mouth, knowing he was still looking at her.

"Don't be sorry, darlin'." It was a deep, luscious rumble. "That just made my day."

They were interrupted as the plane accelerated to takeoff speed. She felt the pressure of the G-force against her chest as they were lifted into the air, swinging around San Francisco Bay below until everything began to resemble a miniature scale model of Silicon Valley.

After they leveled off, the stranger extended his huge, callused hand, flexing the tat on his forearm, and said, "Hi. My name is Tyler Gray."

"Kate Morgan," She lay her palm against his and enjoyed the warm squeeze he gave her. She could feel what those fingers were capable of.

He was the first to withdraw his hand. He clutched his right thigh as he cleared his throat, licked his lips, and began speaking with a croak until he paused to clear his throat again. "Having a sister who writes romance is kind of embarrassing. I don't normally tell people about it."

"I'll bet."

"Most of the time on her covers, they cut off my head, so all you see is, well, my chest and a little below."

"I noticed."

Where in the hell did that comment come from?

"I'm happy to do it for her."

"For her. Sure. Nice of you to do it for your sister." It was her time to tease. Was he blushing? "You're actually blushing, Tyler Gray. Do cover models blush?"

"When we're affected."

That one was going to have to hang in the air a bit until she could figure out what it meant. *Affected?*

"Sometimes I do a shoot with a model. Things can heat up, even though I don't know the girl."

Did she want to hear this?

"I imagine it can affect her, too." *The girl would have to be blind!*

"Well, sometimes funny things happen. I'm sure you can imagine."

She could. She really could. And her mind shouldn't be going there at all. Not. At. All.

The pause between them felt a little awkward. "What brings you to Portland, or are you going on further north?" she asked.

"I'm going home to spend some time with the folks before—" he hesitated. "I'm in the military and I deploy in ten days."

"Ah." So that hard body was beginning to make sense. And his longer hair triggered a realization. She'd read enough romances to peg him as a Special Forces guy. "I'm guessing you do something dangerous."

He seemed to like that statement. "Some would say so." He was studying her reaction like his life depended on it. Without her meaning to, her eyelids fluttered and she found herself looking at his smooth, full lower lip, the clenched jaw muscles bunching under a day's stubble, and the swallow that moved his Adam's apple down his powerful neck. He had exactly the body parts she loved to see in a man. The soft lips that could give pleasure, the eyes that wouldn't waver from her face. Honest, and relentless. Full of courage and unflinching. She liked men who would look back and not hide their attraction.

Because that meant she didn't have to hide hers.

And there it was, like a dragon coming to life, the danger, and the power of getting swept away. The fantasy coming to life again, transporting her from where she sat, on a plane to visit her sister before her upcoming wedding, to the edge of an adventure, next to a man, God help her, she wished she could get naked with.

CHAPTER 2

Navy SEAL Tyler Gray was heated up with testosterone like he sometimes got just before a firefight overseas. The urge to act with swift resolve and commanding force was a little misplaced, since he sat in the middle of a bevy of heavyset travelers cocooned in their seats. Some were falling asleep, some were talking nervously. Babies cried and kids wiggled. But Tyler Gray had the biggest hard-on he'd had in weeks.

It was damned inconvenient, but the lady was affecting him in such a lovely way, and he was absolutely powerless to act on it. His libido was heightened, cheering for a total lack of control in a breakout move that couldn't accomplish anything but alienate her for all eternity. He understood the urge to mate, to procreate. Boy, did he have that in spades at the moment. In fact, he almost felt fated, like characters in some of his sister's steamy vampire books.

The woman next to him had an athlete's body, slim in all the right places but not too muscled. She had a firm grip, and, in spite of herself, when he'd grabbed her hand, he felt her answer his strength with her own. Did women understand how much of a turn-on that was? He shouldn't be thinking about all this, but he couldn't help it. She was telling him she could handle his intensity, that she was capable of feeling the full force and power of his body as he pleasured her. He was usually careful. Was he misinterpreting things? Damn, he saw that, if she was willing, this kind of woman would let him take them both to heaven and hell and back without a breather.

Holy fuck. Stop it, Tyler. You have no right here.

Of all the fucked up ideas, he'd given her Janice's book, too. What was he thinking? So now sex, reading sex, modeling with a half-naked woman selling sex, was front and center in their discussion. And she'd made that comment about him doing something dangerous. He normally didn't like to mention it to a woman he'd just met, and he'd learned not to brag about being a SEAL, but for some reason he wanted to tell her. If she asked again, then he'd tell her. Maybe it wouldn't scare her off or make her cling to him like a rag doll. Either one of those reactions was a total turnoff.

No, he was snared in the net she had no idea she was casting. And he wanted to be caught. Her hair, her warm eyes, and the scent of her perfume, the way she smiled, crossed her legs, and laughed. Whatever it was she was dishing out, he wanted more. A lot more.

But when he chanced a quick glance down at that huge crystal on her fourth finger, he realized it was pure folly. Someone with lots of money had made a spectacle of his claim on her. Most of his buddies could ill afford a plain gold band, and that's always what he expected his wife's ring finger to wear some day. He saw the rock on her finger as evidence he couldn't measure up in the financial department.

But she *liked* him. He knew she did. They had great chemistry, for sure. He'd be very sensitive to any little change or shift in her attitude telling him to back off, but that's not the message she was giving him right now. So, he'd play along a little while longer and just go with it.

She didn't disappoint.

"I'm visiting my sister. We're going to do some fun things we haven't done in a while."

"Girls' night out?" he asked before he could check himself. *Damn.*

She had that delicious wrinkle on her forehead and her lips were all bunched up and kissable. "Not with my sister. Ew."

"Sorry." He forced himself to stare at the back of the seat in front of him. Out of the corner of his eye, he saw her tilt her head that way ladies did, just before they were going to ask a question. When they played with him, fishing for an answer or a reveal, without wanting to be direct.

"So you grew up in Portland?"

It was an answer he could have given without looking at her, but it gave him the excuse, and, damn, the more he looked at her the more he liked what he saw. "More or less. My parents went to Reed and UW, art majors, hippies. We moved around a little at first, but settled in Portland. They've been there over twenty years, so I guess it's home, although San Diego is where I live now."

He was feeling he'd told her too much, so he inhaled, their eyes still locked. Her expression was one of pure delight. "My parents were hippies, too. Do you have all that great music around?"

"Yep. And the posters. They still like incense and candles."

"Oh, yeah, and when the oldies come on..."

"My dad still does a mean air guitar to anything by Jimmy Hendrix."

"I love listening to the Moody Blues. *Knights in White Satin* sort of puts me in a dream state," she said lightheartedly.

"My mom still has her ticket stubs to a Beatles concert in LA."

"My mom has all the Avalon Ballroom posters, and the early Haight-Ashbury ones. What a time they lived through!"

Her dancing eyes were so beautiful. He wanted to tell her so, but didn't dare. Instead, he said, "A lot of people don't really understand those times. I probably wouldn't have enjoyed some of my parents' extracurricular activities, but I'm glad they had that time." He searched her face, saw her nodding.

"Like they had their whole life ahead of them. They were just being young and crazy, and they'd find their way eventually, but for then, during those times, they just wanted to live and to..."

She stumbled on a word. He knew what that word was: Love. It was a good word to stumble on, because it meant she gave it consideration. That she didn't think it was a word that should be thrown around carelessly. He liked that about her.

Now she was staring at her hands in her lap, thinking about something. He hoped he hadn't said something wrong to make her pensive. Then he noticed her eyes had filled up with tears, which worried him.

"Hey, you okay?" He wanted to touch her, lift her chin, get as close to her face as she'd let him, but he stayed put, with the empty seat between them. Something was definitely bothering her.

"Doorways. I'm sensitive to doorways."

It was a strange phrase, and he wasn't sure he understood her properly.

"You are here," she said, with her right hand outstretched, palm up, "and then you go through this doorway and now you are different." She demonstrated it by cupping her right palm and swishing it through the air, to mate with her left.

"Changes. You are talking about life-altering changes." He wanted to keep the conversation and her flow going.

"Yes!" She looked up at him.

"Things like getting married," he whispered as he looked at her lips. He couldn't help it. Nor could he help licking his.

Why did he have to go bring that up? What kind of a stupid gene had suddenly possessed him?

"Exactly like getting married," she said to her lap.

And then he knew she had niggling doubts. She wasn't rushing through the doorway to that new life. Something was forcing her through it. He was fairly sure it wasn't her heart.

There was no way he would touch that. It wasn't a place he belonged. It was someone else's story. He pulled his eyes from her face and settled the seat back, staring up at the ceiling.

"I must have said something wrong," she said, her face once again cocked at an angle. She was watching his profile.

"Nope. Thought maybe I did," he said, but he closed his eyes and tried to focus on anything but the granite between his legs.

"I offended you, and I'm sorry."

"Nah. Just not a place I've ever been to before." He thought maybe he sounded too harsh, so he turned to face her. "Hard for me to relate, is all. Never even got close to that step."

"I understand."

Were his ears playing tricks on him?

"An important piece of advice?" she continued.

He shrugged.

"Don't do it until you are sure, really sure." She turned away and stared out the window.

He watched the way her hands twisted in her lap, the gentle slope of her shoulders as they rounded so she could take a private moment, facing the window. Her silky brown hair, with tendrils that curled at the back of her head where she'd brushed against the headrest. She was like a delicate flower he wished he could comfort. He had an intense desire to protect her from whatever she was headed for that clearly wasn't good for her.

But that wasn't his decision to make.

The stewardess was making rounds with coffee and water. Kate turned, and he could see her eyelashes were glistening wet. She ordered mineral water with lime. He ordered a beer.

The plastic glass with ice cubes and lime floating on top was passed to him, and he in turn passed it to her, their fingers touching slightly. As they brushed against each other she glanced at him and then refocused on the little drink.

Lifting it to her mouth, she closed her eyes and inhaled the scent of lime. He was turned on by the sheer bliss on her face. All he could think about was what it would feel like to kiss her like the man she deserved. Like the man he wished he were.

CHAPTER 3

She knew it was barely an hour flight to Portland. When the cart came around for more drinks, he bought another beer and asked for another mineral water with lime for her, without asking her first.

He made her feel, in spite of how brief their conversation had been, like he'd actually *seen* her in ways her fiancé Randy never had. Of course, he probably couldn't miss her crunching the ice. Just as she thought of it, he stopped the attendant to ask for another plastic tumbler of ice without liquid, and presented it to her with a Cheshire cat grin followed by a wink.

"You're too cute. My nerves that obvious?" she asked.

"As obvious as an RPG." He must have seen her eyebrows lift. "Rocket Propelled Grenade," he whispered, as if it was a closely guarded secret.

"So when I said something dangerous, I guess I should have put the adjective *very* in front of that?"

"Not today. And not most days." He grinned at her. Nice, straight white teeth, those bright blue eyes that sucked her right into his psyche. She had the sudden need to be his best erotic fantasy.

And what's up with that? She never thought about sex when she was with Randy. From the very beginning he'd been almost awkward around her, seemingly afraid to kiss her. She'd found it kind of sweet. In time, he grew on her.

But compared to this man next to her—who was clearly a man and not a boy, even though Randy was five years older than she—her attraction was to the feral, pirate essence of Tyler, and not to the sweet side of anyone. Dangerous and more than a little risky.

Her mind was going all sorts of places with this fantasy. It was a continuation of the excitement she felt every time she—what was that about, anyway? Every time she left Randy for a day trip, for anything longer than the time between breakfast and lunch or lunch and dinner? They were inseparable in Healdsburg. Every restaurant in town wanted their business, and they never had to pay for their meals, either. Just having them seated at a prominent table up front was an endorsement that would pay off big time, even if the restaurant didn't carry the family wines.

With this guy, she wanted a back room. Some place private, with oilcloth table covers and a waiter who would not interrupt them every thirty seconds to bring water or butter or ask them how their food tasted. Maybe she'd splurge on a margarita, or a jelly jar glass of Randy's—

How stupid of me!

He'd been watching her and she'd been smiling ever since he gave her the ice, even when he talked about the thing he was obviously most comfortable about. So, she decided to use it to gain some surer footing.

"So you're in the military, and you enjoy it," she said and crunched down on some ice.

He nodded watching her mouth.

"You're Special Forces, I'm thinking."

He frowned but didn't take his eyes off her mouth. *God, if he tried to kiss me, I'd let him. Just to find out what he tastes like.*

She had to look away, because she'd become aware their faces were moving closer together. That was a very dangerous sign.

Down below, green patches of ground were dusted with clouds resembling puffs of smoke. Ordinary, regimented life was going on right under her. And she was having an out-of-body experience with a hunky guy she didn't really know.

She heard him adjust his seat back and sigh. When she looked up, he'd closed his eyes and was perhaps slipping into a catnap.

Good idea. She pushed the button on her seat, leaving the unfinished mineral water and ice on the tray in front of her, closed her eyes, and tried to collect herself. Her head lolled to the side, and when she opened her eyes a crack, he was staring at her, at all the places he shouldn't be staring. She watched him. Was he that starved for someone of the opposite sex? But he'd just come from San Diego. And he was deploying soon, he said. So surely there were girls after him in San Diego.

Long-legged girls with long blonde hair, not brunettes from Santa Rosa who never got out in the sun.

It was reflex that made her lick her own lips and then open her eyes. She took in the full measure of his gaze. He wasn't casual, or matter of fact, though she suspected he spent most of the day practicing that persona. No, he was what she would have to call needy.

She fully understood it. Because she was the same.

Kate put her elbow against the back of the seat and propped her head to look at him. "So, you're a soldier, and you're going overseas."

"Yup."

"How long are you going to be in Portland?" She didn't look at his eyes, but examined his veined hands, still resting his powerful thighs. He didn't wear any rings, but had bands of barbed wire and Celtic inkings all over his forearms, plus some tattooed frog prints that extended from his wrist to his elbow.

"Five days," he said.

Five days. Why was that important? For starters, it was just enough time to get in trouble, and not enough time to get to know someone. But why was she even thinking that? Her life course was going in another direction, even though her body and perhaps part of her heart sensed there was someone else out there for her.

Could she do this? Marry Randy, when the sight of someone new stirred her so? Was that an indication perhaps of second thoughts, disguised as a sexual fantasy? Was it about being a bad girl, breaking out of her well-organized lifestyle, or the realization that she'd be chained to someone who might not bring her true happiness? Randy had worn her down. He hadn't bowled her over. Would she grow tired of him the same way, and then regret what she didn't have the courage to do when she had the chance?

No, she wasn't that kind of girl. She'd accepted Randy's loyalty and love when she accepted his ring, when she accepted that, though his kisses didn't exactly curl her toes, there hadn't been anyone else's who did, either. She'd told herself that probably those kinds of guys didn't really exist. Had that been the true fantasy?

Probably not, since here was this guy, who wouldn't answer her questions, who smiled like he knew what she looked like naked, who watched her and understood things Randy hadn't noticed in months of non-stop dating. Wondering these things was hardly the right attitude for someone on the verge of marriage. And it was hardly a reason to begin an affair she'd regret forever.

"Okay, now it's your turn. How long are you going to be in Portland?" His serious look was followed by a quick smile.

"Three days. Just the long weekend. Have to get back to work on Tuesday."

"And you do something dangerous?" he asked.

"Hardly…well, not unless you consider drunk tourists dangerous, anyway. I work in the sales room at my fiancé's family winery."

"Ah. Which winery?"

"Heller Estate Wines. You probably haven't heard of them. Good wines, but a small facility."

"I'm not much of a wine buff. I like beer."

"Actually, they're starting a brewery there, too. Big explosion of them all over Sonoma County."

"Like Portland?"

She laughed at that one. "No. Not nearly as big, but we're catching up. And we have better weather."

"That's for sure. I can remember more than a few rainy days growing up in Portland. Very depressing days," he said as he searched the aisle in front of him. "If you'll excuse me, I'm going to take a restroom break while I can."

"Good idea." She didn't have to ask, but he waited for her in the aisle, holding out his hand so she could grab it and haul herself out of the cramped seat. He walked behind her while they strolled to the center of the plane. She imagined he was checking her out. She noticed the looks other passengers gave her, thinking they were a couple. Part of her liked it.

One restroom was available. He motioned for her to go first. After she was alone in the little cubicle she examined her face. Was this the face of a woman who was going to cheat on her fiancé with someone she'd just met?

No. She couldn't do that. This was just a healthy animal attraction, nothing more. Perhaps she was reading way too much into it, anyway. He probably wasn't nearly as interested as she thought.

Kate made it back to her seat, buckled in and waited for him to return. Nearly twenty minutes went by before he made his way from the cockpit. She heard laughter coming from the crew up front. Tyler nodded to the attendants, who blushed at his attention. He whispered something to the pretty young blonde who had taken their drink order earlier and she nodded.

She didn't want to watch, but Kate couldn't keep her eyes off him. His wild blue eyes and bright smile focused on her completely as he strode down the aisle like some kind of warrior prince, with that swagger that told her he could exaggerate it if he wanted to, but was trying to do "low profile." He couldn't help it. He was drawing attention from everywhere, and all he was doing was being Tyler. Big, bulky, but all-muscle-and-sinew Tyler, with his hair hanging a little curly over his ears that had pinked up at the edges. Was he blushing a bit? About the attention?

"I went through training with the engineer. He washed out during the last phase of it."

"What kind of training was that?" she asked.

"BUD/S. I heard it over the loudspeaker. How many MacConaghys are there who fly jets? I thought it was him, and I was right."

He was still chuckling. The pretty attendant leaned in front of him, a little too close, Kate thought, extending her arm, practically putting her boob in Tyler's face, and handed Kate another glass of ice.

The blonde gave her a pert smile, followed by a "here you go." Tyler watched her hips and butt cheeks all the way back to the forward cabin, like every other male who was close enough to the aisle to observe her undulating progress.

Kate dove into the ice, tipping the plastic cup and spilling a couple of pieces onto her own chest, which Tyler quickly glanced at and then returned his eyes to the front of the plane. His smirk, still facing forward, widened as she ground her back molars on the ice. After getting a thorough brain freeze, she was satisfied and set the cup down. She didn't care what they said about chewing on ice. She was not sexually frustrated, and anyone who thought so had rocks in their head.

She looked at the romance novel sitting on the seat between them.

"Is she a good writer?" Kate asked him.

"Hard to judge. She loves writing them, though. A lot happier when she's working." He shook his head. "You don't want to be around her when she's not. And when she's finishing a book. Those are two times I try to avoid."

"Has she been doing it a long time?"

"Nearly ten years. Makes a solid income. She's a single mother."

"Ah, so she gets to live vicariously through the heroines in her books," Kate added.

"Who knows? She says so. Her ex took off before she made it big. But then, he was a dumbass. Sorry." Tyler lowered his eyes. "She's better off on her own. Besides, she's got designs on a couple of my buds from the Teams."

He darted a quick look at her face, probably to see if she'd picked up his verbal slip.

"So," Kate began slowly, "you're a SEAL?"

"Yes, ma'am."

CHAPTER 4

Before they landed in Portland, they had shared most of their "firsts," which was odd for him, being normally fairly private. First kisses, first dates, first crush, first prom. They conspicuously avoided the first sexual encounter. That was okay with him, although he was dying to know hers.

She'd stopped ordering crushed ice, which Tyler took as a small triumph, not that it really meant anything. But he preferred to think so. He looked at the half-melted cup of ice on the tray table in front of her.

She was light-hearted by nature, which warmed him. He liked uncomplicated, easygoing women. He'd been truthful when he said he'd never come close to getting hooked up with anyone permanently. And the honest truth was, all the guys on the Teams thought he was some big player, but at heart Tyler was shy, not that anyone would ever guess. He sensed she was as well, and something about that pleased him.

"Your sister picking you up?" he asked.

"I'm supposed to text her when I land."

"I've got a friend meeting me. We could give you a ride, if you want."

"Thanks, but I think Gretchen will be there."

She smiled with her fresh face, the matter-of-fact look of her making him wish he could watch her all day.

"Really nice of you to offer," she added.

"My pleasure." He let it roll out and over his tongue before he could hold it back. For a second he thought he saw her eyelids flutter, like she'd wanted to close them and changed her mind.

Once they'd taxied and come to a halt, he helped several people remove their bags from the overhead bins before getting hers down. He caught her sneaking looks at his abdomen, which he sucked in. Her eyes traveled over his biceps and up along his light blue T-shirt, and up under his chin before resting gently on his lips. She was admiring him. No question about it.

He felt a flame flicker to life in his stomach, light and barely perceptible. And something inside his chest felt good. It was his heart.

Passengers began filing down the aisle. He stepped back and allowed her to go in front of him, for all the right reasons, he told himself. He was thinking about the gentleman he was not while he watched her jeans-covered ass sway very slightly down the aisle. She was ample, which he liked. Squeezable, but not heavy. He knew she'd have a perfect shape and would fill his palms deliciously.

The baggage carousel was backed up. Kate was on the phone and appeared to be having trouble reaching her sister. Her frustrated expression ended when they made eye contact again. Then she began to speak to someone on the phone, a little furrow developing between her eyebrows as worry spread over her face. She turned her back to him and finished her conversation in private.

Tyler made a point of looking at his feet, but he used his peripheral vision to watch her swing around and head in his direction. He'd been trained to do this. The monotonous hum of the machinery and the thud as bags deposited onto the turnstile was background to the way his heart quickened, just knowing she was looking at him, and coming his way. He let her wait just a second or two before he let his eyes travel from her knees to that pretty, innocent face he wanted in the worst way to kiss. He couldn't help but smile.

"Um. She's asked me to take a cab. Would it—?"

"Done," he said, interrupting her. "Let's get your bag."

She told him it was a bright red one with a red ribbon. He set his duffel at her feet and worked his way through the crowd to retrieve it for her. Funny how this little mission gave him so much pleasure. How his soul was tickled. He'd get to spend a few minutes more, at least, in her company. And she'd *asked* for it. Her idea, not his. She was someone else's girl, after all. But he was grateful he'd had the foresight to offer earlier.

"Where does your sister live, or did I just commit my friend to driving to Vancouver?"

"I forget what they call it. In the hills overlooking the water. Hundred Thirteenth Northwest or something. I have it in my purse."

"That's not too bad. I think we can manage."

Outside, the air was chilly and he was grateful he'd slipped on his jacket. He felt the buzz of his cell phone and knew Kenny was nearby. Then he heard his best friend's familiar shout-out.

"Dude, you finally did it. You brought a girl!" The tall lanky kid-of-a-man wearing a bright blue Hawaiian shirt, cargo pants and flip-flops grabbed Tyler around the waist and hauled him up off the ground. But he didn't take his eyes off Kate.

"Whoa, whoa, there Kenny," he interrupted. "This is Kate, and we're just giving her a ride."

"I got ya. Well, if you get tired of his ride, you can always try mine." Kenny wore a goofy expression, gawking at the beautiful Kate.

Tyler saw her blush, though he could tell she was trying hard not to, and suspected she was feeling uncomfortable. "We're dropping her off at her sister's."

"Uh huh," Kenny said, obviously unconvinced. He stepped back two paces, giving Tyler lots of space. Then he ran back and punched him on the arm. "You been holding out on me, dude."

Tyler knew Kenny lived vicariously through him. His friend had problems with the female population because he was so shy. His gangly frame reminded Tyler of Coop, actually. He made a mental note to invite Kenny down to San Diego when they got back, maybe arrange a little face time with Cooper, who would appreciate his old friend's knowledge of computers and computerized gadgets.

Tyler rolled his eyes and put his palm on Kate's shoulder like she was a porcelain doll who might shatter under his fingers. "Please don't mind Kenny. He's harmless enough." He saw that she stiffened a bit at his first touch, but then relaxed and rewarded him with a warm smile.

"I understand. Got friends who act be the same way." She wrinkled her nose but her eyes still danced. "They'd get the wrong idea and make a big deal, too."

Tyler gave her a squeeze and then let his hand drop. Kenny was over by his Gremlin, had already popped the hatchback and opened both doors. The men put all the suitcases in the rear, while Kate slipped behind the front bucket seat on the passenger side. Tyler sat directly in front of her next to Kenny, and they headed west.

Kenny was listening to oldies, and the music was so loud it sucked up the dead airspace. Gave Tyler time to think about things, and strategize the next few minutes.

Kenny's dash was covered with glued-on dinosaurs and military action figures, a couple of felt-tip pens on end and a crooked hula girl. He had beads and a miniature Native American headdress dangling from the rear view mirror. His week-old stubble would barely cover the surface of his little fingernail, whereas Tyler's beard would cover his entire face after only three days. Kenny's skin underneath was pearly white, confirming that he spent the majority of his time these days in a darkened room in front of a computer monitor.

Tyler turned down the music and leaned over the old Gremlin's partially ripped black vinyl bucket seats. Kate appeared to be comfortable and slightly amused as she scanned the eclectic car. Looking at the plastic figures on the dash, she pointed, squinting at Tyler.

Tyler leaned into the creaking bucket seat, angling to see her face. "Kenny's an acquired taste, I admit," he said. "But harmless as hell, which is why I like him, right Kenny?" He thumped his friend gently on the shoulder, careful not to distract his driving.

"Damn straight," Kenny sputtered. "I just tell people, 'don't fuck with me or I'll get my Navy SEAL friend to come up here and whup your ass.'"

Tyler rolled his eyes. "Great, Kenny. Appreciate that."

He'd been worried that the vehicle and Kenny's Aloha shirt and state of hygiene had put her off, but she actually seemed to be enjoying herself. He couldn't believe it.

"I think you should buy yourself one of those Hawaiian shirts, Tyler," she said. "It would look good on you."

She warmed him all the way to his toes with her smile. God, she had perfect white teeth. Her fresh face was so kissable.

Kenny had a coughing attack, disguising an unmanly-like giggle. "See there, Tyler. *I've* got my shit together, in spite of what you say. Lady knows her Tommy Bahama shirts."

Tyler cursed under his breath.

Kenny winked at Kate through the rearview mirror and continued to rub it in. "For once you've got a looker, not like those librarians you've been dating."

Tyler wasn't comfortable at all with that reveal. Yes, he had to admit to himself, he liked dating bookish girls who didn't give him any trouble. And he found girls who read a lot had wonderful imaginations, too, which certainly didn't hurt in the sack.

He stared out the windshield until he remembered they didn't even know where they were going.

"You have her address?" he asked, as he leaned his shoulder into the seat and peered over the top at Kate.

Kate handed him a slip of paper she'd prepared. "That's her address."

Under the address was a phone number. It wasn't a Portland area code.

"And that?" he said as his index finger touched the number.

"My cell. Just in case."

Just in case, my ass. Just in case I can't sleep tonight thinking about how beautiful you are. How nice you smell. How cute you look in the back seat of this old beater. Would I be granted this if I asked for it? Even if you're taken?

But he didn't reveal any of his thoughts. "Right. Thanks," he said and turned forward, handing the slip of paper to Kenny.

"No problemo, dude." Kenny stared into the rearview and asked his back seat passenger, "You want to stop and get something to eat?"

"Sure."

Tyler heard the response, and it made him glow. *Sure* was such a wonderful word, really. Totally compliant, willing. Full of possibilities.

"Where were you thinking?" Tyler asked.

"Voodoo Doughnut."

Of course it was Voodoo Doughnut. It was the only place Kenny ate. Tyler just couldn't understand why he never gained any weight.

Tyler leaned back to warn Kate. "You don't want to order the ones with the blue-green jelly centers. Word is they're Nyquil-filled."

"Good to know," she said as she pursed her lips. Her eyes danced. Did she have any idea how attractive she was? A lot was going on inside his chest and other places, despite his efforts to remember she belonged to another man. Tyler could control his actions, but he could not begin to tame his thoughts.

He looked out the dirty, cracked windshield as the city of Portland came into sight. The skyline, it bridges and buildings highlighted in the sun, the bright white clouds filling the blue sky that might threaten rain five minutes later, always made him relax. He was at home here. Not that he wanted to live here. Just that it was home. A place where he could safely melt into his past, and where his eccentric friends and relatives, all of them self-absorbed extroverts, would take some of the attention off him.

In his entire family of hippies and environmental zealots, no one ever had ever gone into the military. But being a SEAL really wasn't *about* being in the military. It was more about being part of a family, a brotherhood of guys he'd die for.

Seemed hard to connect with right now, sitting in Kenny's old Gremlin. Reminders of high school brought back memories of the years he spent unsuccessfully trying to get laid, a time when everything seemed so normal. But he'd been certain even then that death, destruction, and evil were out there. Now he'd seen it overseas. But just because most people couldn't taste it, smell it or sense it, didn't mean it wasn't right here, too. He was just one of those guys who was willing to give his life so everyone else could go around being batshit crazy.

And it was okay with him. It was his job. Even today it was his job, delivering this young woman to her sister's house safely, making sure no one messed with her, that she was protected. He liked opening the door for her, running around to make sure he opened the smudged glass door to the donut shop for her before Kenny could get there. That was all part of his job. And it was something he loved doing.

The unmistakable bakery smell was intoxicating, but would have been more so if it weren't for the heavy metal music in the background and the tat-covered plus-sized beauty behind the counter with a large nose bone and plates in her ears. He hoped she took the bone out at night when she slept.

"Kenny!" she shrieked, and ran around the counter to body-slam his skinny nerd buddy. Her hands were still in plastic mitts, but that didn't stop her from running her crinkly fingers through his hair and placing a lip lock on him that sounded more like a toilet plunger.

Kenny was unaffected, as in embarrassed. Although he actually did kind of blush. Apparently this thing with the lovely lady was a recent development.

Holy God of SEALs, Kenny finally got laid. It had only taken him twenty-seven years, but finally lust had dusted the boy with sugar and put chocolate sprinkles all over him. He was grinning just like those days when they'd get stoned out behind the soccer field and Kenny would look up at the sky and point out animals and people's faces. A goofy, sheepish, yup-I-fucked-her grin. Hence the real reason for the Voodoo stop.

And then he remembered Kate with a start. She had missed all of it and was looking into the glass case, examining some pink frosted mini donuts displayed next to a couple of wilted green salads. But she was more interested in the salads.

"Sorry about that," Tyler started to say, cramming his hands in his front pockets. Shoot, now he was feeling like a goofy high schooler himself. Funny how coming home did that to him. "Kenny—"

Before he could finish, Kate leaned into him and gave him a kiss. Just a quick one. Just enough to make the rock music and the intoxicating smell of sugar and baking disappear. His heart pounded. His face had followed hers as she retreated until it almost caused him to topple. He was desperate for another one.

Wow. Holy. Fuckin'. Wow!

CHAPTER 5

Kate didn't know why she'd done it. The impulse to kiss him was just too irresistible. She'd just crossed the barrier between her ordered, "perfect" life with the man she *thought* she loved, and did something dangerous with someone she barely knew, but trusted.

What in the world was happening?

The warm creases at the corners of Tyler's blue eyes made her heart flutter. Unless she was losing her ability to read men, he'd loved her little surprise kiss, her spontaneity. And, based on the way he'd leaned into her, he wanted *more.*

Then she realized she didn't know what *she* wanted. One thing was certain. She was in serious danger of taking a huge detour. Something that would change her life forever.

She tore her eyes off his face and scanned the case containing dangerous round things covered in sprinkles and powdered sugar. The heady aroma made her want to swoon. Out of the corner of her eye she could see him lean forward, felt him wrap her forearm with his warm fingers. His hand slipped down to her wrist and hesitated while he studied her. She didn't resist when his slid his fingers in between hers, mated them without saying a word. He waited, rubbing the back of her hand with his thumb.

He was asking her a non-verbal question she wasn't sure she'd be able to answer. The confections were safer—way safer—than the blue of his eyes and the warm blush of his lips, if she would but sneak a peek at him. The distraction of their sugary irresistibility would only last so long. She'd have to look at him soon, and that would tell her everything she either did or did not want to know.

She drew her breath in, gaining courage, and looked up to return his gaze at last.

His head was tilted to the side. He swayed like he was going to ask her to dance. His knowing smile and warm eyes seem delighted with the budding of a new relationship looming as large as the little shop. And there was the attraction again, starting at the pit of her stomach, almost like a food craving. Something about him was so right on so many levels, and so wrong on a couple of big ones.

As if he was acknowledging her internal thoughts, mirroring them with identical ones of his own, he nodded slightly. The unashamed way he allowed the lust to show in his eyes as he focused on her mouth again, as he squeezed their fingers together, as she let him pull her to him, sent her ears buzzing and her heart racing. Slowly, their lips met again as old, hungry friends, and this time it was a proper kiss. She opened to him, and she felt his chest rise, his slight moan vibrating in her chest as well.

Then Kate realized the moan was coming from her own throat. She tasted him, exploring the texture of his tongue, the softness and warmth of his lips on hers as they slid and angled the length of hers in play. They dropped their entangled fingers and he placed his palm at the small of her back, pulling her to him as she stepped into his full embrace.

Her palms traveled up the hardened muscles of his torso to the base of his neck, then around, pulling his head down to hers, lazily letting her fingers sift through his hair. He wasn't going to go faster than she wanted to go. Each move she made was perfectly matched with his own, such that they led each other, drew each other together, and savored their shared heat.

Something in the back of her mind was sending up an alarm, as though part of her knew this kiss wasn't wise. But being rational was a distant planet. Kate *wanted* to let herself be carried away, loose the bonds of her control. Being so intimate with this complete stranger somehow seemed as natural and right as smiling.

As their lips parted, and his arms squeezed her waist in a kissless hug, he whispered to the side of her face, "Thank you, Kate. Thank you."

Thank me? For what? Was he thanking her for ignoring her standards? Her loyalty to her fiancé? Or, did he sense that he had a chance at a relationship with her? That this wasn't a casual kiss, or an opportunity taken, stolen from someone else's life. This was something more.

She heard the titters of Kenny and his friend, and Kate blushed about having been so oblivious. She wondered what they must think of her getting so carried away so quickly, and then realized with a start she didn't care. As she peeked at their audience, Tyler didn't move. He was still focused on her face.

Reality began to sink in. As if he read her thoughts, he stepped back, still holding her hand, and addressed the gawking and awkward sounds, like noises from a video game, coming from behind him.

Kate studied his mahogany brown hair, worn a little too long, curling behind his ears and over the top of his shirt, his tanned face in profile—a face which now seemed so familiar to her. He warmly addressed their audience, and she didn't care what he said. She just wanted to listen to him say it.

"Sorry, guys. I guess I got a little carried away with—" Tyler turned to address Kate and his face lit up with another warm smile, eliciting the same from her. "I was not able to stop myself." His lashes fluttered as he dropped his gaze to examine her lips again.

Kenny and his lady friend probably hadn't noticed that Kate was the first one to make the move, initiate their first kiss, but Tyler took the fall for it. At that, her excitement over what could be was more important than what had been. Her future was eclipsing her past.

Tyler's fingers moved a ringlet of hair from next to her cheek and tucked it behind her ear, his thumb caressing her lower lip. She felt the exquisite knotting of her nipples and the ache in her core. She wanted his hands on her, anywhere.

"So much for 'we're just giving her a ride to her sister's,' bro," Kenny said with a smirk.

"And that's still the plan," Tyler said as he drew her to his side.

Now it was Kate's turn to say it. "Thank you," she whispered. He rewarded her with a squeeze and she found herself leaning into him again.

Kenny cleared his throat. "So, just tell Vonda here what you want, and she'll make us some sandwiches, right sweetie?" He gave Vonda a quick peck on the cheek.

Tyler led them over to the corner table after they'd placed their orders, and the three of them sat. Kate watched the eclectic variety of customers come and go. The crowd apparently purchased donuts all day long. Kenny and Tyler bantered back and forth, needling each other and catching up. Kate found herself wanting to hear more about the librarians Tyler had dated, but the conversation stayed strictly away from them.

"I report back next Friday. We do a week of workup," Tyler was saying. "Been preparing hard for this one for over four months."

"Where are you going?" she asked him.

"We have a general idea, but it could be anywhere." Tyler delivered it flat, but then his eyes wandered down the side of her face, over her shoulder and then back to her chest. She felt herself blush. Afterwards, their eyes did not meet.

"Cool. So like Tunisia? Morocco?" Kenny wanted to know. He nodded a greeting to a couple of skateboarders with purple and green hair who had entered the shop.

Tyler shrugged and shook his head. "Even if I knew, couldn't say." He punched Kenny in the arm. "You know that."

Kenny rolled his eyes as he complained non-verbally to Kate.

"Hey, Kenny," Tyler began. "I got a friend you got to meet. Cooper, our corpsman, that's our medic. He's the biggest gadget guy I've met, outside of you, of course."

"Yeah?"

Kate had finished her lunch and sat listening.

"I think you two'd have a good time. You should come down to San Diego, I'll introduce him to you. You can bring Vonda, if you like," Tyler said as an afterthought, winking at the tattooed beauty behind the counter. "We have this lady in San Diego who does amazing tats, works on all of us. A fuckin' knockout, too, named Daisy. She has the softest hands and the biggest—" his cupped hands had gone out in front of his chest until he looked at Kate and abruptly stopped, dropping his hands to his lap.

At the mention of Daisy's name, Kate found herself feeling uncomfortable, perhaps a little jealous. Tyler sighed, apparently deep in thought.

"That depends," Kenny replied, leaning back on his chair and rocking it precariously.

"On what?"

Kenny dropped back forward, placed his palms on the pink, glitter-flake Formica tabletop and stared at Kate, raising one eyebrow. "Is Kate going to be there?"

He wiggled his eyebrows for effect.

Kate found herself blushing again as Tyler's eyes swept from his friend's to her face. Did he see the flutter in her chest? The red blotchy marks there? The flush on her cheeks?

"I dunno where Kate will be," he began in a whisper. "But she's welcome to come to San Diego when I get back from deployment. Any. Time. She. Likes."

She melted into his warm smile, and then looked down. Suddenly, she remembered her sister, who might be waiting for her at the house. “You guys,” she began, “I need to go. How much do I owe?” she asked.

Both men held out their hands, declining. “We got this,” Tyler said.

The road to her sister’s house was winding. Freshly rained-on surfaces of made the green shrubbery brighter, the blue sky more intense, the grey and white billowy clouds more defined. She’d always loved the faint smell of the huge Columbia River as it snaked around the waterfront. Her sister’s house was on one of the prominent hills overlooking rows of trendy commercial districts and warehouses.

She’d been quiet while she watched the wisps of Tyler’s hair blow in the breeze blowing in the little crack in his window. The conversation between the two friends was background noise to her thoughts, which began to darken and become heavier. She was beginning to regret the doorway she’d plunged them both through.

What was I thinking?

Her ordered life was close to perfect, maybe too perfect, she thought. She’d gotten the handsome guy with the wealthy parents who doted on him, and had shown her nothing but affection. Maybe they were a little overbearing at times, like the way Mrs. Heller took over some of the details of their wedding, insisting on using her caterer and ordering all the flowers for not only the reception but the ceremony as well. She could understand the caterer decision, since the reception was going to be held at the family winery, and she needed to be able to work with the staff. But the flowers had been done without even consulting Kate's mother, who had been a little hurt by the gesture, although Mrs. Heller said she'd intended to help.

A small war was brewing between the two sets of parents as to who could provide the most for the couple. Kate knew her parents felt slightly embarrassed they weren't able to promise the same lavish gifts Randy's parents did. To Kate, that was her only concern: how her parents felt. She never wanted to forget where she came from. There were times the Hellers seemed to live in a fantasyland they wanted to suck her into.

But who am I to question all of this? She knew all of her friends, especially Sheila, were over the top excited for her. Randy had long been the one who every one of her friends had wanted to snag, and they'd all tried.

Kate realized he'd chosen her probably because his family and background didn't really impress her, and so she'd paid him little attention until he began courting her in earnest. This had surprised her as much as it dismayed her friends. Settling down hadn't been on her radar, but once she got involved with Randy, things had escalated and before she knew it they were engaged. Everyone was jumping up and down with excitement.

Kate had thought perhaps she'd get excited once it was closer her wedding day. But her fears and jitters were growing instead.

And now this.

Which is why it was so odd she'd made it all complicated and kissed Tyler. And wanted him to kiss her back. Yes, there was a physical attraction there, but her initiating the kiss had come from somewhere else. She decided to cleanse her head of that thought. It was unhealthy. Time to start living in the *reality* that was her life.

She was going to marry Randy Heller in September, like she'd promised, and all would be right with the world. And Tyler would come home from overseas, healthy and whole, to the waiting arms of some other woman.

Not her.

She felt her eyes burn with the beginnings of a cry forming. No way was she going to show that to anybody. She dismissed her melancholy mood as wedding jitters, plus the upcoming visit with her vibrant, overbearing sister and three unruly kids.

The Gremlin seemed to lose most of its power on the last long climb to the top of the knoll where Gretchen's house stood. When Kenny turned off the ignition, a cloud of smoke burped from the rear, drifting over the top of the vehicle and out into the crisp afternoon air.

The house was just as Kate had remembered from her last visit some three years ago. And, true to form, there was a bike thrown onto a hedge by the front door and several bright plastic buckets scattered on the porch. Chalk designs made by little hands decorated the risers of the concrete stairs, holding fast despite the rain. The colorful artwork told the world that the kids were the center of this household.

Tyler turned in his seat as they stopped. "Looks just like my sister's house. Stuff every—"

He'd stopped himself as a plea formed on his face.

"She does the best she can," Kate said with a smile. "I admire her. The kids are happy, even though I know it's tough on her."

"My sister's the same," Tyler nodded. "Except she has a do-nothing ex-husband. But they don't seem to mind." He frowned. "I'm sorry, I didn't mean to imply your sister..."

"No worries. Sounds like your sister has her priorities straight, like mine does. Except mine doesn't write smutty books."

Tyler nodded, got out, and pulled the front seat forward so she could squeeze out of the back. He'd taken her hand and kept holding it while walked to the rear of the dirty green Gremlin. They stood close again. Tyler pulled her up against his chest.

She wiggled her way out of his attempted embrace and frowned. She'd decided it would be best for her to forget the kiss, and the second kiss, and all the fantasies about what could come next, and the way her body felt. She wrestled herself back to feeling a proper blushing bride, even though the face of the groom in her fantasy was now hazy.

Which bothered her.

She heard a muffled "I'm sorry," at her back as she lifted the hatch and began hauling out her bag. Kenny appeared and brushed her hands away. He struggled, but got the big red suitcase out and walked up the stairs with it, Kate and Tyler following.

At the top, Kenny dusted his palms together and grumbled something as he skipped back down the stairs to his waiting car. Tyler stood right behind Kate.

It was one of the hardest things she'd ever done, to turn, which she did, take his hand in hers, and thank him sincerely for the ride. And nothing else. What remained unspoken as they gazed at each other was the longing no doubt they both felt…that chemical attraction formed long before their first kiss. Something had sprouted inside her heart, wanting desperately to grow. Along with that was the ache at knowing she was going to force it to wither.

Because that was the right thing to do. Kate always did the right thing.

"Well," he said as he turned to the side and stared off at the river. "I hope you have a beautiful wedding, and a wonderful life, Kate." He looked down. His face was in line with hers, and if she wanted to, she could lean forward and their lips would meet, since he was one step below her. "It was very nice to meet you," he finished.

"Nice to meet you, Tyler. Good luck on your next tour. And thank you. Thank you for doing what you're doing for all of us. Just know that I for one appreciate it."

"Thanks," he said. "Well at least that's something I can go away with, then." He looked at the door. "Is your sister home?"

"Five minutes," Kate said, holding up her phone. "She just texted me."

"Good. Take care, Kate."

With that he turned and started down the steps. Kate watched his muscular body descend, and her heart felt like it was being stabbed with a dull pencil. "Tyler," she blurted, before she even knew what she wanted to say.

He looked up at her, hands on his hips, one foot on the step above the other.

"We could write. I could write you while you're overseas."

Tyler examined his shoes again. "We could do that," he said as his blue eyes swept up to take in her face. "Don't want to go where I don't belong, though."

It was a dangerous thing to say, but it was the truth of their situation. Where did he belong in her life? A man whose service she was grateful for. A warrior called to do his duty. An honorable man not willing to encroach on another man's girl. That made him even more attractive than the moment she'd kissed him. He wasn't going to complain, or try to talk her into anything she wasn't going to be a full participant in, and she liked him all the more for it.

"I'd like to write you letters. I'd like to hear about what it's like being over there. Whatever you can share."

"More like what's going on here," he said as he pointed to his chest. "And here," he pointed to his head.

"Then I'll take that. Whatever you want to tell me. I'll listen. We'll be friends through our letters, Tyler."

"I'd like that very much," he said. He got out a notebook he kept in his jacket pocket and scribbled down something, then jogged up the four steps until he was just below Kate again, handing her the paper. "Use this address."

She took the notebook and his pen, her fingers grazing his. He stood too close, so close that she could feel his body heat and hear the deep, satisfying sound of his breathing while she wrote her address and handed him back the notebook and pen.

"Here's mine."

"Good. I'll write first," he said. His clear blue eyes searched her face and landed on her mouth again. She thought he was going to cover her lips with his, but he leaned in, angled, and gave her a gentle kiss on the cheek. “Bye, Kate.”

He didn’t look back at her as he rounded the Gremlin. Kenny waved to her and she waved back. But Tyler got in the passenger seat and didn’t turn in her direction as the little green monster sputtered off down the wet blacktop.

Like one of the little monsters glued to Kenny’s dash, a tiny piece of her heart was embedded there, staring at Tyler’s face, begging him to turn around and come back.

But it was not to be.

CHAPTER 6

Kenny shut off the music, which was the first sign, and gave him one of those *what-the-fuck-were-you-thinkin'* looks, just like when they were in community college. It usually involved a girl, but it was the same look he'd given Tyler when he announced he was going into the Navy and the SEAL brotherhood was going to be his career path. And it closely approximated the look his mother had given him later that day, when he told her he'd already enlisted and was shipping out the next week.

"So, Tyler, I gotta ask you. Are we coming or going, here?"

It was a very good question, and deserved an honest answer.

"I have no idea, but one of the two of them. Not going to stay the same, that's for sure," Tyler found himself mumbling.

"Well, all I gotta say is wow. She's a looker."

That lightened his heart. He grinned. Yup, she certainly was that. He knew he'd be thinking about her all night long.

He wasn't too displeased, either. He thought about her long legs and smooth skin, silky brown hair that felt wonderful spilling between his fingers when he'd held her head as they kissed. He even loved the way she sighed and how she shook. Everything she did was a major fuckin' turn-on. Just watching her trying to pick up her red suitcase had been fun, even though Kenny had tried to save her from it. She was *just fine.* That was all there was to it.

And she was going to be okay with writing each other so he wouldn't have to bury her memory. Now, that was something he could do. She didn't know he'd won that poetry contest in high school. The star soccer player who could write love poems. Half the girls asked him out after that one little stint. Nope, didn't mind it much then, and he certainly didn't mind it now.

Then he had the fleeting thought that perhaps she'd given him a fake address. Nah, he didn't think so. That's now he read her character. He could hardly wait. In fact, perhaps he'd work on the first letter tonight. He could post it and perhaps even get a response before he left, if she wrote him right back. That would be a very good sign, right?

The clicking of Kenny's thumb and first two fingers in front of his eyes brought him back to the reality of Kenny's Gremlin. The red Yoda figurine on the dash seemed to be grinning right at him. The hula girl vied for his attention. The yellow dinosaur with the tiger stripes stopped chomping on the green plastic tree branch and stared him down. They were all asking about his next move.

"What's it gonna be, Tyler?" they cheered.

He scanned the audience before him on the dash. *None of your fuckin' business, guys,* he told them mentally. All he heard back was laughter.

"You okay, Ty? I mean, you are *way* more distracted than I'm used to. Like, you're usually ready for World War III, which means I don't have to worry about it. But today, you'd probably walk into a fuckin' Afghani tank and hit your head before you woke up. You can *wake up*, can't you?"

"So I'm thinking about that woman, Kenny. No harm in that."

Kenny nodded. "No. No harm in that. As long as you don't step out in traffic, or forget you're driving or something."

Yeah. Thinking about her was kind of addictive. Made him want to take a nap and dream about her. He needed to be alone with his private thoughts about her. Kenny must have realized he was going there, and nothing would disturb his daydreams, because eventually his friend's incessant banter petered out. When the green monster car pulled up to Tyler's mother's salmon-pink-with-turquoise-trim two-story shingled home, he realized he'd been stuck thinking about what she felt like while she shivered against his chest there in the donut shop.

His mom ran out the front door to greet him, her hands buried in a paint-smeared towel. Her lined face was still beautiful, and her long grey hair hadn't been cut in twenty years. She'd just taken it out of the clip she usually wore when she was painting.

"Oh, sweetie. Thank God you're home." She engulfed him in one of those mom hugs that had smothered him and made him sneeze when he was five or six. He felt how slight she'd become, and for the first time felt, as well as saw, her age.

"You're getting too skinny, Mom," he whispered into her hair.

"Oh stop it, Ty. You know your dad likes me at my dance weight. And you'll see every pound I've lost has gone right to his waistline."

Nope, Tyler thought, that would be your blackberry cobblers and homemade vanilla ice cream.

"Hey, Kenny," she said as she rubbed her fingers through Kenny's hair like she was rubbing a charcoal stain from one of her sketches. "How are the folks?"

Tyler and Kenny's parents had tried to be friends since the boys were in grammar school, but it never took.

Kenny shrugged. "Fighting like cats and dogs, making up like rabbits."

Tyler saw his mom's eyes sparkle. "Well, at least they make up."

"I think it's why they fight," Kenny quipped.

She Kenny as he said his goodbyes and they made a plan to get together the next day for coffee. The Gremlin took off down the hill in a belch of smoke like its namesake.

Tyler put his arm around his mom and pulled his wheeling duffel along with the other hand. They walked across the old creaking porch to the front door and into the "cave of bright and light," as he'd once described it to a couple of his friends.

Funny how he thought about that just now. One time during the BUD/S training, he'd been between Jones on one side and Rory on the other, locked arm in arm. The three amigos all graduated in a class that had been another near-washout. They were lying in the surf on the beach in San Diego, their clothes on, including their combat boots, wet and cold as hell. Shivering and talking about stuff just to stay awake, because sure as shit the water wasn't doing it for them, after only ten minutes of sleep in the last three days of training. Someone had started to snore and he and the guys on either side of him had to run five miles while the others lay back and got wet and sandy.

They'd contemplated pretending to fall asleep, because then at least they could get warm during the run, but a five-mile run at midnight, completely soaked through, with the boots…and besides, the spot between his legs where his wetsuit had chafed would hurt even more. If he took off his clothes, and it would be a full forty-eight hours before he would be able to lose the clothes and take a hot shower, he'd known he'd see blisters the size of his fist, probably good and bloody, too.

So they talked about stuff just to keep each other awake. He described his mother's house in great detail, with all the huge, colorful, abstract paintings, the way the rain pattered against the stained glass windows his folks had bought from some abbey in France on their honeymoon, the smells of strong coffee, and sounds of Joni Mitchel in the background, brightening everything, including his soul…that's what he talked about. The guys gave him hell for the Joni Mitchel comment, which was well-deserved. He couldn't understand her much or the words, but he liked her tone and spirit. And the guys hadn't believed a word of that, either.

He'd have to say his mother was a nester. The opposite of Tyler's simple life, with a definite lack of things to clutter it up. He liked her color and her free spirit, her warmth. It reminded him, every time he walked through the door of this battered, eclectic home, why he did what he did. He was fighting to protect this for all the people like his mother, and for Kenny and his donut love, and all the other people who didn't have to know about the evils out there and the things he and his Team had to do. And because they were so removed from his arena, he hoped they never thought about it, either. That was the way it was supposed to be. Make it so safe, people never had to worry about the safety of their ordinary lives.

He let the colors soak in like sunlight on the beach. He must have sighed because his mom snuggled against his chest and whispered, "You've had a long trip, I can tell. Want some coffee, or do you want to go up to your room and take a nap?"

He did want to be alone, and felt guilty about it. There would be time later for sharing himself with her, and with his dad when he came home from his principal's job. But right now he didn't want to take a nap. He wanted to start writing a letter to Kate, while the thought of her was fresh in his mind.

His mother waved to him as he climbed the groaning, hand-hewn pine steps that wound up the middle of the great room to the bedrooms above. He'd never really thought before about how huge the house was. The grand staircase could host a king's procession as it descended to a waiting crowd of loyal subjects gathered below in the enormous hall. The combined living/dining/family room area was at least five times the size of his apartment in San Diego.

He opened the door to his room. His baseball and soccer trophies still lined shelves built along two walls almost up to the ten-foot ceilings. Posters of baseball players and international soccer stars covered the rest of the wall space, along with a tattered American flag he'd brought back from Afghanistan for his mother. She'd mounted it here instead of flying it out front like he suggested. She told him it meant a lot to her, which is why it took prominence in his bedroom, so she could go in there during his deployments and feel like she was next to him.

He never told her about the two young Marines he'd attempted to rescue that day, or the ten others he had. The kids they'd escorted to a safe building, along with their pretty teacher, who had already lost a hand in the explosion that took out the school. He'd never forget the way she took care of those kids, little girls among them, which they figured was why the school had been targeted. And she hadn't fainted from her serious injury until after they were all safe. She'd used her hijab to wrap around the wound, leaving her head uncovered so she could protect her stump of an arm and stop the bleeding. Or maybe it was so the kids wouldn't have to see it.

His mind wandered back to Portland and memories of sitting at his desk, watching the Columbia River glisten past, looking lazy but vibrant in the late afternoon sunlight, belying a deep spirit buried in the strong current underneath. He'd sat there and written the poetry he hadn't thought of in years.

His memories led him next to the bookshelf with all his favorites starting with the Huck Finn and Treasure Island books he'd read as a child, books lovingly passed down to him from his father, who had taught him the love of reading. He let his fingers travel over the old paperback Star Trek, also his father's, and then some of his own, including a well-worn secret book, *Lady Chatterley's Lover*, which, oddly, now was prominently displayed next to his science fiction collection. That meant that his mother had found it on one of her cleaning days, and it was a message to him that she approved of his choice.

So be it.

He'd loved that book and the beautiful description of a woman's body, the way her passion bloomed for her lover, how she gave as much as he took in the illicit affair that would consume them both. He wanted that kind of love.

He was surprised to find, next to the erotic tome, two spiral notebooks he'd filled with love poems in high school. He brought them over to his desk, removed his jacket, and sat down to read.

I watch you travel on your way to who knows where,
Jealous of the shoes your little feet are tucked into.
I'm jealous of the air you breathe all around you,
Jealous of the boys who flirt with you and then glare at me behind you,
As if they know I like to follow,
Just to smell your perfume.

He blushed at his own words. He tried to remember her name, and then did. Karen. He'd lie awake at night and think about her, and what it would feel like to caress her back, hold her naked against him. It was the vision that got him through high school.

And Karen never even knew he existed. The back of the notebook had several blank pages, along with a letter he'd begun to her. Holding his breath, he dared to go back to that time in his life he'd all but forgotten.

Dear Karen,

I've enjoyed watching you from the shadows and won't reveal who I am, except to say that I think you are the most beautiful woman I've ever met. We are graduating soon, and I know we probably won't see each other much, if ever, but maybe we could have one dance at Project Grad night. If I came up to you, would you give me one dance? If I showed you who I was? I'm not a creep, or someone you have to worry about. I'm just writing to tell you I will miss seeing your pretty face every day during the week, and hope…

The letter wasn't finished. He remembered he'd been interrupted, but forgot why. He'd never dropped the letter into her locker. And she hadn't attended Project Grad that night, either. Who knows, maybe if he'd told her, if she'd gotten a mysterious letter from an admirer, she would have come. And maybe it would have changed the trajectory of their lives.

But no. He'd made a different choice. He wasn't going to let that happen again.

He found an unused page in the back of the notebook, smoothed his hand over the lined white paper, and began to write.

CHAPTER 7

Kate waited on the front porch of Gretchen's home, watching the waterway below and listening to the sounds of late afternoon boat traffic. The constant commercial noise and the way the river meandered on its way out to the ocean was comforting. Life was back in order and would go on as planned, even though her life felt, after this morning's plane ride and adventure at the donut shop, chaotic.

Gretchen waved as she maneuvered her car up the steep driveway along the side of her house. Kate heard car doors slam and the voices of Gretchen's three girls. The back door banged, and she heard the patter of little feet racing towards the front door. Angela, the youngest, barely four years old, struggled to open the heavy wooden door of the large two-story bungalow. Her face was streaked with smudged Indian war paint.

"Auntie Kate!!" the little one squealed as she ran to her and embraced Kate's knees. Clover and Rebecca, Angela's two older sisters, hovered in the doorway, waiting for the hug fest to end. Clover appeared to have grown nearly a foot, and resembled her handsome basketball player father.

"What's the matter with you guys? Clover, Rebecca, get over here," Kate commanded. In two long steps, Clover traversed the distance between them and bowed her head, giving Kate a tentative hug. The girl was nearly Kate's height. Rebecca pushed Angela out of the way and took her place at Kate's knees.

Gretchen appeared next and walked over to complete the group hug.

"Sorry about the mix-up. Angela's preschool had an event I forgot about." She turned to her daughter. "Angie, you need to wash that face now. Part of your war paint is already somewhere in my car or in the house or—" she checked Kate's pants to be sure she hadn't been slimed. "Oh good, you're unscathed."

Kate shared a grin with her sister. Despite curly hair that went everywhere, her lack of makeup, and the ripped jeans/fluffy sweatshirt ensemble, Gretchen looked happy. Happier than she'd seemed in years.

"Looking good, Gretchen. You have your spark back," Kate said.

The comment didn't get past Clover. "Mom's got a new boyfriend," she said around her braces.

Good for you, Gretchen. "Ah, so that's what it is." Kate examined Clover for evidence the new man was a problem for her. It had been a very public divorce after her dad, the awesome professional basketball player, had been outed doing shots and disco dancing with a coed about half his age. Up until his indiscretion, if it could be called that, he'd been the golden boy of the family. She was proud that her sister refused his attempts at reconciliation and only accepted a minimal amount of child support, even though he had at least a seven-figure income. Gretchen had told her she wanted him to feel as useless to their lives as she had felt when she saw the newspaper photos of him, bare-chested, dirty dancing with the blonde.

"Come on in. We have so much to catch up on," Gretchen said, wrapping her arms around her girls, who lovingly hugged her back. Kate was glad to see again that her sister had the family she'd always wanted, even without the guy. In fact, she was a bit envious of her sister's happiness.

"Let's get Aunt Kate's bags up to the room," Gretchen said, and immediately the bevy of girls took everything and preceded Kate up the carpeted stairway to the top floor.

They had moved her into Clover's room. A poster of Justin Bieber was prominently displayed on the wall, along with some posters of her dad in a Trailblazers jersey. Kate noticed a number of ribbons and small trophies. "Way to go, Clover!" she said to her niece as she pointed at them.

Clover stared at the ground and shrugged, embarrassed.

"She plays basketball, but loves volleyball even more," her mom said.

Before she could stop herself, Kate blurted out, "Thank God." The girls snickered and her sister handed her back a smirk.

Kate felt the need to explain. "I was just thinking she's her own woman. Not to be following along in her dad's—" She realized her slip and began to shake her head, angry with herself.

"Kate, best to stop digging now you've gotten that hole started."

"I'm sorry, Clover," Kate said.

"It happens," she said with a shrug "I'm used to it." Her voice wavered and Kate could see she'd hurt her feelings. She put her arm around the lanky preteen. "You're nothing like your dad in all the wrong ways, and everything like him in all the right ones."

And that seemed to make things okay.

Gretchen and the girls left Kate to unpack and get adjusted while they went downstairs to make an early dinner and begin their homework. Clover's bedroom window looked out over the waterfront, and Kate wondered what Tyler was doing right now.

It was time to journal, she decided, and got out her notebook. Out of nowhere came a welling up of sadness, and she fought tears that poured out uncontrollably anyway. What was going on? Looking out over the glistening waters of the Columbia as it rolled slowly past, it hit her.

She didn't want to marry Randy. The prospect was like a lead weight around her neck. All of a sudden it was clear to her that going through with the wedding would be the worst decision she'd ever made.

Holy cow. How come I feel this way?

It hadn't been the kiss, the attraction to Tyler, which had triggered this feeling of dread. It was because her decision had finally been revealed in the light of day, and in the sunlight it didn't hold up. It wasn't what she wanted. It was what her parents wanted, what Randy wanted, what her friends wanted, what his parents wanted. Everyone wanted it except her.

Her pen stopped before she could commit anything to paper, as if writing it down would make it permanent. Or that someone might read her second thoughts. But they were more than second thoughts. This was real dread, real fear she was about to make the biggest mistake of her life.

She closed her eyes, and all she could see was Tyler and his blue eyes. Damn him! She tried to relax, shoo him out of her thoughts so she could examine her feelings for Randy uninterrupted…and yes, there it was. She found a lot of obligation, but not any desire or love of any kind. Was she doing this for all the wrong reasons? Had she sold out? The idea made her feel nauseous.

Kate abruptly stood up, slipped on her shoes, and dashed down the stairs to consult with Gretchen. Growing up, they'd been confidantes, and she'd always been able to tell Gretchen things she couldn't tell their mother, even though she knew her sister would tell her on her if it was really important, or if she was pressured. Kate needed sisterly advice and Gretchen's level head.

Gretchen must have sensed something, too, because she turned down her music and laid down her knife. Of course. All she'd ever had to do was look at Gretchen and she'd know something wasn't right.

"Were you nervous before you married Tony? I mean, so nervous you considered…"

"Breaking it off?"

It sounded so harsh, so permanent when Gretchen said it. "Well, not exactly." Kate avoided eye contact, even though Gretchen was watching her closely while she moved around the kitchen, not taking her eyes off her face. Then when their gaze met, Kate's tears welled up again.

"Ahh, sweetie," Gretchen said as she darted around the counter to hug her. "What's happened?"

Kate brushed the tears away with her palms, and then the backs of her hands, but the torrent wouldn't stop. Gretchen's gentle hug while she rubbed the tops of her shoulders just made the tears flow faster. Finally she pulled away from her sister's embrace and took a deep breath. "I'm just having huge second thoughts. I don't know why I didn't think about all these things sooner. I'm thinking I'm not ready. I mean…" she peered at her canvas slip-ons. "Did you question your decision to marry Tony? Really question it?" After she said the last sentence she had the nerve to meet Gretchen's concerned stare.

She saw how her sister studied her, looking for a crack in the veneer, something she could point out that would make her realize she was being foolish, something that would instantly change her attitude on the subject. She was hoping for some word of advice that would put it all into perspective so she could laugh at herself and move on with her plans.

But the look Gretchen gave her was all concern.

"From your appearance, I'd have to say to trust your gut. What do you think is right, Kate?" Gretchen was cautious and Kate could feel the tension, making the hair at the back of her neck stand at end.

"I'm not sure."

"Sort of bad timing this that one, sis."

"I realize. And I can't honestly say when I will feel okay about it." She hoped Gretchen would give her a sympathetic look, something to ease her pain. She wasn't that lucky. Her sister paced back and forth, wringing her hands, and then, as though she'd forgotten to do it sooner, pumped some hand cream into her palm and began rubbing her fingers together. She brought the lemony cook's moisturizer over and squirted a generous dollop into Kate's palm.

As the two sisters looked down, working the cream into their skin, Gretchen whispered, "How long have you felt this way?"

"I think for a while. But it really hit me on the plane up here. I felt like I was breaking out of jail, Gretchen."

"On the plane. Why would it raise its ugly head on the plane?"

Kate hoped she wouldn't have to reveal any of her trip, or her conversation with Tyler, but she did feel guilty, and it must have shown in her eyes, because Gretchen immediately seized on it.

"Who is he, Kate?"

CHAPTER 8

Kate,

I hope you don't mind if I just jump into the letter-writing thing. Thought maybe if I got this right off to you, I'd have a chance to read yours, too, before I go. No pressure, though. I know you have family things you are doing and I don't mean to intrude on that time.

I was just sitting here thinking about how meeting you happened so easily, it was like we'd known each other for a long time, and we picked up right where we'd left off. That never happens to me. Even before I joined the Teams, I was a pretty private person. Actually, I think I'm just naturally shy.

So it's pretty funny how much I want to know everything about you. Hope that doesn't make you nervous. I'm not meaning to be inappropriate, but I'm curious. What do you see as your future? Not that anything is wrong with working in your family's winery, but what would you do, if you could do anything else? Hope this doesn't offend you. If so, I'm sorry. I just wanted to know.

For me, it's pretty simple. When I get home from deployment, I do all the things I love doing. You'd probably find it boring, but after I get back, I want to just play in the surf, have some beers with my buddies on the Teams, and play some soccer wherever I can find a game. We get all smelly and play indoor soccer with some of the Mexican guys who clean our clocks. Seems to help take me down a peg or two when I get to feeling like Superman and savior of the world. Kind of an occupational hazard.

And of course it makes a difference if we have wounded or guys who didn't come back. That doesn't happen very often, but it happens. Those returns are different. We are under high stress over there, and when we come home, well, we just want to be normal and blend in like one of the regular crowd.

So one day, when I retire from the teams, I'd love to have a little farm, something small enough for me to work on my own. Got a couple of friends who might help me. Maybe plant some grapes. Do you know anything about planting grapes? What kinds are best for the climate in San Diego? Of course I don't know if I can afford anything there, so would maybe have to go someplace less expensive. I was thinking I'd take some correspondence courses from UC Davis if they have any. Steer me any way you can, if you know of something I could take online. I usually have some sort of internet connection for part of our deployment, and being able to do something like that takes my mind off the boredom.

Speaking of which, my mom always likes it when I say I'm bored. Then she knows I'm not in firefights or high-risk missions. All the same, everything is risky these days. You probably know the motto we use, "The Only Easy Day Was Yesterday." That's us. Never looking for a softer, gentler ride, because it doesn't exist in our field.

Wow. I've said a lot more than I intended to. Just nice to have someone listen to what's going on with me, especially someone so beautiful. Your fiancé is a lucky man, but I guess all the guys say that to you.

Well, it was nice meeting you, Kate. I hope I haven't said anything that scares you away. That would make me very sad.

He ended the letter with a smiley-face frown next to the word *sad*. He inhaled and scrawled his signature in big, flowing letters, hoping she'd think he felt more confident than he was actually was.

He looked it over, correcting spelling errors and changing one word back and forth a couple of times. He wished he'd written it on something nicer than the binder paper he'd found in his old desk. But that would have to be it for now. He'd post it in the morning—then he had a thought.

Leaning back in his chair, he smiled at his new plan.

CHAPTER 9

Kate and Gretchen hashed over all of Kate's fears after she briefly described her chance meeting with the SEAL. Her sister didn't pry until they'd discussed the reasons for her hesitation about going forward with the wedding. It was all focused on why the matchup with Randy was wrong for her. But it became obvious a huge part of her decision was due to meeting Tyler.

"So, what's he like?" Gretchen asked.

Kate leaned forward and lifted her coffee mug from the table, clutching it between her palms and savoring a sip of the now-cold liquid. She knew Gretchen was assessing her. "He's handsome, of course."

"Of course."

"He's gentle, but has something about him that's strong. Really strong."

"Well, he is a SEAL."

"Yes, but it's something else. I guess confidence is what I'd call it. He's, like, controlled."

"It's how they train them."

"No, it's more than that. He isn't just walking through life. He *lives* it. He embraces life. Living is precious to him."

Their eyes met for a second and then Gretchen looked away, giving Kate the respite she needed.

"We talked about all sorts of things in the hour plus plane ride. Afterwards he gave me—well, his friend gave me—a ride here. We stopped and had some lunch on the way, and, well, it was just like I'd known him my whole life." Kate waited for Gretchen to face her again. "It was seamless…does that make sense? Like I didn't have to do some big adjustment of myself just to be around him."

"Men who are trying to be charming, and who are good at it, make women feel that way all the time. Doesn't mean it's real. There are a lot of fakers out there. I've met a lot of them, unfortunately." Gretchen became pensive and stared down at her linked fingers as her elbows rested on her thighs.

"I've told myself dozens of times this uneasiness with the wedding plans has nothing to do with Tyler. I've searched deep inside, and I have to say honestly those feelings come from something I knew, but wasn't looking at. Talking to Tyler, even though we didn't talk about my future plans, brought all that to the surface. Does that make sense?"

"It does. Doesn't make it any easier."

"No."

"You say anything to Mom?"

"Of course not. I've hardly begun to think about what it means."

Gretchen stood, going to the kitchen to turn off something on the stove. The girls were being boisterous upstairs, arguing over something. She went to the base of the stairs and gave them a reprimand and ordered them to wash their hands and faces and come downstairs for dinner.

"So, what are you going to do?" she finally asked.

"I'll just take the weekend to think about it all. I don't want to talk to Randy until I have my thoughts organized."

"That'd be a good plan. Kate, I sure hope you know what you're playing with, here. A lot of money has been spent on this wedding already. If you're just having the jitters and later you change your mind, well, I can't say as that's never happened before, but you'd be putting a lot of people through things they might not forgive you for. Hell of a way to enter into a new family, know what I mean?"

"I agree. But right now, I'm not sure I want to go forward. I'm really not."

"Well, we have a problem, then."

"Yes, we do."

In the middle of dinner, Kate got a call from Randy. At first she didn't want to take the call, but Gretchen looked at her like she had sprouted green horns, so she pressed the answer button on her cell. As Randy started in, Kate slipped up the stairs and into Clover's room, closing the door behind her. She sat on the little bed and looked up at the posters of her ex-brother in law.

"...and so we thought maybe a carriage ride through the vineyard would be a nice touch. But that would mean the flowered archway you wanted would have to be moved. I met the driver, and the horses are gentle."

Randy talked on as if nervous to allow Kate to say a word. She realized he hadn't once asked her how the flight was, and she hadn't texted him to say she'd arrived safely.

Randy noticed her silence and lack of agreement and then asked, "Kate, are you okay?"

It took a long slow breath before she felt ready to respond. "No." It was all she could say.

"Are you ill?" he asked.

"No."

"Wanna tell me what's going on?"

Do I? Will I feel differently in the morning? Will I wake up in the middle of the night and realize I've been a fool?

Something welled up inside her. With strength she didn't realize she possessed, she began. "Randy, I'm rethinking this whole thing. I have to tell you that I'm not at all sure I'm ready to move forward."

"What? Over a carriage ride in the vineyard? If that's what's bothering you, Kate—oh, my God, that's no problem for me. Being a little dramatic, don't you think?"

"It's more than the carriage ride. I've been thinking about this for a while. I'm just not ready. I want to do this when I'm sure, Randy. I need more time."

His tone got reproving. He was curt, responding with a bitter, clipped attitude. "Mom and—"

"This has nothing to do with your mom. You family's lovely, Randy. Really lovely."

"So it's me?"

"No."

"You don't like how I've been making plans you think you should be making? No problem. I'll back off until you get your little hissy fit out of the way."

"It's not like that, Randy."

"Not like anyone isn't worrying about your cares, your likes and dislikes. For Chrissakes, Kate, everyone is doing their best. Fuck, if I'd known you'd get so upset over these plans—"

She didn't want to hear any more. "Randy, let me think about all this and call you in the morning, okay?" She knew she was about to say something she surely would regret.

"No, dammit. Don't you think you're being a little selfish?"

Yes. I'm being selfish about what kind of life I want to lead. "I need to mull things over a bit more and get them in a state where I can communicate to you more clearly. I don't want to say anything that would hurt your feelings," she continued. Although she knew no matter what she said the next time they talked, the damage had already been done. He was already hurt.

"And you think I can just sit on my hands and wait until you have the whim to call me and tell me you're in a better mood? God, how selfish, Kate. How inconsiderate. How ridiculous. Everyone has been working so hard for you. Waiting on you hand and foot. You're not even grateful—"

"Randy, stop."

"No, I fuckin' won't stop. You've got to get hold of yourself and buck up. I'm dealing with a lot here. We have a lot going on at the winery, and this big fuckin' wedding is happening right at season's peak. We're all making sacrifices. Going to cost us a fortune in lost revenue, put us behind in some things, but we're doing this for you. For us."

"Randy, don't go into that right now. I appreciate everything you and your family are doing—"

"And your family, Kate. You're mom has been spending money she frankly doesn't have on this wedding. Kind of inconsiderate of you, if you ask me. Of course, you haven't—"

"Randy, I'm calling it off."

There. She'd said it. That got him to stop talking as he sputtered on the other end of the phone, backpedaled, and then got syrupy sweet. Kate could feel the icy steel of his anger brewing. She realized then that he'd always had that edge to him that forced her to be and act and do certain things the way he wanted her to do them, that he liked to exert some subtle control over her, like he was the teacher and she was the student. But she didn't want to be a student. She wanted to be an equal partner. She now knew Randy would never allow her that.

"If you could just give me a day or two to think things over, perhaps you're right, Randy. I just need some time."

"No." It was his turn to say it. "No, absolutely not. You have to decide today, right now, what it is you want. You have to make a choice, Kate. A lot is riding on this."

Like what? What is more important than doing the right thing for my soul? It becoming very clear that Randy's vision of their relationship and her own were totally opposite. He was demonstrating he didn't care a bit for hers. And she knew as sure as she was alive that she didn't want to have anything to do with his.

The silence on the phone didn't bother her, because she knew what she was going to say.

"Then it's no, Randy. Today, I am not ready to marry you. And I certainly understand that if I change my mind, you might not be there for me any longer. I say it with a full heart. I love you. I really do. But I can't marry you."

She should have felt horrible, but she didn't. Kate felt the blood pulsing in her veins, greeting a life of her own choosing. She'd just dashed her future for something she had faith would be out there some day. And *that* wedding day would be totally different.

CHAPTER 10

Tyler was used to the early morning fog. He ran down the hill, across the neighborhood strip mall that housed a coffee shop, past the florist and dry cleaners and a women's gym. Then as he came up the other side, he wound around back to the frontage road overlooking the river. He had worked up a good sweat nearly two miles into his run, especially with the dips and hills, until he came to Kate's sister's house.

Tyler ran past the bungalow, taking a quick peek to see the upper windows were all open, but empty. Downstairs, the same assortment of bikes, plastic buckets and a pink and green dollhouse littered the front yard as it had yesterday. The chalk drawings on the concrete steps had been nearly washed away by rain the night before.

Coming back, he ran up the steps onto the wooden porch and stood for a second, catching his breathe, before he rang the doorbell. At first nothing happened, but then he heard the tap-tap-tap of small feet. A short shadow appeared at the glass window and he heard the large knob being turned with difficulty. As the heavy door creaked open, he was faced with a little princess who had remnants of face paint and freshly applied red lipstick creeping all the way up to her nose.

"Yes?" she asked, in a proper tone for a four-year-old.

"I'd like to see Kate, if she's here."

The door slammed shut. He heard an adult woman's voice on the other side of the glass, and the woman wasn't happy. Then he heard Kate's name being shouted. Tyler let his breathing settle down his anxiousness. The anticipation was killing him. Just before the door opened again, he realized he was practically naked. All he wore were a thin pair of bright blue running shorts and a yellow reflective tank top. And he was soaked with sweat.

Kate's fresh face was a welcome sight. That and the fact that she was surprised but not displeased to see him.

Thank God.

The silence between them was a bit awkward, however.

"Wow, Tyler. You're the last person I expected to see this morning." She leaned forward to look down the street, perhaps looking for a car. "You ran here from your mom's?" Her smile warmed his heart in some of those cold reaches where he'd never felt heat before.

"It really isn't that far. See that bright pink house over there?" He didn't step back, letting her lean very close to him so she could see the row of houses at a distance. He smelled soap and light cologne, and probably the smell of shampoo in her hair. One long lock fell forward and brushed his forearm.

"Not exactly hard to miss," she said as she swept her eyes up and came to stand within inches of his lips, her eyelashes fluttering, her cheeks flushed slightly as she licked her lips and didn't retreat to the safety of the doorway. They were both leaning toward each other in what would have been a kiss when he heard what must have been her sister's voice.

"Kate? Is everything—*Oh*!"

Her sister was a blonde version of Kate, a little taller and thinner, but with the same unmistakable eyes that held a reserve identical to Kate's.

Kate stepped back and introduced them.

"Well, come on in. I feed stray cats. I guess a stray runner or two won't do us any harm, right girls?"

There were cheers happening at his feet, and all five females ushered him in. The house had the same high ceilings and bright spaces as Tyler's mother's house, but wasn't full of colorful paintings. But Kate's sister had a collection of Inuit art, including a large totem. Masks with feathers and brightly-colored, sleek designs in green, red and black hung all over the walls. The collection was substantial.

"You want some coffee, or do you not partake?" Gretchen asked him. She was trying to be matter-of-fact but she was working hard to hide a smile that threatened to break out at any moment. "You want something to cover up?" she added without looking over his bare legs and chest.

"Would you like me to cover up?" He didn't know why he asked that, and worried it would offend.

"Not on my behalf." She cleared her throat. "Girls, let's let Aunt Kate speak with her friend here in private, okay? Let's get him some coffee."

The youngest daughter brought Tyler a beach towel. "Mother doesn't like sweaty men to sit on our couch." It was delivered with stern reprimand just as the towel was shoved into his groin.

"Thanks," Tyler said. "So noted."

He followed Kate to the living room until she whirled around abruptly. Good thing he'd maintained a two-foot distance in case he'd misread her earlier body language. She was about to say something when he reached into his pocket and produced the letter he'd written last night.

"I thought I'd deliver this in person, since I was in the area." She took the note and their fingers touched but didn't move away. He hooked his forefinger over hers and pulled her hand to his chest, crinkling the letter between them. "And the truth is, I couldn't wait to see you again."

Her glance down to his hungry mouth was all the encouragement he needed. He closed the gap between them quickly and pressed his lips to hers, drawing in her sweet softness. He involuntarily moaned when he felt her open to him. His next move was going to be to reach around her waist and pull her against him, but a voice to the side called a halt.

"Okay, I didn't see that. If Mom asks, I'm going to say I didn't see that. *Thank you Gretchen. You're welcome, Kate.* And here is your coffee, sir."

Tyler loved Gretchen already. She reminded him of some of his Team buds. He secretly loved women with big mouths who were not afraid to dish out their opinions, sometimes inappropriately. He liked them fearless. Gretchen was all that and more.

He held his hot mug in both hands and for a second felt a little self-conscious as Kate examined the coffee like it was entrails that revealed her fate. He set the mug down.

"Where were we?" he whispered to the side of Kate's face.

"You were going to kiss me again," she said as she kissed his neck, ran her tongue under his chin, no doubt tasting the salty sweat that had collected there. He wished he'd had a shower, but it didn't seem to matter to Kate. He placed his palms on her cheeks, eased her back a bit so he could examine her face.

"Kate. Kate. Kate. What are we going to do with you?"

She stood there with her blue eyes searching his and said not a word.

"I have to ask. What are we doing here?"

"You came to deliver a letter to me," she said again in a throaty voice. "I didn't expect the kiss, but now that I've had one, I want another. Would you mind?"

"Not at all."

He wasn't going to let any heat escape between them. He drank from her lips and, even as he wondered how she could be the kind of woman who was engaged to another man and be answering his kisses with her own, he pushed his worries aside.

But then he just couldn't ignore that dull thud in the pit of his stomach. He dropped his hands and stepped back.

"I'd like to talk a little, Kate, if you don't mind?"

"Sure. No problem." She brought the towel over and spread it on the couch for him, gave him his mug of coffee and took a seat perpendicular to him.

Tyler took a sip of the delicious home-brewed elixir and studied her again. "So, I have to ask you. You said yesterday you were engaged." He studied his coffee. "You know, where I come from that means something. And it means I have no business being here, and probably shouldn't have come in the first place."

"But you don't understand."

"Okay, then help me understand, Kate."

"I've been plagued with second thoughts for a month now. When we talked on the plane yesterday, the world somehow shifted for me. I mean, I realized I was just kind of going through the motions with this wedding."

"Okay. That's kind of hard to believe, but go on."

"Gretchen and I talked until early this morning about it, Tyler. My fiancé called me last night and we sort of had words. Well, he had words. I told him I wasn't sure. He kind of went off on me. And, well, the bottom line is that we broke it off. I'm not sure..."

He could see it was painful to talk about, which was a good sign, Tyler thought. God knew he didn't want to fall for a girl who slipped in and out of fiancés the way some slipped in and out of beds. He knew that wasn't the way she was, so was glad for the confirmation. But it still niggled at his insides.

"Then he just wouldn't give you the time to think things out? That what you're saying?"

Kate nodded, looking down at her lap.

"He's a fuckin' idiot." Tyler winced at his language. "Pardon me, I didn't mean it like it sounded."

Kate remained silent. Nodding, she said to her hands, "I think I know what you meant." Then she lifted her eyes, smiled, and said, "No, Tyler. I've been the one who's been the idiot. And now I've hurt a lot of people."

"Hurt?"

"My mom, his mom—everyone's been making plans for months. Paying for things. No one realized—heck, I didn't realize—I was so ambivalent." She started nodding again. "I'm noticing things now I didn't see before."

Tyler found some discomfort in her words. He wasn't sure he liked being even part of the reason for her broken engagement. He started regretting he'd allowed himself to get entangled. And now he was beginning to feel like he'd been partially responsible for hurting all those people, people he didn't even know. What fuckin' right did he have to go jumping in, causing chaos? Maybe coming over to the house this morning hadn't been such a good idea after all.

Gretchen poked her head in. "You want to stay for breakfast, Tyler?"

"No, thanks, ma'am," Tyler said as he stood. He was getting stiff from the lack of a good stretch. He shook out his legs, picked up his coffee and took it to the kitchen. "Thanks so much for the coffee. I'm going to head out now."

"Stay," Kate said to his back.

"No, Kate. I'm going to go finish my run, get clean, and then I've got things to do with Mom."

It was feeling hard to say goodbye, but that was what he was going to do. He had to do it, even though he was tempted to continue with the lovely Kate. He just couldn't step on the other man's toes. And yes, even if the fuckin' guy was a complete idiot.

At the doorway he said the words he knew he had to say. "I think we got a little ahead of ourselves, Kate. You're in some confusion, and hell, I'm just a dog, a military guy getting ready to leave. I think I jumped the gun a bit and I'm sorry that I—You know, things are simple for me. Pretty girl wants to kiss me. But marriage, all this stuff you've got to decide, I don't want any part of that, Kate. That's not my place."

He could see her lower lip tremble.

"Look," he said as he held her upper arms, keeping her a good distance from his chest. "I'm sure if you call the guy, he'll have thought things over and, well, you know how it goes. In a day or two, you'll be so happy to be together, you won't know what hit you."

"No. You're wrong." She wouldn't look up at him and she was stammering a bit. It nearly broke his heart. Like a brother, he drew her to him, held her secure but didn't rub or initiate anything.

"You're a sweetheart, Kate. The guy must be crazy for you. And crazy out of his mind at the thought of losing you. Give him a chance. Go make up and have a nice life." He pulled her away from him and tipped her chin up with his thumb and forefinger.

Oh Jesus, those lips! What was he going to do? Oh yes, he was going to be the warrior he'd been trained to be. Do the right thing.

He was going to walk away. Forever.

But he still hoped in a week or two maybe he'd get a letter.

CHAPTER 11

Kate spent the day trying to dodge her sister's questions. She dialed Randy's number several times and didn't get an answer but left the same message, saying she was sorry she had hurt him, and to please understand her indecision. She begged for time. She begged for patience.

She knew he was avoiding her call. And just what was she going to tell him? Her decision not to go forward with the wedding was still unchanged. And as difficult as it was to bear, she was still glad Tyler hadn't inserted himself. He was right. He didn't belong there. Not now. Maybe not ever.

She called her mother.

"Oh, my God, Kate, you'd think the winery had gone up in flames, the way those people—" Kate could always tell when her mother was upset with the future in-laws because she started to call them *those people*—"have been acting. Like I'm supposed to fly up there and knock some sense into you."

"I'm sorry, Mom."

"So, I gotta ask you. What the hell is going on? And couldn't you wait to tell Randy in person if you had questions? Call a family pow-wow?"

"That's just it, they'd try to talk me out of it."

"Well, yes, because that's what we do for people we love, Kate. You're out of your head if you think we don't want you to marry Randy. He's perfect for you."

But I don't love him, Mom.

"Did he say something, honey? Did he offend you? Give me some kind of clue here, please. I'm drowning in questions."

Kate watched her sister walk into the room, drying a bowl. Just the fact that Gretchen had appeared gave her the support she needed. "Mom, I'm not sure I love him. I'm not sure he's the right one for me."

"Oh, Lord save us. You gotta be kidding me, Kate."

"I'd give anything if—"

"When did this happen? When did you first start feeling this way?"

"It just came on me fast, Mom. I guess getting away from everyone, up here, where I could think—"

"Gretchen isn't doing one of her anti-male talks again, is she? I'll wring her little neck—"

"No! Mom, listen." She glanced at her sister's worried face. "No one has said anything to me."

Gretchen rolled her eyes, knowing their mother had made a comment about her. She shook her head disgustedly.

Kate's mother was speaking urgently and fast. And she was getting angry. Finally Kate had to interrupt.

"I. Don't. Love. Him."

Her mother sputtered and erupted in a spate of words Kate couldn't understand, but eventually calmed down.

"That's enough of that talk, young lady. You get your butt back down here to California. You tell your sister to put you on the next plane available."

"I can do that myself, Mom. I'm a big girl."

"You've done quite enough already. Kate, what were you thinking? I don't understand what could have made you change your mind."

"He's just not the right one. I care for him, mom. But I don't want to *marry* him. Haven't you ever had second thoughts?"

There was a pause that disturbed Kate. "I never had any second thoughts about your dad. Not one."

"Well there, you see? I do, and I need time to sort those doubts out. Randy won't even return any of my calls. I've tried all morning."

"I think he's trying to arrange a plane to come get you."

"Great. I'll be a hostage. At my own wedding."

"It's not like that, Kate."

"No? Well then, what would you call it?"

"You have the wedding jitters. You're confused. They want to help."

"No, Mom. They want to pressure me. Don't let them do this."

"I'm sorry, honey. I can't control those people any more than you can."

"And you want your daughter to marry their son anyway. Why is that, I wonder?"

After a brief hesitation, her mother sighed and said, "Yes, honey, I do, because it's what's best for you."

"I'm not going to do it. You know me. The more they push, the more I'll resist."

She knew her mother wouldn't be able to disagree. Kate was legendary for her stubbornness.

"Okay, I've got Marsha calling on the other line. Can I at least tell her you're coming home and will discuss this with Randy in the next day or two? Can I tell her that?"

"Yes. I don't want any private planes coming up here to fetch me. I'll take the next commercial flight out I can. Probably tomorrow."

Her mother sighed. "Okay. I'll tell her. Call me back later tonight, okay?"

"Will do."

Kate slumped into a chair and began to bawl her eyes out. Gretchen was at her side.

"I'm so sorry, sweetie. God, I wish I could be of help here, but just know I feel for what you're going through." She rubbed Kate's neck and shoulder, and then dropped to her knees and gave her a hug. "You'll do the right thing, kid. You always do."

"Except this time I've really botched it up."

"No, Kate. Really messing up would be marrying the wrong guy. Trust me, I know a lot about that."

Randy did return her call later that evening, but she was in the shower. She played back the message and was grateful she hadn't been able to catch his call live. What he said made her blood boil.

"Kate. What you're doing is a big mistake. A big fuckin' mistake. We have treated you with respect and you show none in return. My family has welcomed you into the fold. You have to understand this is a huge inconvenience for everyone. The functions they turned down so they could have everything ready for us—that's real dollars and cents, Kate, not some fantasy."

He paused, then continued his rant. "You live in some kind of fairyland where everything has to be perfect and that's not the way life is. Do you think I'm one hundred percent happy with everything about our relationship? I'm not. But do you think I let these doubts or thoughts interfere with the planning, or the fact that I'm committed to you? Yes, I'm committed to you. Or at least I *was* until you pulled this little fiasco.

"Now I don't know who you are, Kate. You're not the woman I thought you were. I just never thought you'd pull this kind of stunt."

The rest of the call droned on until he'd used up all the message time. Kate was furious.

She sat at the desk in front of the window and pretended she could see through the dark to the Columbia River winding slowly past. She felt cold. She was in shock. As she twisted in the chair, Tyler's letter, which she'd forgotten, fell out of her pocket.

Her heart was racing as she carefully unfolded the binder paper and read his letter. And then she knew what she had to do.

She couldn't wait for morning.

CHAPTER 12

After dinner, Tyler checked in with his LPO, Kyle Lansdowne, double-checking orders and making sure there were no changes to their deployment.

"We're good. They're saying prepare for six but we might be home in four," Kyle said. "How's it hanging up there in Portland?"

"Good. Mom's got a gallery function tomorrow night. Kenny's batshit as hell. Thinking I should bring him down there and give him some time with Cooper."

"You don't want to do that, Tyler."

"Why the hell not? The rain up here is melting his brain. No sunshine."

"Cooper's got the little one now. And he's about as sleep-starved as he was during BUD/S. Libby's cool and just as fine as ever, but Cooper. Oh. My. God. You'd think this baby was made out of porcelain the way he's so careful. Won't let any of us hold the little sucker, either."

That was good news. "Glad the baby came before we deploy."

"Roger that, Tyler."

"Shit, Lanny, I'm sorry." Tyler was referring to the fact that Kyle's wife, Christy, was going to deliver their second while he was on deployment. It wasn't certain he'd be given leave to come home for it, since it depended on what they found when they got overseas.

"No worries. She understands. Sucks, but she understands. But as for Cooper, and having his first, I'm not sure we could have gotten him to go otherwise."

"Bet the girls are loving the baby, though." Tyler noticed his voice faded as he spoke.

"You okay?" Lansdowne asked.

"Yeah." Kyle knew all the members of SEAL Team 3 like they were blood brothers, which, in a very real sense, they were, since they'd spilled blood together. Even the wives stuck close together. The babies would play together. The community would close ranks around the new mom and child and try to fill the void left by Kyle's absence. Tyler wondered how they did it.

"You gettin' laid?"

Kyle always wanted to know if his guys were regular.

"Shit, Kyle, I just got here."

"So that's a big fuckin' no, then."

"As a matter of fact I met a girl."

"Fuck's sake, Tyler. What are you waiting for, a marriage proposal?"

That comment stung more than it would have before yesterday. Before Kate and those couple of kisses in the donut shop, and the one today at her sister's. God, he wished he'd met her before that Randy dude had. He dismissed that thought as unhelpful. "She's engaged."

"Well, then you're wasting your time. Or am I getting something wrong here?"

"She's confused."

"Of course she's confused. She met you, and now she's weak at the knees in love with her SEAL fantasy man. Get out of Dodge, Tyler. Leave her alone and get some real booty that won't make you feel all guilty. We don't want any of that coming up next week, you understand?"

"Of course I understand."

"Okay, I gotta go."

"Tell Christy hi for me."

"Will do." After a brief pause, Kyle added, "And Tyler?"

"Yes, sir?"

"Go get fuckin' laid."

It had never seemed like such a burden before, but he didn't want to just run out and find a girl to have sex with. This change surprised him a little. All he could think about was Kate. Darn it all. He was going to have to wait at least two weeks for the military mail to catch up to him, since he knew wasn't going to stop by her sister's house anymore. Not that he wouldn't look out the window and try to find it. He'd already discovered he couldn't see the house from his mother's, but he'd tried all afternoon just the same, and always came up with the same result.

He also prepared himself for the real possibility she wouldn't write back.

Whatever. It was out of his hands. She was probably out of his league anyway, he thought.

He fingered the notebook he'd started in high school, and the unfinished letter to Karen. He wondered what happened to her. He did a search on Facebook and couldn't find a listing, which probably meant she had a married name now, not the one he knew in high school. He wasn't allowed to have a Facebook page because of what he did, but he'd set up the persona of a twenty-year-old college student and used that account to surf the internet.

He searched the winery where Kate worked. The pictures were lush with views of golden rows of grapes and large oak barrels. There was a family photo of the Hellers and Kate wasn't in the picture, which Tyler thought very odd. They had three boys. Handsome ones. He didn't know which one was the fiancé but he secretly hoped it was the middle one, who was a little chubby.

Now why are you thinking that way? He understood he felt more than just a little competitive with the guy who'd gotten there first and now was blowing it, in Tyler's opinion. But then perhaps he'd feel the same way if the roles were reversed. Women confused him, mostly because he didn't want to hurt them, so didn't engage fully. He'd never found that right one, like he'd told Kate on the plane yesterday. Was that just yesterday? Wow.

Something in the way she looked at him just melted the crust he'd formed. Somehow she had gotten inside that veneer, and he'd just jumped right in. Was stupid, but kind of satisfying, in a way. No, not satisfying. Exciting. Whatever she could give him, no matter if she wrote him every six months, he'd take what she'd give, and he'd not ask for anything more. And he wasn't going to do anything more until she made up her mind.

Besides, by that time, she'd have moved on to a cowboy or a fireman or some other kind of hero. Yes, that might explain it. She had a fascination for heroes. She had her orderly life all planned out, and then he had to waltz in and shake things up a bit. Kind of like what they did overseas with the Snatch N Grabs. Just stir things up and see who runs where and to whom.

He would wait, because somewhere inside he knew it would be worth it. No matter how long it took. All the right things had happened, despite all his good intentions. He'd just wait it out and have faith in a future he had no fuckin' control over.

Instead of turning in, he pulled out another of his sister's steamy romance novels and began reading. When he got to the first sex scene he skimmed it, then took a shower.

He wondered if there'd be any cute girls at the gallery party tomorrow night, and he set his sights on perhaps meeting someone nice there. He hoped he wouldn't wind up in the morning looking at someone's green or purple hair.

No champagne for you, buddy. He was going to make it a sober night. Besides, the audience at these events was already interesting enough. Alcohol enhancements were rarely needed.

CHAPTER 13

Kate was at the front door of the pink house at nine o'clock sharp, hoping she hadn't missed Tyler. His mother greeted her warmly and invited her inside while she got her son. She had on a smock with paint smudges all over it, and her long, silver hair was fixed to the top of her head in a rhinestone clip. With her large brown eyes and her deep red lipstick, she looked like a paint palette herself. Soft music was playing in a sunny great room which was covered in large paintings full of brilliant, abstract shapes resembling jungle flowers. She could smell strong coffee brewing and secretly longed for a cup.

Tyler was in jeans and a white V-neck T-shirt, but barefoot. His shiny, deep brown hair had been hurriedly finger-combed. He did not look like he was happy to see her, and she began to wonder if she'd made a mistake.

"You woke me up," he said.

"I'm sorry."

Tyler's mother disappeared into the kitchen, and he offered her a seat on a heavy leather couch covered in patchwork quilts.

"I just came by to give you this." She reached in her shirt and pulled out the folded letter she'd tucked into her bra. She blushed as she handed him the warm paper.

He studied the folded note before he said anything. Kate immediately thought about leaving, sure that her visit had not been wise.

Then he surprised her. "You wanna go to a gallery party tonight? My mom has a showing, a big champagne reception. I don't know if you like those types of things, kind of boring, but—"

"I'd love to go." It was out of her mouth before she had a chance to think about it.

"Okay. Well, I was going to go for a run." Tyler was looking at her lips again, and she was pleased it had the same effect on her it did yesterday.

"I'm off to the bookstore," she said truthfully. "Think I'll pick up a couple of your sister's books, too—"

"Oh, I have several here you can *have*. Did you finish the one I gave you?"

"Yes. Last night."

"Wow. You're a fast reader."

"She's a great writer."

"I'll tell her you said so."

"Good."

The distance between them was awkward. The small talk wasn't helping, either.

"Tyler. I'm sorry I put you through all that stuff yesterday. Can we just start over, sort of hit the reset button?"

"I don't think there is a 'we' in there, Kate. You are engaged." He looked down at her hand and it registered on his face that she had removed her ring. "Wow, so, I guess you didn't exactly patch things up with your fiancé."

"Ex-fiancé. I think that's probably the kindest term I could use. I'm not so sure I'll even have a family or a job to go home to, but he's definitely my ex." She shrugged, deciding to toy with him. "Not that it matters, or anything."

"No," he shrugged.

She heard him hitch his breath a bit, and thought perhaps she'd stung him slightly.

"I mean it doesn't matter, if that's what you want." He seemed shy and uncomfortable.

What is it I want? I want something I don't have right now. I want something else.

"Why don't we meet downtown after you get your run in? I'll go to Powell's and we'll meet at Mother's? You can have a big breakfast after your run? My treat? My way of making amends."

"Kate," he started.

"Just breakfast. No big, deep discussions, okay? Then we can meet later at the gallery."

"Okay, then." It seemed to satisfy him. He held her letter in his right hand as she exited the front door and ran down the steps to Gretchen's second car with two kiddie car seats strapped in the back.

She thought she'd be the first to arrive at the restaurant but found him waiting in the lobby. His hair was slicked down from his recent shower and, as he gave her a peck on the cheek, she smelled his cologne and felt a fresh shave. She liked that he'd worn a dark sports jacket over his jeans.

They were ushered to a corner and given brunch menus. The restaurant featured mix and match plates, silverware, chairs and tables, with an eclectic assortment of paintings and plaques, as well as bookshelves filled with dog-eared paperbacks. The espresso machine screamed. Steam clouded the windows. The Sunday brunch crowd had dispersed somewhat, so the tables around them were vacant.

"My mom loves this place," Tyler said. "She has some paintings here somewhere." He turned and examined the walls.

She watched his profile, the way his Adam's apple moved when he swallowed, how full and long his eyelashes were. The thickness of his chest and neck seemed almost more so today, though covered in clothes. "I can't find them," he said after he'd searched the walls he could see from where he sat.

"Maybe she sold them."

"That could be. She's getting very popular now."

"How long has she been painting?"

"Ever since I was little. I've always seen her with paint streaks in her hair."

"Sort of like my little niece, Angela. She is constantly playing dress-up."

"Ah, a budding makeup artist."

"Yes. Or perhaps a painter as well. Gretchen's got her hands full."

"What about her husband?"

"Ex-husband."

"You guys send 'em away don't you? This a sisterly trait? Your parents are still together, I think, right?"

"Right. And no, I wouldn't exactly blame Gretchen's divorce on Gretchen. Her ex is Tony Sanders, the basketball player."

"Okay."

"And he didn't exactly honor his marriage vows. It was all a little too public for Gretchen. And the girls."

"Okay, so perhaps it's not a trait."

"No, definitely not." Their eyes met. The chemistry between them was there again, making her ears buzz.

She asked him about his deployment and he told her what he could. Fact was, he knew very little about it. He talked about the BUD/S training, about some of his single friends, and what it was like living in San Diego after being raised in Portland.

"I couldn't live here," she said. "Too cold and not enough sunshine."

"On that we agree. I think San Diego is perfect. Only varies about ten degrees. Ever."

"Sounds nice. I've actually never been there."

"Then consider yourself invited." His smile warmed her. It was becoming something she needed more of, the more he dished it out.

Without making a promise to visit, she asked him if he'd ever been to Sonoma County, where she lived.

"As a matter of fact, yes. Got a friend who has a small vineyard. A former Team guy."

"Really?"

He chuckled. "What, you don't think we retire, go do other things, I mean ordinary things like ordinary people do?"

She liked the dance in his eyes and the dimple on the right side of his mouth. "That's not what I was thinking," she said.

"Then what were you thinking, Kate?"

If she were honest, she'd have to say that she was thinking how nice his kiss had tasted, how hard his chest had been when he'd pulled her to him with urgency. How she wanted to see his bare shoulders again and the muscular thighs she'd looked at yesterday. She was thinking—no, feeling—what it would be like to make love with him. And she didn't dare tell him any of that. So she said nothing.

He shot a quick glance down at her mouth again and then dropped the subject as he stared out the window. A light rain had begun to fall. "Bad day for a walk," he said.

She watched his profile. "I don't know. Makes everything smell fresh and clean. If we had an umbrella, a walk might be nice."

That got his attention. "I think my mom has one in her car we could use."

Their eyes met again. Her heart was racing. She laced her fingers together on the tabletop and he placed his large hand over her hands and squeezed. The intimate gesture tugged at her heart. The place between her legs began to throb with need. It was so foolish to want someone as badly as she wanted him right now, but she just didn't care. Something powerful was overtaking her body, and she was going to surrender to it, no matter what the cost.

"Come on. I have an idea," he said.

Outside she was squinting up at the droplets of rain when he pulled her under the eaves of the old restaurant and kissed her hard. She lost herself in the way his tongue played with hers. Her thigh rubbed against his erection as she moaned into him, melting and giving herself up to his passion. One hand cupped her head, fingers digging into her hair as he squeezed and pulled her face into his commanding her mouth and uncorked something wild inside her.

"Oh, God, Kate. You've got to stop me."

"Why?" she whispered into his ear.

"Because I can't stop."

"I don't want you to."

"It isn't wise."

She put her fingers over his lips. "Shhh. I don't want to hear about what's wise. Give me what you can, and let me decide if it's wise or not."

He laughed, throwing his head back.

"What's so funny?" she asked.

"I wanted to give you more time. Kate, I don't want to be the rebound guy. I don't do that."

"For a guy, you sure think a lot." She scrunched up her nose and waited until he understood she was messing with him.

He laughed again, studying her face, focusing on her lips again. "Ah, fuck it," he said as he kissed her again, wrapping his powerful arms about her waist and pressing her against his length.

Within walking distance there was a boutique hotel he knew about. The elevator ride to the third floor was a blur. The anticipation was killing her. Her panties were wet, and she could feel sweat pooling between her breasts. Her nipples ached against the fabric of her bra. One of Tyler's hands had snaked up under her shirt, and he rubbed her back, and then headed down inside the back of her pants.

The elevator doors opened and he took her hand, leading her down the hallway. They had a room at the corner. Due to the vintage nature of the hotel, the inside was barely big enough for the queen-sized bed it contained. The musty smell of the old hotel was comforting, as were the sounds through the open window of traffic swishing past on the street below.

He removed his jacket and approached her, helping her off with hers. She pulled up his T-shirt. Prominent right over his heart was a design of a compass with thorns and other Celtic designs in the borders.

"So I'll always know my way home," he whispered. "So I'll follow my heart."

She kissed him there, then rubbed her check against it, listening to his heart.

"It's there, honest."

"I'll say." She reveled in the sensations as her palms traveled the rippled surface of his abs and chest, over the smooth tattoo and his nipples, pulling the cotton T-shirt up and over his head. She tasted him under his ear, at his breastbone. His hands held her rear and squeezed, then urgently tugged at the button and zipper of her jeans to slide them down her thighs. She pulled her top over her head and watched him bend down and kiss the tops of her breasts, slipping his hot tongue under the bra to find her nipples. Her stomach muscles clenched under his ministrations.

Her bra fell loose and his palms cupped her flesh, pinching her nipples, suckling and pulling at them, giving her exquisite pain. She worked on his button fly, and after a few seconds they were both completely naked.

"I have something, unless you—"

"Thank you," she said.

Reaching into the pants at his ankles, he found a foil packet and sheathed himself while Kate ran her hand over the hard ridges of his member, squeezing him, reaching back and squeezing his balls, which made him gasp.

He brought her closer to the bed, then crawled up on it and leaned back on the headboard, his cock at full attention. She followed right behind him, seating herself over him and feeling his palms slide over her thighs as he gripped her hips and sank her down over him. She was so wet, the friction of his size stimulated her insides and ignited her libido. He ground her body over him, raising her up slightly and then plunging into her deeper.

The relaxation of the tension between them and the way they eased into the feel of their bodies against each other was delicious. He moved one palm to the small of her back, arching her forward so he could lean up to her breasts and suckle. The deeper he seated inside her, the more she wanted him. Her muscles held him, squeezed his shaft as her body rocked and stretched to receive him deeper still.

She held her hair atop her head, arching and grinding her torso, riding his cock. Then she released her hair and balanced herself on his shoulders, looking down at him while she rose and fell, as his hands gripped the sides of her hips, as they gazed into each other's eyes. He bent forward to taste her lips and draw more moans from her. She began to shudder as she rode him with a slow rhythm up and down, undulating and grinding when she had him fully inside her.

He deftly withdrew and flipped her over onto her back, spread her knees, and sucked at her labia, devouring her juices.

His hot tongue rimmed her opening, and then sank inside. He sucked and bit the top of her thighs, running his teeth over her delicate flesh and making her cry out. He scooped his arm under her, arching her breasts toward him, kissing her neck, covering her lips and then plucking and running his teeth over her nipples. She felt like an instrument he played, working her body, which was fine-tuned and more than ready for him.

She urged him to come inside her again, raising her knees up against her ears. His thick cock found her opening and eased inside, then began a back and forth motion, picking up speed. He scooted them to the edge of the bed, holding her wrists above her head with one large hand. The intensity and depth of his penetration was new for her. He released her wrists and immediately dropped her hands to his butt cheeks, squeezing them and pulling him deeper inside her. The powerful muscles of his ass and lower back tensed and released in the quiet hush of the darkened room. With one hand she found the spot where he was rooted inside her, and she ringed his shaft with two fingers, squeezing his balls gently with the other fingers as he rammed inside deeper and deeper.

She felt the low vibration of her long orgasm beginning deep inside, until it traveled the length of him. Her internal muscles clamped down on him, held him as she spiraled out of control. She dug her fingernails into his back as the orgasm rocked her world, until she could feel him spending inside his protection.

His heartbreaking cry at the loss of his control spurred her on. She found his mouth and their tongues clashed as she inhaled whatever she could gather from him. It was simply not possible to get enough. A violent series of spasms overtook him as he jerked several times and then collapsed onto her chest.

Her heart beat wildly, pounding blood into her ears and the tips of her fingers and toes as his chest pressed against hers, matching every undulating movement she had with one of his own.

And then he was done.

"God, Kate," he whispered.

"Shhh," she lovingly whispered into his temple. "Stay inside me? Rest, Tyler, rest inside me." She brushed the back of his head with her fingertips, following down his spine, and then over his butt cheeks. His powerful lower back muscles still moved him within her and sent little delicious waves of further pleasure. She never wanted it to end.

As their bodies finally unwound from each other Kate realized a new, beautiful chapter had opened in her life. A romance she'd only read in books was manifest in flesh and blood with her this day. All she wanted to do was take his passion and give him more in return.

CHAPTER 14

Tyler hadn't allowed himself to sleep, although he needed it. He wanted to remember her, the way she dreamed, the way her little finger twitched, the way the back of her hand brushed her forehead as she mumbled something in her dreams.

Dream of me, sweetheart. Bring me with you.

And just as he knew he could do this every day of his life, he also knew she was not his to take. The dark reality that she was confused, that there would be other powerful forces in Kate's life who would exert pressure over her and make her question this afternoon of beautiful sex, made him shiver.

It would have to be worth it, he decided. But he couldn't help hoping somehow this thing between them could work.

He felt a pang of regret that he didn't have more than just a few days—not nearly enough time to develop a proper relationship with Kate—before he had to ship out for several months. And he'd have to be prepared for the Dear John letter he would most likely get. He'd seen what it did to guys overseas who didn't prepare themselves for that eventuality. As much as they trained men to do the things they did, falling in love and getting stung by a relationship, and then coming unraveled while trying to save your own life and the lives of others in the killing fields, was one of the toughest things about being a SEAL.

He'd seen good men have to leave the Teams because of a breakup at home. God, he didn't want that to happen to him. But he wouldn't be there to talk with her, reason with her, make her understand how incredibly wonderful and perfect she was for him. He didn't know how to grow a relationship, but he sure as hell knew when an existing one was so totally right.

While training was the solution to always being prepared, with love, and he was absolutely sure that's what this was, the solution was to let it bloom, let her come to him with all the intensity she could muster, because God knew, he wanted that with her. And if she didn't have it, she just didn't have it. There was not a damned thing he could do about it.

It was going to be Kate's battle to fight on her own. While he was over there fighting the bad guys, she'd be home fighting for them.

Her warm, soft derriere fit against him as he spooned himself behind her and held her while she slept. Their second lovemaking had been less urgent, but even more beautiful than the first. Her delicate, feminine side was reaching out to him, trusting him with her heart. He felt it pull on him with golden tethers he willingly submitted to. Whatever happened in the next days and weeks or months to come, he knew he'd always love her like no other before or after. He was hoping she'd be his last lover, if she'd have him. But that was going to be a delicate negotiation.

His thumbs over her nipples must have tickled her because she turned in his arms and faced him.

"Tyler, tell me exactly how many days we have left before you have to go."

"I leave day after tomorrow."

"That's not enough time."

"You're right, Kate. But it's all we have."

"I want to just stay here, then."

He laughed at that. Yeah, there was a part of him that wished for the very same thing. "You know that's not possible."

"I didn't think it was possible to find this," she said, and then kissed him. "Or this," she caressed his cheek with the backs of her fingers. "Or this," she undulated her mound against his length and—*hallelujah, yes* there was going to be a round three.

They lingered in the shower too, and decided they'd keep the hotel room for after the party. Kate planned to go back up to her sister's to get ready, and Tyler would take care of some errands for his mother. After some long kisses and near clothing malfunctions, Kate left, and Tyler was left to watch her drive away.

At six o'clock sharp Tyler presented himself at Gretchen's. Kate had obviously been crying, so when she slipped upstairs to get her purse he decided to open the subject with her sister.

"Look, Tyler," Gretchen said, "I don't know much about you, but what I do know is pretty good. However, you're not out of the woods yet."

"Gotcha." He liked her honesty. Made it easy to be with her. He never understood why women had to cover up what they were really feeling by lying.

"I'm going to tell you she's paying an awful price for this."

"This? I'm not doing this."

"Beg your pardon? Are you blind?" Gretchen said to him without expression.

"I don't understand what's going on here. You asking me to step away, is that it?"

"Hell, no. And it wouldn't do any good anyway. What I'm saying is that, if you mess with her heart, I don't care who you are or who your buddies are, I'll find you and kick your ass."

Tyler chuckled. Gretchen didn't.

"Then you wanna tell me what's going on, Gretchen?"

"He's coming up on the corporate jet. And she won't meet with him."

"Who?"

"Randy. He wants to take her home with him."

"So what does she say?"

"Well, let's see. There was this little comment about a hotel downtown I'm not supposed to know about, so when the guy shows up at my door tonight, I don't have to tell him she's in a hotel with another guy. I'm not happy about this situation. Those people don't give up, Tyler."

"Like I'm some piece of meat." Kate's voice shot through the room.

"Kate, honey, maybe you better meet with Randy. This party isn't as important as that. You owe it to them."

"So now you're on their side?" He could see her tears were threatening to erupt again.

"No, I'm on your side. I didn't know about this when we made our plans today."

"Neither did I."

"But now you're tied up. Honestly, Kate. You should have called me. If you're still here tomorrow—"

"If I'm still here tomorrow? What kind of a comment is that?"

"Honey, I'm just saying we didn't know this, and now the situation has changed. You can't just duck away. I'm not going to let you do that, Kate."

"He's right, Kate," Gretchen added. "Even if you just tell him in person what you told him over the phone, you can't ignore the fact that he's coming up here to see you."

He could see she understood there wasn't a choice. "Kate, we'll talk in the morning. You call me tomorrow. I'll still be here."

Reluctantly, he left without giving her a kiss or a hug. And he hoped it wasn't the last time he'd see her. He'd remember her standing at the foot of the stairs in that killer red dress, her hair flowing about her shoulders, unbelievably beautiful, but miserable.

On the way to his mother's gallery, he called his LPO.

"I need a word, Kyle."

"Shoot, but make it quick. We're expected someplace and Brandon is in one of his moods."

"Okay, the lady I mentioned."

"Who is engaged."

"That one, yes. I love her, Kyle."

"Fuck me, Tyler. Bad. Very bad timing. You shouldn't be doing that."

"It's done, the deed is done. I'm asking for advice, here. Should I just leave, forget I met her, just come back home?"

"Probably. Is that what you're going to do?"

"Shit, no. Her fiancé is coming up in a chartered jet to talk some sense into her. My mom's gallery thing is tonight, too."

"Yeah. You better get home tomorrow. Be there for your mama and then get your butt back to Coronado where you belong. Dammit, Tyler. When I told you to get laid I didn't say to go lie down in a snake pit."

"I just—you're right. I fucked up."

"So, make it right."

He whispered, "Yeah. Thanks, man."

The gallery was buzzing with people when Tyler arrived. He grabbed a glass of champagne immediately. As soon as his mother found him, he was paraded around the room like a stuffed toy.

He was introduced to not one, but two young ladies with purple hair. Later, he stood with his father while they watched his vibrant mother talk to buyers and the gallery owner, describing her paintings and her process.

Tyler watched his father, a quiet man, thoroughly enjoy following his mother around, soaking up her animation and her love for what she was doing. It was then he realized how deeply his father loved her. He didn't have to be with her in the limelight. As long as he was the man who took her home.

He wondered which man Kate would choose.

And either way, it would be fine. Somehow, he'd find a way for it to be fine. After all, there would always be the letters.

CHAPTER 15

Randy's rented car pulled up to Gretchen's porch. Kate's hands fluttered nervously at her waist. She put her shoes back on, took a drink of water, and waited for the doorbell. Gretchen had taken the girls to a movie to give them some privacy.

She opened the door and saw Randy's miserable face. He made a step towards her and she backed up. "Not ready for this, Randy. We need to talk first."

He had one hand on his hip and the other tunneling through his hair, a worried expression blooming just on the edge of anger.

"Then I'll take you to dinner," he said formally.

"You don't have to do that, Randy."

"Humor me, Kate." He examined her hand and saw that she'd removed the ring.

"Wait here," she said as she dashed upstairs. Retrieving the ring from her cosmetic bag, she brought it back down and placed the sizeable rock in Randy's palm.

"Kate," he tried to keep her hand in his, but she was quicker.

"I can't marry you, Randy. I just can't."

"But why? Is there someone else?"

Is there someone else? Someone else with blue eyes, someone who made her feel wonderful just standing next to him? She wasn't ashamed of what they'd done. She was ashamed she'd allowed herself to go along with a wedding and a life that she never should have agreed to in the first place. Would this be something she could explain? Suddenly the fog began to lift and she realized what she had to do.

"Randy, come. Let's sit."

Over the course of the next few minutes she explained her hesitation, without saying anything about Tyler. Because she wasn't calling off the wedding because of Tyler. Tyler had never made any promises. They had no plans. And that was the honorable thing for him to do, too.

"I don't want the life you can offer me, Randy. It's a generous, wonderful life, and you deserve to be happy with someone who truly wants to share it with you. I apologize for being so selfish and not understanding that this is not the life I want to live. It isn't fair to you, your parents, my parents, and it isn't fair to me to try to pretend, play a role I don't want to play. I don't think I ever did, Randy."

"So what changed your mind?" He was detecting something.

"I watched people on the plane. I see my sister's life here without a husband. I think about all the things I'd like to do with my life. What you want? It's your life. Your parent's life, their winery. But it's not what I want to do with my life."

"What do you want to do, Kate?"

She smiled. "Maybe write steamy novels, Randy. I don't know. I might go back to school. The point is," she slid over towards him on the couch and took his hands in hers, "I'd be taking the space someone else should occupy. And that someone else would love you and work with you and give you everything you deserve."

He looked down at where their hands joined. Though he spread his thumbs over her knuckles, she didn't reciprocate.

"I care for you and your parents. I thank you for your devotion to me, for everything they've done for me. Everything *you've* done for me. But I'm not the one who should be marrying you, Randy. I'm really not."

She held his gaze until she saw moisture in his eyes as the realization sank in. She had spoken her truth, and Randy understood it.

Tyler was on his fifth glass of champagne, and he was tipsy. The stuffed shrimp and mushroom buttons were nice, but not substantial enough to keep him from getting drunk. He told himself it wasn't about Kate.

What will be will be. The little phrase was bumping around in his head like a bee in a Mason jar. His father finally asked him where Kate was, the girl he said he was bringing to introduce to them.

"Gone. I think she's gone, Dad."

"Nonsense. Fashionably late. Women like to be fashionably late."

But then another hour went by, and after Tyler checked his phone to see there was no call from Kate, he began to understand she wasn't coming after all. And in a way he was glad. Glad that perhaps she was finally going to live the life she had mapped out before he met her. Before he got in there and messed things up, as he'd told Kyle. He'd told himself he was ready for either consequence, but somehow this one was a more bitter pill than he'd expected.

He grabbed a bottle of champagne and retreated to a quiet corner, where his drunkenness wouldn't be a spectacle or reflect negatively on his mother.

The sound of his mother's voice nearby got him to sit up and carefully place the bottle under the chair he was sitting on. It did no good. She saw it anyway.

"There you are," she said.

"Yes, Mom. I'm right here." Dizziness hit him harder than he'd expected. Thinking back on what a beautiful day he'd had in the hotel room with Kate, he realized they'd skipped lunch, and the finger foods at the gallery were a poor substitute for dinner. He leaned his back against the wall and his mother split into two.

Great.

Except that the other vision of his mother was wearing a red dress, and her long hair wasn't grey. He squinted, not sure he was seeing correctly.

"Kate?" he said slowly.

She looked down at him, bemused. "You don't hold your liquor well, Tyler. I guess I'm going to have to teach you."

"I didn't eat."

"Yes. I remember," she said as she winked at his mother. She leaned in and planted a kiss on his lips.

That's when he knew he'd be okay.

"Tyler, I'm going to take you down the street to the pancake house, and you're going to sober up," she said.

"Oh, yeah?" He was feeling masterfully giddy and ready to spar. "Or else what?"

"I'll fuck your brains out drunk, if you can get it up."

"I can get it up." He did like her comment. He realized after he'd responded exactly what she'd said. "Hey, you said a nasty word."

She leaned into him, allowing him a good look down her low-cut red dress. "That depends on who you're talking to."

Her chest mesmerized him. Before he could reach out to touch her, she had moved to brace him under one armpit, helping him stand. "I like your tits," he said in what he thought was a whisper, but he noticed several guests nearby looked in their direction.

"Tyler, you need to straighten up and walk out of here like a soldier." Cupping her palm to his ear she whispered, "And after you sober up, you get to play with my tits."

"Deal," he said.

CHAPTER 16

They played footsie while he ate his pancakes. He drank three cups of strong, black coffee and was beginning to think he had sobered up sufficiently, since he found himself regretting his drunkenness. All the same, he didn't want to drive, so they walked the ten long blocks, miraculously without rain, until they reached the steps of the little hotel.

A recording of a French singer was playing in the background while they made their way through the lobby to the elevators. Tyler had threaded his fingers through Kate's, with a grip he softened when she shook her hand in front of him. He wasn't going to stop holding it, but he relaxed.

Their room had been left with the sheets tangled, which looked sexy as hell. Kate slipped off her red shoes and her dress, but left her pearls on, and her red undies.

"I like those," he said, pointing to her red bra and panties.

"I kind of thought you would. Bought them on the way up to Gretchen's this afternoon. I knew I was going to borrow this dress."

"I like the dress, too, but I like those better."

"Come here, Tyler. And take your shirt off first."

"Yes ma'am."

He removed his shirt and pants after kicking off his shoes. He stood before her in his boxers with the American flags on them, his compass tat bulging proudly over his heart.

"Nice touch. I wear red, but of course you had to wear the red, white and blue," she said to him. "But you can leave those behind, too."

"Glad to." He slipped them down his thighs. His erection bounced to attention. He remembered the little square packet in his pants pocket, since he'd spent the evening checking to be sure he hadn't forgotten and let it slip out onto the floor for all to see. After sheathing himself, he crawled up on the bed and nestled Kate in the pillows as he kissed his way from her lips, down her neck, between her breasts to her belly button. While his tongue played there, he slipped a finger along the waistband of her red panties and removed them, exposing her soft pink pussy.

He sighed. "Now that's a thing of beauty," he said as he inserted one fingertip and watched it disappear inside her. Kate moaned and spread her knees wider, arching her pelvis up to his mouth. Her sweet juices sent an electric jolt to his cock.

She pulled at her bra, squeezing herself while his fingers rubbed over her nub.

He was becoming familiar with her body, even though the sun had barely set on their first encounter. It was like she was made for him, and he knew he could please her, rock her world as she so deserved. He climbed up her writhing body, drawing her face up to his and whispered to her mouth, “I love you Kate. I can say that now.”

She hesitated, watching him.

“You don’t have to say it back—”

“But I do.” Her fingers brushed over his lips. She pulled at his ears and sifted through his hair. “I think I fell in love with you on the plane. It was like you were the one I was always looking for.”

“Me too,” he said. “I knew it instantly. Never happened to me before.” He kissed her as she wrapped her knees around his waist. When he was positioned to enter her, he stopped. “I wish I didn’t have to go the day after tomorrow.”

“But you’ll be back.”

“Yes, nothing could keep me away.” He thrust deep, loving her sudden inhale as she accepted his girth.

“Tyler,” she said between kisses, “I’ll write to you every day.”

“Every day, baby. I’ll write you back. I’ll be with you every day through your letters. Those letters will bring me back to you, sweetheart.”

“Yes.”

“And Kate?”

“Whaaaat?” Her head was thrashing from side to side, her body straining toward him, toward release.

“I write good letters.”

CHAPTER 17

The farewell was harder than she'd imagined. They'd spent every second they could together, and most of that had been in bed. As she watched him walk through the gate and wave to her from the other side of the barrier separating them, and then board the plane to San Diego, she held her breath so he wouldn't see the sobs threatening to erupt. She so wanted to be strong. To give him the confidence he really didn't need. The idea that a SEAL would need her to show a stiff upper lip was ridiculous, of course. But that didn't mean she didn't want to show it. Give him everything she had that was strong.

The bow he gave at the top of the stairs before he disappeared into the metal cylinder of the prop jet that would whisk him away—maybe forever—delivered the final blow. She wobbled backward and knocked into a man sitting in a wheelchair, almost falling into his lap. He sported a Navy cap, and when she saw him she felt as if God was twisting her heart in her ribcage with a set of pliers. There were no accidents, she thought, as it hit home that Tyler could come back damaged, come back without legs, or arms, or with some other disfigurement. And he'd still say he had done what he wanted to do. That it had been worth it.

And she'd have to agree. It would be worth it. As long as he came back to her. She'd take him in any condition, just as long as he made it home.

She made her apology to the Navy vet, and turned back to the window, watched the plane taxi down the runway, the nose and windshield heading full into the sun. With that golden kiss and in front of the backdrop of grey-blue skies full of clouds, Portland's usual condition, he lifted off and her heart felt like it was flying behind desperately trying to catch up.

She returned to Gretchen's car in short-term parking, turned on the ignition and heard the pinging of her cell phone messaging:

Love you, Kate. I'll write every day. Every day will be one day closer to coming home to you.

She answered him, *Miss you already. Painful. Is it possible to love someone too much, Tyler?*

She waited, but there wasn't a response. He was probably out of range. She'd have to get used to this. It would be something she would have to learn about herself. It was cruel to discover something as wonderful as their new love, only to have to live without it.

A young couple walked by, kissing, arms entwined. Her flowered backpack was slung over his right shoulder. They were oblivious to the rest of the world. A plane could drop from the sky and they'd not notice, she thought. The moisture that flooded her eyes and blurred their outlines obscured their image.

Leaning her forehead against the top of the steering wheel, she let the tears finally come. She let her chest sob, her constricted throat gasp for air. She cried like a little girl, but with the depth and pain of a woman. Images flooded in, of walking hand in hand with Tyler in the rain, the way he'd sprawled at his mother's art show with the bottle of champagne at his side. The way he looked that day when she opened Gretchen's front door and found him standing there and her heart leapt out. How he looked in his running shorts, the flavor of the compass tat over his heart when he was arching his hips into her.

But the pain of the separation was way more significant than she'd thought it would be.

It took a couple of minutes for her sobs to subside. With her renewed composure, the sounds of the running engine made themselves known, and the reality of where she was seeped back into her being. She sat with her feelings as she drove out of the lot, paid her fee, headed to the freeway and back to Gretchen's.

She guessed there'd be some messages there, too. There were about ten on her cell phone from her mother, and a couple from Randy. She started playing them back.

"Okay, Kate. I'm not in the habit of chasing my grown daughter around, but in this case, I'd sure like some assistance. Just wish you were here to help me field some of the questions. Am I doing the right thing by telling people the wedding is on hold?"

Kate knew they all believed she'd change her mind. She also felt some shame and guilt over making her parents, especially her mother, battle the Hellers alone. She decided to call her mom first. Randy could wait.

"Tell me some good news, Kate."

"Everything's fine. I'm fine. Gretchen and the girls are fine."

"Where are you?"

"Driving back from the airport."

"You landed?"

"No. I'm in Portland still. Took a friend to the airport."

The pause on the other end of the phone shouted volumes. "I see," she said curtly. "This 'friend' have anything to do with calling the wedding off?"

"Indirectly."

"Oh, right. How stupid of me. God forbid you'd fall in love with someone else while being engaged." The acid of her tone did the job. Kate felt the hairs at the back of her neck stand on end. Her reaction was swift but she worked to temper the bite she wanted to take out of the phone.

"It wasn't like that, Mom. You know me."

"Do I, Kate? I'm beginning to wonder."

"Were you ever unsure, Mom, about marrying dad?"

"You asked me that question already. What difference does it make, Kate? I'm not the one who said yes to Randy, you are. You're the ones who told everyone you loved each other. It wasn't my idea, and no one forced you to make that decision. I hope no one is forcing you now." She sighed. "And for the record, no, I never doubted my decision to marry your dad. Not for a minute."

Kate thought of the safety and power of Tyler's arms. She missed him so much, and he'd been gone less than an hour. With each passing minute the distance between them grew, leaving her cold and sad. But the strength of the love she felt for him warmed her. Gave her courage.

"Kate?"

"Mother. I'm in love. Deeply, truly in love. A love like I've never known."

"Oh. My. God."

She laughed to herself. "You act like that's a bad thing. I would think you'd be happy for me. To finally find the love of my life. It wasn't Randy, Mom. I don't want to miss that chance to grab the brass ring, the whole fairy tale. I want it all, Mom. Wouldn't you want that for me, Mom?"

She could tell her mother was crying silently. The deep breathing she did to control herself was a dead giveaway. Then, in a soft voice, her mother surprised her, "Yes, Kate, I do want that for you. You have no idea how I want that for you. More than you'll ever know."

"Mom?"

"Come home, Kate. We have much to talk about."

"I will. I've got reservations for tomorrow morning."

"Text me the information and I'll pick you up."

Her mother hung up in an uncharacteristic non-sign-off, her voice subdued and, Kate would say, pensive. Hurt. Her usual, "Love you," was conspicuously absent. Kate wondered what private spaces her mother had that she obviously had never shared with her. She hoped the breakup with Randy hadn't triggered something painful from her mother's past.

Or was it something about Tyler?

Are you happy, Mom? As much as she could concentrate, the answer always came back, "Yes." So what could it be?

Kate almost drove past Gretchen's house. She braked quickly and turned carefully into the teensy driveway, which was stuck between two older concrete walls and barely big enough for a compact to fit through. The car following behind her nearly rear-ended her and honked in irritation as he sped down the street toward the row of houses where Tyler's parents lived.

She thought about Tyler's mom, a handsome woman with the long, grey-streaked hair and exotic features enhanced by colorful makeup and big, bright jewelry. Just as Kate hadn't considered checking in with Gretchen or her mother, Tyler hadn't spent much time with his mother or father. Since he'd come to Portland to say goodbye to his family before his deployment, they'd probably feel as robbed as Kate's. Maybe more so.

Gretchen wasn't at home. Her car wasn't in the driveway, either. The back door was locked and Kate hadn't thought to ask for a key. Of course Gretchen couldn't be expected to wait on her, be at her beck and call. She and Tyler been so involved with themselves it hadn't occurred to either of them. She got back in her car and waited.

Watching the hillside behind Gretchen's house, she focused on the structures poking out from behind flowering rhododendrons, which easily stood ten feet tall. Roses and bright green new shoots waved to a rhythm of life she hadn't noticed before. The calm green, rose and peach of the gardens soothed her, as if they were smiling down on her from an old friend's face. She felt part of something growing, even as she experienced the pain of its absence.

No question about it. This was love.

Kate had drifted off to sleep when she heard Gretchen's car round the top of the driveway and park in front of her garage doors in the rear, her brakes squeaking. Like an exploding grenade, the doors opened and her three nieces came running toward her without closing their doors behind them.

Gretchen had a stern look about her as she picked up two packages in her trunk, carrying them with a ramrod straight back. She slowly made her way over to Kate, who was surrounded by her three exuberant daughters.

"Glad you managed find your way home," she said with a twist of sour in her voice. "And you can still walk."

It could have been a funny comment, but it wasn't delivered that way. Kate was reminded, again, of how her actions had caused others around her some inconvenience and worry about her safety.

"I'm sorry, Gretchen. I'm just—"

"Save it." She showed Kate "the hand" briefly from under her packages. Kate took one of the bags from her sister's arms and walked next to her, careful not to step on little feet as her nieces unwrapped themselves from her one by one.

"He's off. I leave tomorrow morning."

"Good," Gretchen flatly.

Kate decided not to test the prickliness of her sister and to just get through the afternoon and evening without harsh words. Having her sister understand her was too much to hope for yet. But it was a possibility.

She had a few hours to figure out how to handle the Hellers, her job and Randy. Then she'd make her amends to her mother, and find out what she was hiding.

CHAPTER 18

"You talk to Mom yet?" Gretchen demanded. She was making a bunch of noise putting away the groceries, and then snatched the large brown package from Kate's arms. They hadn't made eye contact since the driveway.

"Yes, just about an hour ago."

"How's she taking it?"

What about me? Why don't you ask me how I'm taking it all?

"She said we have to talk."

"I'll bet."

"So is there some kind of deep dark secret here? Something she hasn't told us? That's what it feels like, anyhow."

"I'm not touching that, Kate," Gretchen snapped. "On your own, kid. You made your bed. You get to lie in it."

"Interesting choice of words."

This irritated her sister, who turned and finally leveled one of her you're-not-going-to-get-away-with-it glares at her. "You know what you've done, don't you?"

"Sorry, Gretchen, I think I know exactly what I've done, but apparently I'm missing something."

"He's a total stranger, Kate. You've had monkey sex with a total stranger. And for him, you've given up a dream with Randy—not that he was the catch I would have chosen, but my 'choosing antenna' is bent, as we all know."

"Gretchen, that's not fair. You've done a wonderful job with the girls, with your life. You're a great mom. Tony wasn't a bad choice."

"Just not husband material. But I digress. Kate, you went off with him and spent days doing the wild naked thing," Gretchen leaned in closer and whispered, "And not a word of this around the girls, either. I find out they know you shacked up with some guy for two days at a hotel in downtown Portland and I'll disown you myself. Hear?"

"I get it. No worries there."

"Well, you should be worried. You use protection?"

"Come on, Gretchen."

"So the answer to that is a resounding 'no' then?"

"Not fair."

"Not fair to your body. What the hell are you doing?"

"Falling in love."

"How things change. Just a few years ago they would have called it falling in *lust*."

"Funny."

"Honestly, Kate. Are you okay?"

The stinging sensation at the back of her eyes distracted her. Something in her chest felt like it was melting. She wanted to say something, but was worried it would just sound like a whine. She remembered what she'd texted him.

Is it possible to love someone too much?

Her phone pinged with a message. Glancing at the screen she saw the message at the top. He'd answered her question.

Not if it's me you're loving, Kate.

She'd closed her eyes and absorbed what he'd told her. The little text took away the hollowness in her chest. But only a little. When she opened her eyes, Gretchen was glaring at her.

"It was him," she admitted.

"Well, I sure as hell knew it wasn't Randy." Gretchen's demeanor was still prickly.

The phone pinged again. *Can I call you?*

Sure she texted back.

"I'm going upstairs to take this call," she informed her sister.

The phone rang while she was near the top of the stairs. She ran down the hallway, entering Clover's room. Her niece was sitting at her computer desk.

"Hello?" Kate heard the familiar husky voice of Tyler. "I'm here."

"And I'm still in Portland," she said as Clover rolled her eyes and unplugged her pink laptop. The lanky teen pushed past her.

"That's good. Would have worried if you were headed for the airport. Except if you were coming here, of course."

Clover slammed the door behind her.

"Everything okay?" he asked.

"That was my niece, Clover. I've been staying in her room. I came here to talk in private, but she was on the computer. She's gone now."

"I can call back."

"Don't be silly. I need to talk to you, Tyler."

He paused. "Not sure I like the sounds of that."

"I just meant that I needed to hear your voice."

"Me too." He whispered.

What do you say to someone you barely know, but feel like you've known him your whole life?

Tyler filled the space between them. "So, what's tomorrow look like for you?"

"I called my mom on the way back from the airport."

"Oh? How did that go?"

"About what I expected. It was hard."

"Yes, I imagine. I'm curious, Kate. What did she say?"

"Do I know what I'm doing? Why haven't I been in communication, you know, all stuff I deserved hearing. You and I got so caught up..."

"Yes, we certainly did that."

"Not complaining or anything."

"Didn't take it as such." His breathing was heavy. "Now your real life is creeping back. Now you'll have to deal with all those people. Wish I was there to help you."

"Me too."

"I could come up next weekend, if I can get away. Or, you could come down."

"No. If I still have a job, I'll have to work all weekend, like I promised. Might not be able to spend a whole lot of time together."

"I'll take whatever I can get." His sexy voice was getting raspier.

"I like being missed. I like having to urgently steal away minutes with you. You should capture me and whisk me away." She was surprised at her own comment. So much had changed in the few little days since she'd met him.

"That sounds nice, baby. I promise to be gentle."

She found herself laughing in spite of the heartache.

"That would be fun. I'd like to introduce you to Sonoma County. My parents. My friends."

"Sounds serious." The low timbre of his voice made her shiver. "Miss you, sweetheart. Only been a few hours and I miss you already."

"This is serious for me, Tyler."

"And for me, baby. Can't wait to learn all about where you grew up."

"Then come this weekend. I'm not sure I can last any longer than that without imploding."

"I'll work on it. It's the last weekend before deployment, and sometimes they want to keep the Team together. Easier if you come down here. But I understand you've got your job."

"Which I don't want anymore."

"But you have to finish it off clean. Besides, I'll be gone at least four months. Better count on six. You'll need that job to support yourself until—"

The awkward silence crashed like an iron barbell. What was their future? And was he thinking that way? She hoped to God she wasn't misreading him.

"Until I can sort out what I'm doing with my plans up here." She thought he'd appreciate being let off the hook.

"Yes, baby. We'll take it one step at a time."

"But in the meantime, I am going to miss you something fierce. I think one way or the other, we should try to see each other one more time before you go. That way…"

Now it was time for her to create the awkward silence.

"We'll know the trajectory," he whispered. "You can't plot the trajectory when you only have one point of reference. You have to have two events to plot the direction of the distance between those two points."

"Well said." She was in awe that his steely resolve could creep back into their conversation, but he still could remain loving, soft and normal. Hell, not normal—fantastic and downright irresistible.

Clover popped her head inside the room. Kate held up a finger. "Look, Tyler, I'll call you back later. Just nice to hear your voice."

Clover's eyes got huge and the crease between her brows deepened.

"I'm imposing on my niece's privacy," she continued.

"Later, Kate. You know I love you."

"Yes," she looked up at Clover who was giving her a shoulder full of attitude. "Me, too. We'll talk soon." She was worried he would find her signoff too impersonal as she hung up.

"Tyler? You're talking to Tyler?" Clover asked.

"You know I am."

"What about Randy?"

And that was a very good question. One she was going to have to deal with tomorrow.

Time to buck up and deal with my real world, just like Tyler said. It was an apt way to put it. While looking at her niece, she realized it would not be an easy task, but even if Clover no longer looked up to her, it was still the right thing to do to set the record straight with her.

"I'm not in love with Randy. I'm in love with Tyler."

Clover plugged in her pink laptop and sat on her bed, bouncing as she did so. "I don't ever want to fall in love. Look what it did to Mom. Look what it's doing to you, to Grandma. To everybody in this family. Like everyone's gone batshit or something."

CHAPTER 19

Tyler stopped by Gunny's Gym before he made it to the apartment. As he expected, Kyle, Cooper and Luke were working a little PT. Sanouk was cleaning their new display cabinet and setting out the branded tee shirts, and plastic water bottles, as well as Team fundraising patches, Gunny's Gym mugs, and SEAL logo survival bands for kids' summer camps. Even a new vending machine with enhanced mineral waters and natural fruit drinks had been added.

The Chinese reflexologist and masseur sat on his table, arms crossed. Gunny's utility closet had been converted to a private treatment space, and the door was ajar while the ancient man waited. A colorful poster of the bottom of a foot was tacked to the wall behind.

Kyle started in on Tyler first. "Hey, if it isn't lover boy. I hear you got bitten by the love bug real good up in Portland."

He had to laugh at that one. "Yeah, I did." There was part of him that was proud of the fact that those two satisfying days with Kate seemed to have given him some mental clarity. His life now was more complicated, and he surprisingly liked it.

Holy shit, I can do this.

"Things still a mess, then?" Kyle asked. He threw down the rusty iron hand weights, which bounced off the rubber mat, too close to Coop's foot.

"I don't care who you are, Lannie," Coop shouted. "You fuckin' nail my toe and I'll kick you in the butt with my good one and make it come out your other side."

"Roger that, Coop. My bad. So, Tyler, got everything *nailed* down?"

The rest of the contingent started with the catcalls again.

Best he just admit it. "I'm in love, fellas. It finally happened to me."

Coop stood up quickly, came over and put his lanky arm around Tyler's shoulder. "Just so you know, what happens next is you ask her to marry you so no one else takes her while you're gone."

"Wait a minute Coop, he's only fuckin' known her for less than a week. You think that's smart?"

"Since when are we talking smart, ladies?" Luke said.

Cooper dished it back to Luke. "Hey, I think you getting married was the best fuckin' decision you ever made, Luke. Now for step two, if you're lucky, you'll be back in time to see your new little one."

And then everyone got quiet. Coop removed his arm from Tyler's shoulder. The unspoken fact was that Luke's wife,

Julie, would be delivering while they were deployed. And no one liked that one bit.

It was Kyle's opportunity to say something, if he wanted to. And naturally he did. "Shit, fellas, I was thinking we'd be all wrapped up with this caper in thirty days and be back home. Besides, you know how strong Julie is. I was there for Brandon. Maybe little miss pink wants to come into this world without her father's tatted arms holding her."

"No shit, Luke. A girl? You're having a girl?"

"And all of you get to keep your hands off her when she arrives. That goes for Julie, too," Luke said to the group.

Tyler worked into a rotation and had Luke spot him. He waited for a space to engage Kyle in a private conversation.

"You okay, Ty?"

"I'm fuckin' pretty damned good, except I got a favor to ask."

"Shoot."

"I know we had plans to get together this weekend with the girls and families. But, I'm wanting to go up north one more time before we deploy. Any chance of that?"

Kyle tried to hide a frown that threatened to breach his normal poker face. Tyler wondered whether he shouldn't have asked, but he had to.

"You single guys have it a little tougher on that score. Can't bring just any someone to the gatherings, and if you go solo, I know it's not much fun, especially if there's some place you'd rather be. I get it. Believe me I get it."

"Appreciate that, sir."

"So tell me if it's worth it. You real serious about this girl? And any chance it will fuck you up before we leave—not that we ever know anything before it happens. Especially with women."

"Roger that, Kyle. But from where I'm standing, it would be worth it."

"Then you know if that's the case, she'll wait. It will work out anyway. You gotta ask yourself if it's time to put down the fantasy loves and start dealing with the hellhole we're landing in over there in a couple of days."

"Yessir. I know that. And I still want to go. I mean, I'd feel bad if I got home and found out she'd had a change of heart."

"This the girl who is engaged?"

"Was."

"You interfering with her life, Tyler?"

"Absol-fuckin-lutely, sir."

Kyle placed his hands on his hips, dripping sweat from his chin and chuckled. "You're a horn dog, just like me. I couldn't take it slow, either. But hell, Christy loves it that way."

"Kate's the same, Lannie. She's the one. I know she is."

"Then you go on Friday. You get your butt back here Sunday because Monday we prep and we're outta here."

"Thanks, man."

Tyler turned to leave the room. "Excuse me, sailor," he heard behind his back.

Kyle had squinted up worse than his old drill sergeant at Great Lakes, the guy that practically made him pee his pants that first day when he was a speck of shit in training to be a tadpole.

All the Team guys had stopped. Luke was wiping his face with a towel.

"You finish your PT, you hairless frog. You get your body right with the SEAL gods, okay? And then you go run off and get your dick polished."

After he finished he joined the other guys in wiping down the equipment, spraying the vinyl and chrome parts with Amornpan's new sanitizer, which was laced with a faint lavender scent. Aside from the fact that the gym was cleaner and more organized and smelled a hell of a lot better, she hadn't changed it much from when Gunny owned it. The spirit of the old man was still there, as if he was waiting just on the other side of the air intake grates near the ceiling.

The "no digital anything" still ruled, except for the scale, and then only because it was too easy to fake the old-fashioned weighted ones. The iron dumbbells suffered from advancing rust. The mats had the same worn patches where hundreds of Team guys had grunted and scratched to find their footing as they sweated their way to optimum performance. So they'd be ready for anything. Be ready to die with honor, if it came to that.

Getting strong was what you did. It was how you got your mind prepared for the rigors of the unknown. So you could be counted on to do your part when it was needed. There were never any second chances, unless you were planning on spending eternity in Heaven. Tyler would rather spend it in Gunny's gym, or in Kate's bed.

He telephoned the airlines and got a flight out Friday evening. It was a non-stop to Santa Rosa, which was more expensive, but he didn't want to waste a minute of time with her by getting stuck on a freeway from San Francisco.

He left a message for Kate and she returned his call while he was unpacking and doing laundry at his apartment.

"That's wonderful, Tyler. I can hardly wait. I'll pick you up."

"Maybe we can go someplace Friday night, go over to the Waterwheel Inn?"

"No, sorry, that won't work. I have to be at work early Saturday and Sunday. Gotta maneuver my way out of there."

"I'll get you to work on time. You don't trust me?"

His dead-sexy, raspy voice made her tingle and she giggled in spite of herself. "Okay, if I still have my job. They haven't fired me yet, that I know of."

"Baby, we don't want that, do we?"

"No, I guess not. They'd probably have told me by now. Or maybe I'll get a 'you're fired' message tomorrow when I pick up my paycheck."

Tyler knew what that was all about. Randy and his family were not giving up on her. And that was going to make this weekend even more important. His instincts were right. He was going to do everything in his power to make sure there was no way Kate would ever change her mind.

He would be up against an enemy who had the luxury of time on his hands, could afford to wait for Tyler to make a mistake. And that was just not ever going to happen. He was going to make damned sure she understood how much they needed each other.

CHAPTER 20

Kate's flight was delayed, so when she finally got back to the Park N Ride via the Airporter, the day was nearly over. Randy had dropped her off when she went to Portland. No one was there to pick her up now.

She dialed her best friend, Sheila.

"Holy shit, Kate. What's happening?"

"What do you mean?"

"I mean Randy has been, like, throwing things all over the tasting room. Yesterday he dumped four cases of wine over, just crashed right into them like it was on purpose. His dad gave him a public scolding and Randy was seething. I mean, I've never seen him so mad."

A thread of unease snaked its way through Kate's belly, up to her throat, triggering her gag reflex.

Sheila's breathing was deep and breathless, like she'd been running. Kate waited a little too long to speak up. "You okay?"

"I called off the wedding."

"We heard. Why did you do that, Kate?" Her voice was whispery and incredulous.

"I don't love him."

"Geez. When did you figure that out?"

"Look, can I explain it all later. I have a favor to ask. Are you working today?"

"Was going to go in at three. Why, you need something?"

"Oh, was hoping I could bum a ride. Can you pick me up?"

"Where are you?"

"The Park N Ride by the Fairgrounds. I could call a taxi if it's a big imposition—"

"Don't be silly, Kate. I'll be right there." Sheila hung up.

Kate sat on a cold bench in the shadow of the concrete freeway overpass. Wind whipped around her ankles and up the back of her neck. She zipped her jacket and flipped up her collar. Her thoughts became melancholy, even though there was excitement in her belly at the thought of Tyler would come to see her.

Recalling the days before she left for Portland, which now seemed like a decade ago, she was glad they'd left her car at her cottage, rather than over at Randy's. In fact, Randy hadn't been available the night before she left, so he'd picked her up that morning to take her to San Francisco. It would have been awkward if she'd needed to go over to his apartment to get her car.

She got out her cell to see if she'd missed a call from Tyler. It was a blank, black screen. She knew he'd be busy, especially since he was getting off a little early to catch the Friday flight.

She texted him to let him know she'd landed. Then she did the same to Gretchen. Gretchen had answered with a *Good luck.* She was certainly going to need that.

Sheila drove up in a new Volvo just as Kate was putting her cell back in her purse. She wheeled her weekend bag over to the back as her friend popped the hatch.

"Wow, Sheila. You musta got a raise. Beautiful car."

"New to me. Leased."

"A big step up from your crusty old Volvo. The one with breast cancer around the headlights." Kate belted in.

"Well, don't you look like the cat that ate the canary?" Sheila said, winking. She'd put a bright red rinse in her hair. Her tank top was skimpy, showing off her pierced belly button, but her jeans were slightly baggy, with rolled up cuffs lined in pink flannel that matched the pink shoelaces on her black lace-up boots with paisley designs on them. Kate didn't think she'd be going to work that way, but then Sheila was known as being a rather free spirit.

"Your hair's different," Kate remarked.

"Time for a change."

On their way to Kate's place, Sheila pumped her for details. Kate attempted to keep Tyler's name out of it, but somehow got caught up in the barbed wire of Sheila's clawing interrogation.

"Tyler? I used to know a guy named Tyler. He was just my type, too. Loved to screw all day and all night."

Kate blushed. She could have been describing her Tyler.

"He didn't live in Portland," Sheila said.

"My Tyler's from San Diego. He's a SEAL."

Sheila's head whipped around nervously, then she recovered her composure. "Nope. Definitely not the same guy. A SEAL, huh? All I can say is that he must be pretty incredible if you'd toss Randy off the boat for someone else. When do I get to meet him?"

"We're working on it."

"You gotta work this weekend, kiddo. We got some big parties coming in. I'm working too. No time off, I'm afraid."

"I know." The comment didn't sit well with Kate, but she didn't reply. She watched the tree-lined streets along the route home. The salt and peppering of manicured as well as unkempt homes in the neighborhood she lived in. The large Victorian in front of her cottage was painted light moss green with green trim. Her cottage, nestled behind the main house under a fruitless mulberry tree, was yellow. Sheila parked on the street and set the brake.

It was the first time Kate noticed Sheila had gotten a tattoo on her right shoulder. The cluster of burgundy grapes surrounded a red heart with the words *Wine Lover* scripted inside. She turned and Kate also saw Sheila was wearing heavier eye makeup than she was used to seeing. Sheila's glance through half-lidded eyes was mischievous.

She leaned toward Kate, flattening back the collar of Kate's fuzzy jacket, patting it at her shoulder. "When are you going to talk to him?"

"Tyler?"

"I love that name," she whispered. Her eyebrows jiggled up and down and her speech was syrupy sweet, but well controlled. In a low sexy growl, Sheila said, "Randy. I was wondering about Randy. Or were you going to avoid him altogether?"

The smirk after her statement seemed condescending to Kate.

"I suppose I'll see him this tomorrow. They already had me on the schedule, but when I looked online yesterday, they'd booked me for tomorrow and all though the weekend."

"That's because I agreed to do the night inventory, Kate. I figured you didn't want to spend your first day back in a dark, dusty wine cave with Randy. I got your back." Sheila winked.

Kate was grateful she had been spared that trial. "Thank you, Sheila."

"De nada."

Kate rolled her weekend bag down the short driveway, past her SUV convertible to her front door. Sheila waved through the clean windshield of her Volvo and was off. Before, it would have been a grinding of gears and a cloud of smoke. Kate was happy for Sheila's new car.

Glad to be home at last in her own space, she unpacked. The cottage was perfect for her. Built originally as a wine storage building, the thick walls were cozy and warm in the cool months, and on a day like today, when it was hotter than usual, kept the little place cool. She'd left just one window ajar to take the edge off any stuffiness.

First thing she did was put on some satellite music and shed her clothes, heading for the shower just as some sad viola music began. She could barely hear it over the spray of the fresh water as it sluiced over her body and successfully triggered her reset button. With her hair washed and fresh makeup applied, her dirty clothes tossed into the stacking washer-dryer, she poured herself a tall glass of ice water and gulped it like it was the last on earth. Mail had been placed on the dining table, which she thought was odd, since it normally fell all over the floor through the slot. It meant someone had been inside her place, and then she remembered Randy had a key. Today was payday, so she decided to go up to the winery and check her box, go to the bank, and get everything ready for the rest of the week. She'd get her key from Randy, too.

After checking her face in the mirror over the sink, she grabbed her keys, locked the front door and headed for her car.

No one appeared to be home in the big green house when she drove out. She barely saw the couple, who lived there only part time, since they lived in San Francisco and used this place as a weekend getaway. In fact, it seemed like she hadn't seen them in weeks. They like to go on long overseas travels, so she figured that's where they had gone. She actually knew their gardener, Jose, better than she knew them.

The ride to the winery was beautiful, winding through vineyards bright green with new growth. There weren't many tourists, since it was a Monday. Come Friday and all through the weekend, strangers with expensive cameras, sports cars and purses, wearing sweaters tied across their shoulders, shaded by floppy straw hats and winery baseball caps, would casually stroll down the sidewalks and shops of Healdsburg. In their attempts to look local they looked anything but. Their dollars, however, helped keep the town alive, and that was a good thing, especially for a family-owned winery concern. The Hellers were good at entertaining tourists, making them feel they, too, were part of the wine industry family. In a life that seemed distant now, Kate remembered she'd been the top seller of wine club memberships, adding to her already sizeable bonus from telephone wine sales.

She never thought of herself as especially good at selling, but in this arena, when all you had to do was be decent to people and tell them the truth, she excelled. Now she was going to have to do the sell job of her life.

Except it didn't matter if they let her go. So why was she so nervous? And then it hit her. She was more worried about how things would be if they kept her on.

CHAPTER 21

Tyler had agreed to give three newer Team guys a tour of the community grounds and some of their haunts downtown. He'd also agreed to take them to Timmons's office, where the man was packing up his things, preparing for retirement. His replacement had been posted a month ago, so Timmons had very little to do. After twenty years in the Navy, most people figured he'd be happy to take off the last few days.

But they were wrong. It would have taken Timmons another week to extricate from his office. All the walls were covered in framed pictures and news clippings with some memos attached with yellowing tape. Cloth campaign swags and foreign flags were tacked to the ceiling or screwed into the plaster walls. A tiny Polaroid picture of Saddam Hussein in handcuffs, looking rather scruffy and unkempt, was nearly buried under an Arabic banner with his picture on it. These things chronicled several of the large and small missions

SEAL Team 3 had been on. He had Kyle Lansdowne's graduating class from BUD/S, all ten of them. Three were still serving, and all on his SEAL Team 3.

The new guys, T.J. Talbot, Frank Moore and Ollie Culbertson were fresh out of the Army long course Corps School at Ft. Bragg. They looked like freaked-out baby goats darting into each other, trying to help the Chief and to understand his instructions. Timmons was not very clear, and they weren't listening much, so it was a giant clusterfuck. Tyler knew how they all felt. Everyone was nervous about the next phase of their deployment: Timmons to a loveless marriage and a wife obsessed with her doll collection, and the new guys to their first encounter with Dr. Death. Though the goals were vastly different, all four of them were distracted as hell.

"So Chief, you want to toss any of this, or are we packing it all up?" he asked Timmons.

"Son, that's what garages are for. My wife's informed me that will be where I offload all this shit, and where I get to store it, since none of it will ever find its way into our house." He'd been emptying a drawer one pencil at a time, checking the length of the pencils and condition of the erasers to see if they were worth keeping. Tyler watched the others try to look busy.

"That's a shame, sir," Ollie said stiffly.

"Oh hell," Timmons said as he straightened and dumped all the pencils into a garbage can, "I'd rather be in my man cave in the garage anyway. At least I don't have to sit on plastic, and I don't have to worry about farting or getting crumbs on the floor."

The new guys chuckled and gave Tyler the checkout look, to be sure it was okay to laugh at the Chief. For just about everyone else, retiring would be heaven and the Navy was hell, but to Timmons it was the other way around. Tyler hoped he'd be able to survive his years away from the base.

The new guys had been trained in that way all the SEALs were. They shut up and just did their jobs. There would be time enough for play, but right now, after the initial awkwardness of packing away Timmons's life like he was dead and everything was being shipped to Goodwill, the men settled down and took turns doing different things. T.J., the tallest, was pulling things from the wall and upper bookshelves, while Ollie taped together the bottoms of new boxes from a local office supply store. Frankie and Tyler wrapped the glass-framed items in bubble wrap and taped them secure with packing tape. Tyler kept a close eye on the nearly two-foot statue of a frog with the surfboard, the sixth such statue Timmons's Team boys had bought or replaced for him.

Tyler grabbed the piece. "Timmons, I'm getting nervous watching this thing wobble every time you walk past that file drawer. You mind if I take care of him first?"

"Go ahead. Put him on top after you wrap him." Timmons pointed to a half-filled box. Tyler could already tell there was no way the statue would fit.

"Sir, I'm going to put this in your car. Toss me your keys," Tyler said to his Chief. Timmons grumbled something under his breath and did as requested. Ollie came along, carrying a full box taped shut which Timmons had labeled "stuff."

"Poor dumb shit," Ollie started, then darted a quick glance at Tyler in alarm. "Sorry, Ty."

"No worries, Oliver."

"That's Ollie, sir. My real name's worse than that, so I like Ollie, if you don't mind."

"Someone play a practical joke when you were born, Ollie?"

"Something like that. I think they took one look at me with my big ears, and said, 'Nope, doesn't belong in this family.' I was adopted."

"You and T.J. have that in common, it seems."

"Nah, he was never adopted. Foster care the whole way. Tough way to work it. But made him the man he is."

They placed the box in Timmons' truck, but laid the frog statue on the passenger seat.

"What about Moore?"

"Pretty much Ivy League. Great family. He's a real gentleman. Got himself a real nice girl who gets him kind of confused, if you know what I mean."

"I get your drift." Tyler knew exactly what that felt like. He hoped this weekend would cure some of his trouble concentrating.

They continued filling and carrying out boxes until Timmons's car was filled to capacity. Then they moved on to T.J's. pickup, first filling the back, and then stuffing the king cab seat full. Tyler couldn't believe all this stuff had actually fit in the Chief's office.

Ollie ran ahead of him back into the two-story office building that had formerly been military housing. Interior bathrooms had been decommissioned to serve as storage closets. Timmons had stuffed his storage closet full as well.

"Think we're going to need more boxes, fellas," Timmons barked.

"I'll go," Frank volunteered.

Timmons handed him a twenty from his wallet. "Think we'll need another roll of bubble wrap, too, son."

Tyler examined the walls. T.J. had just removed the picture frames from the walls, and the stack on Timmons's desk was nearly two feet high, with two more large moving boxes stacked with unwrapped frames standing up like poster board in an art store. "Geez, Timmons. Had no idea you had all this shit. You'd need to rent a hall to put all this crap up. A Timmons family museum."

"That'll fuckin' never happen." Timmons looked over the project with fondness, unlike everyone else. "I'll sort through them and pick one or two to display. But the rest? They'll just sit there until my wife carts them off to Goodwill or the Salvation Army. If I could, I'd be buried with all this." He chuckled to himself. "Now wouldn't that make a movie? A man with this huge burial plot big enough for all his man stuff no one else gave a flying fuck about."

"Maybe your daughter will want some of these things," Tyler answered.

"Love her to death, but Cassie's interest in the military stops and starts with you guys running down the beach. Besides, her apartment is nearly this small," he said, stretching his arms out to the sides.

"And does she like dolls too?" Tyler asked.

"Hell, no. And she thinks her mom's nuts, God bless her."

Tyler let the new guys escort Timmons home with his stash. They'd have to come back tomorrow to finish the details and sweep clean the office. He returned to his sparse apartment and thought about what he should to do to make it cozier. He'd need a couch. A recliner for watching TV. He wondered if Kate ever watched TV. Then he wondered what her favorite programs were. He might need to get cable to entertain her. But not yet. Not until he was back from deployment.

The bed was good, though. King size. He hadn't scrimped on that one, although it cost nearly a month's pay to get it and the boxed spring, which sat directly on the ground. The "panther eyes" black fuzzy blanket had seemed just the thing at the time, but now he wanted some new sheets and perhaps a comforter. Girls liked comforters, he thought. Something in a print, not too feminine. Maybe something in a fresh green.

His bathroom towels were a dingy grey and had strings of cotton hanging down that would need to be trimmed. Hell, he needed new, fluffy towels. If she ever visited him, he no way would he allow her lovely flesh to be wiped down by these grimy, scratchy rags. Something again in a light green color would be nice, or ivory. That wouldn't look too feminine. He also didn't want to catch hell for decorating from Luke or one of his other best buds. No, solid, neutral colors were the order of the day.

He knew he had lots of adjusting to do, but he'd take it little by little. One thing at a time. Since he'd fallen in love before, everything was new, and when new things came along, it was best to take them one at a time, let each thing settle in.

He didn't feel like going out tonight, so sat on the bed, propped the pillows and grabbed a bad of paper, and settled down to write Kate a letter he could post tomorrow morning. Maybe she'd get it by Friday night. If not, he'd read it to her on Saturday. He wanted to communicate with her in the intimate way his mind worked when he put words on paper. Somehow, the act of writing softened him, helped him pour out his soul.

Kate,

I'm lying here on my bed thinking about you. Long before you come visit me here, I plan on making some changes so this place doesn't look so depressing. It's a typical bachelor pad. My mom would love helping me get some color into this place, and maybe lend me some of her paintings. Funny how I never thought of these things before now.

I'm aching to see you again. You make me feel wonderful, like a high school kid again. I'm noticing couples everywhere and I miss you. I feel your hand in mine, the softness of all those places on your body I love to kiss. I can't help it, I'm a guy and a certain body part misses you too. Hope that doesn't offend you. But it's the truth.

We helped our liaison officer close down his office and move home to retirement today. Was kind of sad, really. The man has been here the entire time I've been on the Teams, sort of the guy who kept us out of trouble and helped if we needed any special favors. And we checked in with him, not as much as we do our LPO, that's our Leading Petty Officer, who goes with us on missions, but he was the guy at home who ran interference for us.

But it is sad that he's going home to what I feel is an early grave. He has a daughter who doesn't live with him, but his wife is a complete nut job. We get the impression he won't have it easy being around that woman so much every day. Hope he can find more time to be with his daughter. Maybe that will happen.

Sorry, didn't want to write about a downer. But it did make me think about what would be next for me if I ever got off the Teams. None of us like to think about that, and the word is if we start thinking about it, we're already halfway out. I'm not ready yet to give up this community. There are things I'd miss. Most guys don't usually stay in very long. Only a handful. But today I don't have to think about it. All I want to do is dream about what we'll be doing when I see you Friday night.

I can hardly wait.

Don't bother writing me back. I want you to tell me in person. LOL. Until then, I'm going to think real hard about what that will feel like and sound like.

Tyler

He quickly scribbled the address Kate had given him on the outside of a small white envelope, found a stamp, ran downstairs and mailed it after making sure the mail hadn't been picked up yet.

CHAPTER 22

There were only three other cars in the visitor parking lot, so Kate pulled in next to one of them instead of going behind the building and parking in the dusty gravel employee lot.

The afternoon had warmed up so much she was grateful her newly-washed hair was still damp, but inside the twelve-foot carved oak doors of the tasting room the air was nearly ice cold. She'd worn a sleeveless silk top over her black skinny jeans, out of respect for the black and white dress code of the winery staff, but now wished she'd worn a sweater. Luckily she didn't intend to work; she was just going to drop by the office and check her employee box for her check and perhaps a notice of some kind.

She found neither. The Sheila looked up from her books and seemed surprised to see her.

"Oh, Kate! I thought you wouldn't be in until tomorrow," she said over the top of her red rhinestone reading glasses. Kate had never noticed she wore them before.

"Changed my mind. You have my check?"

"I'm sorry, Kate. I didn't—"

"Hello Kate."

Kate whirled around and there was Randy, leaning against the doorframe. His arms were crossed across his chest, his hands in leather gloves. Over his shoulder Kate saw Sheila's shake her head from side to side, eyes wide and rolling. "Randy! You scared me to death."

Randy dropped his arms and walked deliberately toward Kate. "Nice to see you, sweetheart. You look ravishing." His eyes were sparkling, but a little too wild for her. Kate picked up he was nursing some serious pain, and perhaps more than a small amount of anger.

He stopped in front of her and allowed a slight glance up and down her body, just enough to notice she was wearing black and white. One eyebrow rose. The smile that sneaked across his lips was an afterthought. "I thought you'd want the day to recover from your exertions of the weekend."

Anger flared like a hot poker up her spine. There was only one place he could have gotten the information about her meeting another man: Sheila. Her friend looked down, examining her paperwork, shrugged and sighed without making eye contact.

"I was on the schedule until this morning. So I came in to handle the open enrollment forms and get my paycheck."

"So you intend to work for me still?"

"Well, ye-es. I didn't hear otherwise. Forgive me if I'm wrong. I just assumed—"

"I convinced my folks to keep you on until we could get all this sorted out. But that was before I learned you've been screwing someone else."

Sheila straightened her spine and made her rolling office chair squeak, apparently deciding she wanted to be anywhere but in the room between the two ex-lovers.

"That's not fair, Randy. I'm afraid it's a little more than that."

"Really?" he asked. "So you've known this guy, what, more than four days, then?"

"I'm not comfortable talking about it right now. Can I just get my check and perhaps we could discuss this when your parents are present? After all, I do work for *them*."

Randy and Sheila exchanged a look. "You wouldn't even have a job here if it wasn't for me, Kate. You sure as hell know that, don't you?" Randy's expression was smug. Not bitter.

Kate didn't want to pick a fight. "Randy, I'm not here to cause a scene—"

"You think this is a scene?"

She looked around the walls, as if hoping to see some opening, a window she could fly out of. The oppressive adobe walls of this fortress, a former storage yard during the Mission period of California, pressed against her and made it difficult to breathe. As much as she wanted to keep the peace, Randy would be in charge of the conversation, and whether or not it escalated. She could only hope he'd decide to be reasonable.

She allowed him to walk close enough that she could smell his wine breath. She'd remembered at one time thinking it smelled pleasant and didn't mind the way his speech slurred when he talked to her in a low rumble. But today, his behavior triggered warning bells. She didn't like that he might be slightly drunk and therefore out of control.

"I gave you everything, Kate. My heart. My family's support." She saw him searching her face, felt him twirling her hair between his two fingers. "They accepted you as one of their own. I wanted to build my dynasty with you. My kingdom. You were going to be my queen."

Hair at the back of her neck bristled. Their lips were close to touching, and she looked him honestly in the eyes, unafraid. Before she stepped back, she said, "Wrong girl."

She wouldn't have said it if he hadn't been so creepy with the pseudo-affectionate messing with her hair, the lack of respect for her space, like he owned her. She wanted to make sure, in front of a witness, the message was delivered: *I'm done.*

He did have a deer-in-the-headlights look to him when she distanced herself safely. His eyes blinked. From her peripheral vision she saw his left fist tighten at his side and then release. He'd inhaled, filling his lungs with what he wanted her to think was courage. The transparent act did little to cover up the anger she saw lurking there as his breath hitched slightly.

Kate's heart was pumping wildly. The standoff felt dangerous, a quiet before the storm sort of thing. Then she remembered her key.

"I need my key back, Randy. I don't want you to go over to my place without me there to let you in. Understood?"

He squinted for a second before answering. "I've not been inside your place since before you left for Portland. I don't do snooping, Kate. Up until recently, I had no reason not to trust you. Nothing I needed to check up."

Kate knew it was a lie, but let it slide.

"All the same, I want it back. Please."

Randy rocked back on his heels and produced a cluster of keys from his front pocket. Removing his leather glove, he detached her red key from the rest of them and handed it to her.

"Before you ask me, this is the only copy I have, Kate."

She felt a little sheepish she'd planned to do exactly that. But she had. She still was convinced he had entered her place while she was gone, since Randy was the only one who had a key other than her landlords.

"Thank you," she said softly. And then she remembered her paycheck. "Sheila doesn't seem to have my check. Is there something I've not been told?"

Randy returned a sly smile. He was feigning compliance, agreement. "Unless Dad and Mom made a decision without consulting me, you're still employed here," he said. He leaned over to Sheila, and in his most seductive voice said, "Sheila, darling, would you mind giving Kate her check, honey?"

Sheila blushed. Kate felt sick to her stomach. She knew Randy had delivered it in an attempt to make her jealous. The opposite happened.

"Sorry, Kate. When I spoke to you earlier, I didn't realize you were coming in today. I was working on quarterlies and figured I'd book the salary in next month's figures, but no worries."

"But I'm always paid on the fifteenth. This is the fifteenth," Kate replied.

"Like I said, I'm sorry!" Sheila's eyes got wide. "It will only take me a couple of minutes, if you both will leave my office and give me some peace and quiet."

"See there, Kate? No conspiracy. Just a misunderstanding. All a misunderstanding." Randy had recovered some of his composure and was syrupy sweet again. She darted a look at Sheila and saw her tiny shrug. Was there an ounce of disappointment there? Kate wasn't getting anything from her, which was surprising.

"I'll be right outside in the tasting room. Just holler when you're done," Kate had started walking to the bar, Randy following behind her.

"I'll need the check signed—" Sheila shouted to Randy's back. Randy reversed course and quickly returned to stand behind Sheila, placing a palm on her shoulder and leaning forward.

"Sure, and then she'll be on her way," he whispered.

"Thank you, Mr. Heller," Sheila said with a tease, and another unmistakable blush.

Sheila did as she was told, producing the checkbook register. Randy's scribble took up several square inches.

"How about one for me?" Kate heard Sheila ask.

"Oh, fine," Randy said with a flourish and signed a second check. He threw the pen down and left the office, walking toward Kate and then turning to go another direction without looking back at her.

Sheila presented the check to Kate. "Sorry about all this. He'll calm down. We're all having to put up with him a bit."

"Self-absorbed jerk," Kate said.

Sheila sighed and looked off in the direction Randy had disappeared. "But he's our jerk. Something still loveable about him, don't you think?"

Kate had never thought Sheila was interested in her fiancé, but today it was as obvious as a billboard.

"Sheila. You have something to tell me?"

"You mean, have I been fucking your fiancé?"

"Sheila!" Kate blushed.

"No worries, Kate. I have my eyes on much bigger fish."

Kate walked toward the exit. "Thanks," she said as she held up her check.

"Don't mention it. Call me, okay? I want every detail of your new beau."

Kate agreed, but walked out of the tasting room sure Sheila wasn't the friend she'd believed she was. It would be a cold day in hell before she'd bare her soul to that woman ever again. Her friend had jumped ship, and Kate hadn't made up her mind which team Sheila was playing for now.

Something told her she would need her allies close and tight. And she better be sure who they were. It would be better to not have any than to have a couple you trusted when you really shouldn't.

CHAPTER 23

Tyler and the three new men helped Timmons with the last of his boxes and cleanup, as had been requested by their LPO, Kyle Lansdowne. He'd reported his concerns to Kyle regarding Timmons's state of mind. "We got a problem, sir."

"Not the first time someone has retired, only to find out their whole world got downsized by the wife," Kyle told him.

"Just hard to watch." He began to tell Kyle about their encounter with Timmons's wife, Dottie.

They'd brought the last of the boxes over to Timmons's house while Ollie stayed behind to sweep out the office and do some much-needed cleaning, even though the Navy would bring in their own cleaning and paint crew soon.

A single bay door to a three-car garage was open. Timmons was seated on a pile of boxes, bent over another set of boxes, three deep and running the entire long side of the bay. Timmons's pickup had been evicted from its place and was parked on the street.

Carrying a double stack of boxes, Tyler almost set it on the wrapped statue of the frog surfer, which irritated him. This marked the second time in as many days he'd almost destroyed the statue, and though it was replaceable, doing so had cost the team so much, Kyle had indicated perhaps they should have the next one bronzed, thereby extending its useful life. The expense for that, unfortunately, was prohibitive. Tyler set the boxes to the side first and then handed the wrapped statue to Timmons.

"Sir, I've almost destroyed this thing twice now. You should take it inside, where it will be safer."

Timmons clutched the bubble-wrapped object like it was a favorite toy for a boy of ten. "Thank you, son. I appreciate that." He looked around for a place to put the surfer frog, and then paused and said, "I'll be right back." Tyler watched the gentle giant approach the back door of the house, leading to the inner sanctum of Timmons's wife, whom Timmons had told them was having a bad day. When his Chief struggled to open the door, Tyler was there in an instant to help. He saw too late the oily footprints left on the laundry room vinyl. Timmons had easily opened the lightweight door to his living room and was two steps inside on a light grey carpet.

As soon as the handle clicked shut at Timmons's back, he heard the shriek he knew was coming. For a second, he thought Dottie had thrown a dish at Timmons, but then realized she'd probably pushed him back into the doorway, sending the bubble-wrapped frog sculpture flying. It was apparent it did not fall on carpet. The distinctive sounds of glass shattering were painful to hear. T.J. and Frank immediately stood to attention as if they'd heard an explosion.

And it turned out it was an explosion of epic proportions.

Tyler was careful to tiptoe around Timmons's marks on the flooring, and leaned inside the doorway. Timmons was on the floor next to the door, looking dazed. Dottie had thrown a pot—and from the size of the welt on Timmons's forehead, it was a heavy pot—at the man. To his right, Dottie was sorting through the shattered remnants of a glass curio cabinet filled to capacity with dolls. But the bubble-wrapped frog statue appeared unhurt, lying amongst the wreckage intact.

He knelt to look after his Chief's forehead, where a large purple goose egg had formed quickly and begun to bleed at one corner. Dottie's level of violence towards her husband surprised Tyler so much he kept a wary eye on her while he attended to Timmons, making sure she didn't pick up another weapon.

"Geez, sir. She really got you," he whispered to the Chief.

"Oh that," Timmons slurred. "Just a scratch."

Tyler asked him questions about what day it was, if his back hurt, things like that in soft, gentle, and what he hoped were soothing tones. Timmons was still shaken, but coherent.

T.J. was a fuming torrent of speed as he crossed the room, not giving a rat's ass about re-spreading the Chief's footprints across the light carpet. He pulled the package from the mortuary of broken dolls and mirrored shelving and got in Dottie's face after he'd secured it.

"You fuckin' bitch. You don't have the right to lay a hand on that man," he growled.

Tyler jumped up and had to restrain him, although he was fairly sure the SEAL wouldn't make good on his physical threat. "Not helpful, T.J." He pulled the big SEAL back by the arms. T.J. swung his powerful shoulders and extricated himself from Tyler's grip, swearing under his breath, but not advancing further on Dottie.

Dottie peered back at T.J. with some alarm, but there was no mistaking the hatred she felt for her husband. Timmons sat there motionless, tears streaming down his face.

Kyle was obviously moved by the story. "Holy hell, Tyler. We can't let him stay there with her. She'll kill him."

"It looked that way to T.J., too. I'm not sure I'd go that far, Kyle. T.J. has stayed behind to keep checking him out until we heard from you."

"He should get to a hospital, Tyler."

"Refused. Already asked. Dottie left in a huff. Timmons is safe for now, but we gotta do something."

"I'm going to send Coop over there to check him out. I think he needs a hospital. He could have a concussion he might not wake up from, Tyler."

"Yessir."

"You're still there, I take it?"

"Yessir."

"T.J. or Frankie have their kits on them?"

"I think T.J. does. He never goes anywhere without it."

"Okay, then. You guys restrain him if you have to, give him something if you have to…but be careful. And get him over to Emergency like yesterday, hear?"

"Yessir."

"And Tyler, you keep the statue for now. No sense complicating things and it might feel the brunt of her anger when she comes home and finds she can't pound on her man."

"Roger that."

They'd gotten Timmons admitted, convincing him by showing him the size of the welt on his forehead. The cut did appear to need a couple of stitches, too. And because blood had been shed, a report had to be made to base security, who advised them not to call the local police, who would normally have jurisdiction.

But at the Emergency Room, the friendly doctor who treated him called the police himself, and Tyler knew charges would be brought against Dottie, whether Timmons wanted it or not. No question about it. She'd assaulted her husband with deadly force.

So much for retirement. What a fuckin' first day of freedom. Now he fully understood why Timmons had been so apprehensive about the big day. It also made sense he'd been trying to do it slowly, take as much time as he could, to lessen the impact on Dottie's household. Tyler was only glad he and his buds had been there for him. The man had been solid toward the whole team for the ten years he was their liaison.

After Timmons was admitted and settled in his room, Tyler let Timmons use his cell phone to call his daughter Cassie. He knew Cassie was a strong young lady now, and a good judge of character, having hung around the SEALs throughout her growing-up years. Cassie would get it. Tyler was glad Timmons would have an ally.

He and T.J. drove to a local Starbuck's, picked up something to eat and some strong coffee. He placed a quick call to Kate, who picked up on the first ring.

"Hi, baby. Good to hear your voice," he whispered. He could feel the tension of the last couple of hours falling away just at the sound of her breathing. Just being on the call with her was a safe island to him.

"Oh, God, Tyler, this has been a horrible day."

"Me too, sweetheart. So, you go first."

He felt some of his tension rise again at the description of her former fiancé and his demeanor.

"Stay away from that guy, Kate. I'm smelling something really bad there."

"Oh, he's wounded, and—"

"You know wounded bears are the worst. Don't mess with him. Just stay away."

"Oh, I intend to. I do go to work tomorrow. Don't think he'll be there because he's working the cellar tonight with Sheila."

"All the same, if he comes to your house, you call the cops. Promise me you'll take precautions."

"Of course I will, silly. I just overreacted. Probably made this bigger than it needed to be."

"No. You didn't. You be careful. Promise me. You gotta promise."

"I will, Tyler. Now what is your news?"

Tyler didn't want to tell her about the altercation, abiding by the age-old tradition of keeping family business within the family. Though there might be something in the newspaper about it, he doubted Kate would ever know, and decided it was more than she should have to handle.

"My stuff looks pretty stupid. Like a paper cut, in comparison."

Her laugh was like fresh water washing over him. Such a delicious experience, to be bathed in the beauty of her voice.

CHAPTER 24

Kate called her mother and agreed to stop by for that talk Kate was dreading.

Louise Morgan had dark bags under her eyes and Kate could tell she'd been crying recently. She gave her mother a powerful hug, squeezing the woman who had always been her kind confidant, and noticing she had lost weight, and was a little stiff.

"You're losing too much weight, Mom."

"I'm fine. All this wedding stuff is..." she walked to the kitchen to pour two glasses of ice water, which was their custom. "I don't do well with all this planning, and now the unplanning." Her sad eyes looked up at Kate as she handed her the frosty glass.

Kate found her eyes welling with tears she couldn't help but let fall. "I'm so sorry, Mom." Now she was in her mom's company, she finally realized the intensity of her feelings about the mess Kate had created. Kate chastised herself for not realizing it sooner.

But the dull ache in her belly, that warm glow of a new love, a new relationship, wouldn't be trampled, even with the obvious evidence of her mother's pain.

They both drank in silence, standing in the kitchen as they often did.

Mrs. Morgan took Kate's hand and led her to the living room, where they sat in overstuffed chairs at forty-five degree angles.

"So, tell me about him," her mother said.

"I met him on the plane. It was like we instantly knew we were right for each other."

Kate's mom leaned back in her chair and looked up at the ceiling. She slowly lowered her gaze to look out the picture windows to a garden full of flowers beyond. Her expression was vacant, as if she was caught in a daydream.

"Mom?"

Mrs. Morgan shook her head slightly. "A chance meeting on a plane. What are the odds?" She smiled and pulled at a tiny piece of thread from the denim of her jeans at her thigh.

"Yes. That's exactly it."

"And he feels the same way?"

"Yes. I've invited him to come up this weekend. He deploys on Monday."

"Deploy? He's in the military?"

"He's a SEAL, mom. A specially trained—"

"I know what a SEAL is. I haven't been living in a cave here."

Her mother's sharp tongue surprised her. She decided to go slow. "He leaves for about six months, not the two years most others do. He was flying home to say goodbye to his mother and father, who live in Portland."

Mrs. Morgan sipped her water, finishing it. "What does Gretchen think of him?"

"I thought you'd tell me yourself. I'm sure you two have talked."

"She's tight-lipped on this one, Kate. I couldn't get diddly out of her, which is why I'm guessing this is serious."

"It is."

"Gretchen always has plenty of opinions about men. I knew when I couldn't wrestle a single tidbit out of her she was worried she'd have to eat her words. So tell me about him. You haven't told me anything yet."

"His name is Tyler Gray, for starters."

"Where's he from?"

"All over, I guess. He lives in San Diego now, where his Team is based."

"Okay."

They both sat in silence. Kate filled the looming sound gap between them. "He's not the reason I called the wedding off, Mom. I was making do. I was telling myself I was happy, but I'm not sure I ever was. I think I was doing what everyone expected me to do. Randy has been popular with all my friends for years. When he got interested in me, I just went along with it. Does that make sense?"

"No. I don't know what to say, Kate. It never occurred to me you weren't happy with this decision, or felt pressured at any time."

"I wasn't thinking, Mom. Ever have that happen to you? You just go along with things because you'd already given your word? But what if you were sure you would be miserable? Would you still go along with it?"

"I would say better to figure out the relationship you're in first, before you start another one," her mother said.

"I agree totally." Kate searched her face and saw some sympathy there. Her mother's eyes were pleading, yet kind. Not angry as Kate had expected she would be. "But Mom, I didn't realize it until I got a glimpse of a life I could see myself living. With a man who is the perfect fit."

Mrs. Morgan looked down at her hands, which were folded in her lap. Her head leaned to the side as she raised one eyebrow. "I think you're confused. I wish you'd have come home here before...before..." Her mother stopped and closed her eyes. Kate suspected it was so she would have to feel guilty for making her mother cry.

"What is it, Mom?" Kate said as she took one of her mother's hands and squeezed it.

When Mrs. Morgan opened her eyes, some of her eyelashes were glistening, but, other than that, no evidence remained that she'd been holding back tears. "Oh honey," she said to Kate as she brought her hand up to Kate's cheek. "I've been there. Way before you were born."

With her mother's story still floating around in her head, Kate got into work early the next morning, anxious to get started on the after-the-weekend cleanup that had probably been left for her. While others of the Tasting Room staff usually had Mondays and Tuesdays off, Kate worked. She didn't mind it. Keeping the showroom clean and sparkling was something she did with pride.

The idea that her mother had been in love with someone else before she married her father was like putting peanut butter on sushi. Her mom had met a young Marine who was on his way home for Christmas before his last tour in Vietnam. She told Kate they'd corresponded, even though she had a serious boyfriend she was expected to marry at the time—another man, not her father.

He changed my life that day. I was grateful for his service, but there was something about him I didn't want to let go of. And I should have.

Kate began mopping down the tiled floor of the tasting room while she continued to think about their conversation yesterday.

His letters quickly got very passionate. I felt guilty for not telling him I had a guy. He wrote me every day, Kate.

She stopped and looked around the center where they had hosted so many happy wedding receptions. Hers had been planned for this sunny room, big enough to seat two hundred people, room enough for a small orchestra. She saw the garlands and flower petals everywhere in her mind. Heard music and was dancing slowly, all of a sudden alone. It was Tyler she saw when she looked up at her partner. Tyler smiling down on her. It was a lovely fantasy.

Sighing, she went to find her next chore.

It looked like a small wedding party had taken place last night in the showroom. Several bottles of their reserve label wine were open and only halfway consumed, bottles with a retail value of more one hundred dollars each. One looked like someone had been drinking straight out of the bottle. She saw pink lipstick stains neatly wrapped around the neck like a calling card.

The leftover chocolate truffles left in the refrigerator were gone, as well as a discarded box of chocolate-covered strawberries someone had brought with them. She wondered who would have stayed behind and partied, since it wasn't a normal tasting room day.

She immediately thought about Randy. She wouldn't put it past him to have his own little pity party, and he'd have the added pleasure of knowing it would be Kate's job to clean up after his night of whatever. She had no right to feel put upon, either, since she'd broken off the engagement, but somehow she had an inkling he had done it on purpose.

She ran the dishwasher for the glasses, put all the bottles in a black garbage bag and dumped them in back at the glass recycle. She wiped down the highly polished maple bar top. She'd turned on music, since country-western music was her preferred soundtrack when she did housework.

She jerked and stood up sharply when someone turned it off.

Mark Heller stood nearby with his arms crossed.

"Kate, we've got to talk."

CHAPTER 25

Heller was fidgeting in his chair, stalling for words before he crossed his long legs and folded his hands on his knee. As she watched him tilt his head and smile gently, she thought again that he would have made a good father-in-law. He did seem to genuinely care about people, and about her in particular. And she'd seen him chastise Randy, who had been self-indulgent his whole life, mostly due to his mother spoiling him. But one thing was certain: Heller was the head of the family concern, and would be as long as he was alive.

"Kate, I am so sorry about all this to-do with the wedding. Your new fella kind of surprises me, though. He's a soldier, I understand. He can't do for you what Randy and his mom and I can do for you."

She wasn't sure she was hearing correctly. Was he thinking she would sell out for money? That a life of comfort and privilege eclipsed a life of love? Did the man have ice water in his veins?

She'd gotten used to calling him Mark, but used the more formal term, due to the circumstances.

"Mr. Heller, I'm sure you understand about matters of the heart." She searched his eyes and perhaps saw some vacantness there, a hollow core he didn't usually let people see. Maybe he wouldn't understand about finding and being with a soul mate.

"I care a great deal for Randy," she continued, "and you and your wife have been wonderful to me. As Randy has reminded me many times," she could see him stiffen at that remark. "You have accepted me into your beautiful family with open arms. It is with the same full heart I now must level with you. I don't love your son. I don't think I ever did, and I am so sorry to have put everyone through so much because of my lack of focus."

It was the truth. She delivered it in a matter-of-fact way, trying to keep all emotion out of the communication, and it leached the tension right out of the air. She was proud she'd been honest with him. Maybe that meant the second talk with Randy had a more pleasant prognosis.

"What did he do?" Heller asked, closing his eyes.

"Pardon?"

"Did he mistreat you?"

What an odd statement.

"No, Randy—I don't understand what you mean. I have no complaints there. I never have."

Heller had lost his composure. The veneer of a well-ordered life had melted. For the first time since she'd met him, Mr. Heller looked troubled.

"We thought you'd enjoy working with us in the family business. You seem to be quite a natural in the tasting room. Sales is your thing, Kate. It really is."

Except I'm not selling very well right now. Why don't you understand about love? Where is love in your well-ordered world?

"It's a fantastic opportunity. But it belongs to someone else. I've enjoyed working here—"

"You're leaving us?"

She was taken aback. "Well, I don't have to. No."

"Because we would miss you dearly."

"Well, I wasn't planning on—"

"Harvest will be upon us in three months, and we have all the holiday parties to plan—"

"Well yes, sure I can stay—"

"I don't suppose Randy will be quite up to speed with this big setback you've handed him, but he'll get better in time. I think he'll be right in the thick of things once he fully recovers."

Recovers? Like from a broken leg or bee sting? That kind of recovery? Kate cocked her head, sure that she'd missed something. "Mr. Heller, you *want* me to stay, then?"

"Of course, Kate. We love you like you were our own daughter."

Now she was getting creeped out by Heller. She broke off her engagement with his son, shacked up with some guy for a couple of days, and he didn't fire her *and* he still loved her "like family?"

Holy shit!

Heller stood up, extending his hand. Then he thought better of it. "Oh, hell, Kate," he said as he grabbed hold of her and gave her a hug which she stiffly did not return. "I still consider you part of our family here at Heller Vineyards. And I guess this doesn't change much, then."

He squeezed her and then gripped the tops of her arms while she looked on with incredulity. He was smiling, acting as if nothing had happened. As if all the wedding plans and the money spent for caterers, chefs, stagecoaches and Clydesdale horses was a mere drop in the bucket to him. It was as if she'd cancelled a luncheon date and nothing worse.

Without asking her anything further he placed an arm around her shoulder, "Kate, I'm glad we had this little talk. And I'm so pleased you'll be staying on."

He opened the door to the office and released her to float into the enormous, completely vacant tasting room space, sure that the echo of her thudding heart was shaking the windows.

CHAPTER 26

Tyler brought the frog into Gunny's so it could be properly displayed until Timmons's situation was worked out. His wife had been charged with assault but released. And that meant, thanks to a screwed-up twist of fate, that Timmons would have to stay somewhere else. He hadn't been able to spend one night of his retirement in his own home.

T.J. volunteered to be his babysitter, since he and Frankie had rented a three-bedroom apartment and were looking to add someone from one of the Teams who were just coming back off rotation. That way, someone would be home all the time, and their stuff had less of a chance of walking while they were on deployment.

It was an unwritten rule Timmons would not be left alone until they went overseas. And then someone else's group would be assigned to watch over the man. No one wanted something to happen to the guy to interfere with his retirement.

Timmons was wearing a new pair of Navy swim trunks, running shoes and a tank top they'd bought for him over at the Commissary.

"Don't think I've ever seen you in running shoes, Chief."

"These are cross trainers. No fuckin' way I'm going to go running," Timmons answered back.

Amornpan and Sanouk entered through the back door. "Hey, Sanouk?" T.J. asked. "Can we buy him one of those long-sleeved Gunny's Gym shirts?"

"Nah, fellas, you don't have to do that," Timmons protested. "Besides, having a picture of the Popeye character and remembering old Gunny might make me start to cry, and that wouldn't be very manly of me, would it?"

"What size are you, Mr. Chief?" Amornpan asked. Her pretty eyes were soft and friendly towards Timmons, who turned three shades of pink under the gaze of the still-attractive Thai woman.

"Um," Timmons stumbled over himself as he scurried for the words he was looking for. "XL I believe, ma'am," he said with a slight bow.

It touched Tyler to see the man show respect for Gunny's widow.

She brought the white tee shirt over, unpinned the arms and shoulders and held it up to his chest. She barely came to Timmons's armpits, her long, hot pink fingernails looking like claws on the exotic creature she was.

"I say this one is perfect, Mr. Chief," she said in her lovely, singsong voice.

She lay the shirt against Timmons's torso and walked away. The Chief didn't seem to know what to do next. He looked at T.J., who was shaking his head.

"You can consider this a gift from Mr. Gunny himself," Amornpan said with her back turned, face in profile to Timmons, demure, and, Tyler would have to say, doe-like.

"Then I thank you, ma'am."

Tyler and T.J. darted quick looks between them. After Timmons got himself settled and his future was figured out, Tyler wouldn't be surprised at all if Timmons developed a sudden fondness for gyms, this gym in particular, and the lovely Asian goddess who left her imprint everywhere she went.

Friday couldn't come fast enough for Tyler. He boarded the plane from San Diego and in just under two hours touched down at Schulz International Airport. Kate ran to him as soon as he entered the small terminal. He dropped his bag to welcome her exuberant body slam.

His heart was overjoyed. He'd been heavy with worry that she'd have to call him and postpone their get-together, and he'd have to go out of country without being able to see her one more time.

Her lips were urgent. She clung to him with fierce need, which was just about the biggest turn-on, and something he'd never dared to dream was possible. He felt her need match and melt into his as the sensual sparks flew and his hands smoothed over her satin skin. Her sweet softness and fresh scent, given up to him so willingly, so utterly compliant, made him wish somehow his deployment was over, that this was the homecoming he'd get when he could finally stay for more than two nights.

Two measly nights! It was all they had left. He wanted to see everything about where she grew up, and meet her folks. Even take a good look at her asshole of a former fiancé and let him know that Tyler was the man he'd have to answer to if the guy had any designs on her. Of course he was all in. And, thank the God of SEALs, it looked like she wanted him right there next to her, as tight as they could get.

"Baby, it was way too long. We should just run away," he nuzzled into the hair at her temple. "We could disappear. Wanna disappear?"

That little giggle as she snuggled under his chin, as her arms came up his back, pulling him into her. Her fingers migrated to comb through the curls above his collar, stroking and squeezing. Her hard pubic bone rode his shaft through his jeans. He pressed her there, aching with need, and then just aching.

"If you weren't the man I know you to be, Tyler, I'd take you up on it. God, I wish I had a few million stashed away somewhere so we could do that. But we have this." She stood on tiptoes and placed her succulent lips across his.

"And this is pretty damned good, baby."

"The best."

With one arm wrapped tight around her waist, he practically carried her through the glass doors of the terminal to the parking lot beyond, slinging his bag over his left shoulder. Her feet barely touched the floor. She hung onto his shoulders, using her right thigh to gently balance against his hipbone as he walked. She wasn't light, but he'd carry her all the way to San Francisco if she'd let him. And, heck, he and his buddies had carried telephone poles up and down the god-damned beach at a full run in combat boots without hardly breaking a sweat.

She'd started to get out her keys and he swiped them, giving her another kiss when she showed that fresh smile again. He stowed his bag in the hatch and they drove toward the freeway, heading north.

He found the little town of Healdsburg to be charming, reminding him of some of the villages in the south of France, or New England, where shops surrounded a town square complete with a lawn, gazebo and park benches. The square was a gathering place, and he noted the foot traffic was so thick that maneuvering the car to make a right turn as she had instructed was tricky.

They drove down a wide street with grand houses, most of them early California or large bungalow-style. At a light green mansion, she told him to turn right and pointed around the corner to the back of the property, where he spotted a lemon yellow cottage.

"Nice, Kate. Love it."

"Thank you," she said bashfully. He could see she was thinking about what they'd be doing just as soon as he got them properly naked. He liked that she was shy, that her cheeks had that just-kissed blush on her fair, peachy skin. She stole little glances at him, which set his insides on fire. He'd never wanted a woman more.

She slipped out of the car before he could get to her side and they practically raced to the front door. His hands were all over her backside, and she dropped her keys twice and feigned at swatting his hands down so she could concentrate and get them inside.

Her cottage looked just like he thought it would. Colorful posters and canvas prints adorned the walls, giving it a cheery, bright atmosphere without looking cluttered. She had an antique patchwork quilt on her full-sized bed, which was the only disappointment for him. But it also meant that she wouldn't be able to get away from him all night long.

She dropped her purse and kicked off her shoes before he could get his off. Her cotton top and mid-calf jeans were next to go. He had to work to keep up with her. She won because she wasn't wearing a bra.

She dove under the covers and he followed. Her cotton sheets smelled glorious and felt cool, emphasizing the warmth of her body as she slid into him, kissing him everywhere. She held his thigh between hers, pushing him back into the pillows that smelled of Kate, against the headboard, riding him, leaning forward to moan into his mouth as his hands smoothed over the velvet skin of her ass. She kissed him under his ear, under his chin, between his pecs, and was going to go down on him, but he chuckled, not letting her get there by holding her arm.

"Na-ah, Kate. This time we do it my way."

"What do you mean?" She crawled up his body, pinning his shoulders with her knees and treating him to a good taste of her nipples. She ground down on his chest with her sex, holding onto the headboard with one hand, then leaned back and gasped like a six-year-old riding her favorite merry-go-round horse. But he wasn't inside yet. She was writhing and holding her breasts, watching him with her eyes flashing fire, begging him to lose control. "Is this what you like?" she asked as she again pressed her puckered pussy over his left nipple and rubbed.

"We do all this and it'll be over soon, and then I'll have to rest a bit, sweetheart."

She stopped, her arms and palms covering her full breasts, hiding her beauty, those pink tips of her nipples, from his gaze. With one hand cupping the back of her head, he gripped her scalp, bringing her face to his lips. He plunged his tongue deep, then swiftly pushed her long, beautiful curls away from her ear, kissed her, and said, "I want to fuck you slow, Kate. Make it last. Baby. I need to feel you come under me."

He bit her earlobe and she hissed, pressing harder so he could bite her again.

"Let's slow down, baby," he said, squeezing her breasts before finding a hiding place between her legs. She laid her sex on his palm and undulated, making love to his fingers. One by one he penetrated her wet lips as he began to feel her shudder.

Kate wasn't going to go slow, which meant he had to work harder to help her reach the crescendo he wanted her to feel. Having her shatter beneath him, calling his name, became the most important thing in the world.

He flipped her on her back with a fluid, cat-like movement. Her hands slid up the sheets, diving under the pillows to grip the bars of her headboard. He pulled aside one soft pillow, placing it under her rear to raise her pelvis up.

"Taste me, Tyler," she whispered.

He shook his head. "No."

"Pleeeease," she whined. "God, I need you."

"Slow down and I'll do it all to you, baby. And I'll make it last all night, sweetheart."

She turned her head to the side and moaned into the pillow. He pressed one thumb on her nub and she gasped.

"Not fair, Tyler."

"Shhh, baby. Slow baby." With deliberate figure eights, he thumbed over her nub, bending to tweak the little organ with the tip of his tongue. She tried to raise her hips, to push her pussy into his mouth, but he smiled and pulled back. "Slow, Kate. We take it slow, like this." He rimmed her opening with his forefinger and she tilted her pelvis up towards him again. She rolled to the side and held his hand between her legs and undulated slowly back and forth, making love to his fingers again.

"Yes, baby."

"Need you inside me, Tyler."

Her body in profile, moving back and forth, burying his hand in her soft moist juncture, was a beautiful thing. He smoothed his hand against her ass cheek, gently following the cleft, tracing a line he kissed from her anus to her channel. Pushing the firm flesh of her cheek back, he exposed her sex, the red swollen lips that called to him. He bent and explored the slit with his tongue, sucking on her nub before lifting his head to look at her.

She was trying to make the fingers of his other hand impale her again, but he slid his arm up her torso, between her breasts, reaching around her delicate neck to grip the hair at the back of her neck and whispered, "Slowly, my sweet. Please, Kate, I'm begging you."

She wasn't listening. Her moans fought against his resolve. She was ravenous to be satisfied and Tyler was slowly losing his ability to keep from spilling. He quickly slipped on a condom and rooted himself along her cleft, pushing hard against her from behind, sliding underneath until he was poised at her opening. She angled her pelvis, spreading her underside wider until just his head entered her body.

She arched and inhaled, pushing her whole body against his cock, forcing it inside her deep. "Yessss, Tyler."

So much for being slow. The sight of her quivering beneath him spurred him on. He forced himself in from behind, so deep she made guttural groans of pleasure. Careful and slow at first, his deep penetrations became more urgent and finally he was pumping her hard, spreading her ass cheeks open so he could slip under for deeper penetration.

He felt her internal muscles clamp down on him. She was tight as she milked him. He leaned forward and whispered in her ear, "You like that baby? You like fucking me, baby?"

"God, Tyler. Don't stop. Don't ever stop."

He stopped holding back, thrust several times, and held himself inside her to the hilt. She seemed to flex and then soften against him as she allowed him to penetrate deeper than he'd ever been before. He felt his seed spurt inside the condom buried deep inside her while she shuddered and groaned. He bunched up her lips with his left hand, turning her head slightly to let her have her way with his tongue, which he plunged deep, just as he rode her deep, forcing his hips against her and then releasing.

She wanted to turn, so he moved her left leg in front of him and looped her knee over his shoulder. At an angle he fucked her, which gave him a whole new sensation. She felt it too, as she gasped, her insides vibrating against him. Her hands flew to his shoulders, up his neck to cup his cheeks. "No other place in this earth I'd rather be right now, Tyler. Here. Here is where I belong. Here is where you belong."

"Yes, baby." Her arousal was building again, slowly rising in tandem with his own. Suddenly she broke, pulling him tight against her chest and then pushing him away to arch back, pushing him deeper inside her. He held her, restrained her movements, while she struggled to no avail. The harder she struggled the more she came, the harder he held her, and the more he spilled.

At last he watched her arms flop back onto the mattress, sweat covering her body, which glistened through the filtered glow of the bedroom curtains. Her perfect breasts were wet, sweat streaking down between them as her torso rose and fell with her heavy breathing. One of her hands made its way back to his mouth where she traced his lips with her forefinger, allowing him to draw it into his mouth and suck on it.

He measured his breathing to coincide with hers in perfect tandem. When she moved, he altered his angle of penetration, keeping himself fully seated, in case round two came soon.

But as he suspected, she wanted to snuggle into the space under his chin, leaning into his chest, with his arms about her waist. Her left thigh was riding his hipbone. His hands cupped her ass cheeks and pressed them into his groin.

She was perfect for him. Everything about her was perfect. Her hair splayed all over the bed was perfect. Her perfect mouth and white teeth smiled at him as her eyes danced a seven-veil dance with the promise of future liaisons. Her flawless, smooth, porcelain white skin rubbed against his tough warrior flesh, and he felt as though all the bumps and scars of battle were being lovingly rubbed off him forever.

CHAPTER 27

Next morning, she took him to the little Bistro three blocks from her cottage, bordering the Square. The town was made for lovers, he thought. Funny, now that he was fully in the throes of new love, he saw couples all around him. He noticed stolen glances between men and women he might otherwise have overlooked. His radar was set, fixed on this warm chocolate feeling that somehow just being with Kate would ease the problems of the whole world.

Every time he thought about his Team's upcoming mission, he purposely forced it out of his mind. Kyle had told him it was going to be especially dangerous, even though it would be a short one, or should be a short one. There were still no guarantees.

They'd managed to get the terp, their Afghani interpreter, out after last deployment, which had been an incredible feat. He'd never known the Navy to move so fast to relocate a valued American ally. But it meant the family that their terp, Jack Daniels, or Jackie—which wasn't his real name, but the name they could use in public when they were in the middle of a mission—his family was left behind. With the recent fall of several cities thought to be American-friendly, Kyle said Jackie's family was being hunted, and some of them had already been captured and killed, including the parents of the young lady friend Tyler and the Team had rescued a year ago from an evil warlord.

Now the whole country was overrun with warlords. Chaos was the order of the day. Without significant American forces as backup, the SEALs were being sent in quietly to rescue people trapped in the carnage and extricate them.

Lying in Kate's bed, with her favorite things displayed all over her walls, the sunlight beginning to bring a blush to the sky, the normal stuff of life, he'd have to say, the Juice of Life, it was a banquet spread before him, his to partake of for a few hours.

This was what he was fighting for, so Kate and people like her could enjoy themselves and be kept far away from the death and destruction of an imploding society. He watched the way her porcelain skin rose and fell, her muscled thigh draped across his, the way her breasts felt as she slept against him. Everything about the picture was pure chocolate, warm, and apple pie. The birds began to chirp in a nest tucked under a nearby eave, and still she slept, secure in his arms, as it should be.

He brought his palm up to tousle the hair at the back of her head. She jerked at first, and then softened and gave a delighted groan when she felt him underneath her. Her hand slipped up his neck and then her fingers walked across his lips as she raised her messed-up head with the hair all over everywhere and gave him that sexy good morning smile he'd had imprinted on his brain. He'd remember this every morning while he was away. How she needed him. How exhausted he had been, how so freakin' happy he was to have this woman in his arms. He decided if his life was limited to just these two days with Kate, it would have been worth it.

"You want to get up, get some breakfast, Tyler?"

"Um hum. Whatever you want, sweetheart. Might not be too many good places open this early."

"I can think of something we could do for the next hour or so until the coffee shops open."

"So can I, but you sleep, baby. I love just lying here feeling you sleep on me just like this."

Kate did the opposite. "Gotta get up to work, lover," she whispered. Rising up by propping her beautiful torso with her forearms placed against his upper arms, she let her breasts gently swipe against his, kissed him sweetly, but let it develop slowly, just like he liked it. She teased him, made him advance on her, using their tongues to mingle and taste. His fingers moved down the small of her back, over the dimples at the top of her butt cheeks, down the sexy cleft until he could feel her wet peach.

Groaning and undulating against him, the press of her pubic bone against the large muscles of his thigh, triggering his own need, lit the bonfire he knew would consume them both.

This delicate creature was made for him. He knew he'd finally found home, after all the years of looking in hookup places, in schools, in bars and with friends, the woman of his dreams was begging him to make love to her again, and damn, he was all in. Would be all in until she rang the bell.

After all, he never would.

She insisted on wearing the T-shirt he'd had on yesterday. She didn't have a bra, so her knotted nipples peeked deliciously through the thin white cotton fabric. Sitting across from her at the coffee house, he was constantly aware of her breasts swinging toward him, plump and inviting. She'd slipped off her jacket and the tee had fallen off her shoulder so her bare skin tempted him, too.

Over her coffee mug, her dark brown eyes dared him to be inappropriate with her. The foam of milk on her upper lip stayed just a couple of seconds until her pink tongue swiped it clean. She leaned further forward and gave him a kiss that tasted like coffee candy. The suction of their lips was making noises. They could have been slurping oysters, but it was a coffee shop, with other breakfast patrons nearby, and clearly Kate didn't care. She'd have fucked him on the table if he'd asked it of her. He knew that about her already.

"I'm getting all turned on just watching you drink coffee, Kate," he said, low enough for her ears only. A young woman sitting at the table next to them looked up.

"I can see that. It turns me on when you're turned on, baby."

"No worries there," he said as he massaged her bare foot that had migrated under the table from her clog to his groin. "I love everything about you."

She partially closed her eyes and seemed almost to purr.

"I love touching you everywhere, baby." His fingers slipped up her leg from her ankles to squeeze her calves. "I like seeing you come, lose control."

This time the young woman glared at Kate, not at him, so he chuckled.

Her look of focused need and complete hunger was a thing of beauty. His whole life he'd wanted a woman to look at him like that, with that kind of a fever for him, a flame only he could extinguish. He loved setting her on fire and feeling them both burn.

He drove her to work in her little SUV, their fingers entwined over the center console. The day was going to be warm. Cars were everywhere, even though it was early on a Saturday morning. Shops were being set up, sidewalks sprayed off, cappuccino makers were squealing, runners and cyclists speeding along on their focused quests. He thought perhaps he'd take a nice ten-mile run while she was working. He wanted to explore the beautiful Dry Creek valley floor they were traveling along. Maybe he'd bring her lunch. He could find a vineyard that was private, maybe find a little shady spot with a blanket…

He knew they were close because that deep crease at the middle of her forehead was there, signaling the return to her previous life. Not what her life was going to be like from now on, but her previous life. With *that* guy.

Through the tall pillars marked with a large H logo, identifying it as Heller Estate Vineyards, he drove up the crushed granite drive to the tasting room. It was a modern two-story stone and wood structure, with oversized doors and windows.

Rows of lush, bright green vines were maturing all around them. The soil was dark and freshly tilled. The front of the building had stainless steel containers bursting with flowering plants.

She directed him towards the side, where he parked. He turned in his seat, put his arm around her shoulders and pulled her to him. "Showtime, baby. Go sell some wine."

He could tell the way she lingered in his kiss, she didn't want him to go.

"Shall I walk you in? You want to show me off to anybody, anybody named Randy, perhaps?" He allowed his feral look to descend upon her, including a half smile á la Captain Jack Sparrow.

"That wouldn't be very fair, now would it? Put you in an awkward position?" she said just before she let herself out of the car.

He got out quickly and ran around to meet her, giving her a hug, not letting her go. "I'm not in any awkward position. Besides, I loved all the awkward positions you put me in all night and early this morning." He kissed her in front of whoever might be looking. "I'm thinking of those positions, baby. Those you did for me, those little private lap dances, and I love it."

She was blushing as she took his hand and led him into the snake pit of the tasting room. She didn't seem surprised to see two people standing near the bar. One was an attractive, rusty-red-haired young woman about Kate's age, and the other was a handsome, graying older man. And then he recognized the redhead. They'd had a one-night stand in San Diego. A very drunken one night stand. And the lady had been a blonde then.

Holy fuckin' shit. What were the odds?

Tyler recognized the older man from the website photos he'd studied.

"Mark Heller. You must be Tyler." The man extended his hand and shook Tyler's with a firm grip. His face was hard to read. His lips formed a thin line yet his eyes seemed genuinely warm.

The young lady's eyes got huge as a sly smile curled up her lips. She didn't eye him like girls often did in San Diego at the beach, not bothering with anything but his package. That's how she'd been that night, and he'd fallen for it. But now her eyes flirted with him openly, sending an alarm straight to his gut. She was thinking about outing him with Kate regarding their night of sex. She was toying with him and enjoying it.

"And this is my friend, Sheila," Kate said.

Sheila's blue-green eyes, enhanced by contacts, delivered the cool message that she was available if Kate should suddenly have a change of heart, or if he did. Maybe even hinting she'd be more likely to keep quiet if he'd show her a little attention again. He'd had to work damned hard the first time to get rid of her. She had been such a frog hog to all the Team guys down there, she even broke up a couple of marriages. *Holy fuckin' hell. I'm screwed.*

Kate appeared to be completely oblivious to Sheila's wayward charms. Or maybe it was just the sexual energy those types of girls had—something that translated to men but couldn't be picked up by other women. He'd been a magnet for that kind of woman in the past. They seemed to know he would cave easily, if they came after him. But he would never call them back.

Not ever.

Kate was going to be his forever, and it didn't matter how long or short it was. He wanted her tight against him. He hoped to God he could get Kate alone to explain if Sheila—and was that even her name?—if Sheila opted to play dirty. He certainly knew she was capable of it.

"Nice to meet you, Sheila," he said with a slight bow, ignoring her outstretched hand. Her eyes got murderous but her smile was all vixen. It was a challenge he had totally lost his appetite for and would not accept.

Heller addressed Kate with coolness. "I have some things to go over first, if you have a moment, and then I'll not interfere with your work."

"Of course," she said. Turning to Tyler, "I'll only be a moment. Wait a bit for me?" She gave him a quick kiss on her tiptoes and he whispered yes.

Her innocence caused him pain, especially since the woman he wanted to forget was swaying from side to side, eager to be able to speak with him alone. He wanted to be anywhere but there. Kate allowed herself to be led to a distant office, where Heller waved to Tyler before closing the door behind her.

Sheila was going to take a chance, he just knew it. He'd already had serious questions about her friendship with Kate, just from Kate's comments about her. Now he knew why. He knew the type. Snakes, the worst kind of people on the planet. Male or female they wreaked havoc wherever they went. Sheila was a user. And Kate didn't realize it. Problem was, he had very little time to convince her without upsetting the whole apple cart.

He'd have to deal with Sheila as best he could. Based on how it went he'd be able to figure out the best course of action.

"Tyler, afraid to shake my hand? Afraid to touch my body?"

"Shut up. This is not appropriate."

"Oh you like all kinds of inappropriate. I know you, Tyler. How many times did we do it?"

"It was one night. And I was drunk."

"But I know you remember. I see it in your eyes, and if I'm not—" her eyes had dropped to his groin.

"Not happening. Nothing here for you, Sheila, if that's even your name."

"I'm not offended you don't remember my name, Ty."

"What about *leave me alone* do you not understand? What kind of an idiot do you think I am? You honestly think I could ever want to be with someone like you if I wasn't shitfaced? You're a fuckin' bitch in heat and all the guys knew it. You didn't snag one of them. We all figured it out."

"Just a minor setback. I've moved on. I'm enjoying myself up here, playing the field. Got a little house, some savings. I'm not the penniless tramp you thought I was. Things have changed, and have been looking up for me."

"Glad to hear it. Now keep away from me and from Kate, or I'll tell them what a bitch you really are. I suppose you're going after Kate's Randy, too."

"What do you think? I bring him something he can't get with Kate. You know, I can't help myself."

"I'll bet. Some friend. Stabbing her in the back."

"What do you care? She dumped him for you. I'd say you're playing the same game, Tyler. I like that you move so fast—"

"Don't touch me." He backed up. The longer they talked, the angrier he got. And she loved it.

"What's the matter, Tyler? Did I upset your little world? Your little honey bucket? Like I said, I know you."

"Sheila, I'd like to make one thing perfectly clear." He'd lowered his voice, leaned in her direction in a conspiratorial fashion. She was eager to listen, and stepped compliantly toward him. He could tell she wanted to appear docile, but it wasn't part of her makeup. And her cold, rough spots could never be hidden.

After a long pause, while her chest leaned dangerously close to him, with her not used to rejection, primed and ready to ignite, he whispered, "I don't fuck my lady's friends. And I was never attracted to you."

She reared back like she was going to slap him, but there was no denying he'd delivered the first blow, and there wasn't anything she could do to improve her situation. She turned one hundred degrees of hatred on him with those eyes of hers, enough to make the hairs on the back of his arms stiffen.

But he also saw she got the message. Tyler wasn't here to play nice. He was here to protect the woman he loved—with extreme force if necessary.

He just hoped it wouldn't come to that.

CHAPTER 28

Mr. Heller was uncomfortable about something.

"Kate, I've been looking over some expenses, and we're trying to be careful right now. Have lots of expenditures coming up with the crush and all. Always takes a while before the sales start trickling in. Your pre-release sales have helped us a lot."

"Thank you, Mr. Heller. My pleasure."

"So I've noticed some things, invoices here I don't understand." He showed her a series of printing invoices, catering bills and entertainment receipts.

"I'm sorry, but I don't recognize them," she said. She was surprised they had been presented to her. "You thought I authorized them?"

"Perhaps I got it wrong. I'll check with Randy, then. Not to worry." He added after a pause. "We want to be a little frugal. Cash is a bit tight right now, and we have to make it stretch."

"I understand completely, sir. No problem here. I completely agree. And I'll step up my calling on Monday morning."

"Excellent."

Both Tyler and Sheila were gone. She found Tyler sitting in her car in the parking lot. He rolled down the window as she approached.

"There you are."

"Sorry, needed some air."

"That hard?"

"No, not hard at all. Just get a really bad vibe from Sheila. How well do you know her, babe?"

Kate shrugged. "I'd always thought of her as my friend. But a couple of days ago I just felt…well, don't get me wrong on this, Tyler. I'm not jealous, but I got the feeling she liked Randy. Was a little too familiar with Randy."

"She's no good, Kate. She's bad news."

"You sound like you know her." Kate bore into him, and she could see it was making him squirm.

"I've seen the type before. A real schemer. I'd watch my back around her. She's not who you think she is. Trust me on this. I know the type."

"Tyler, what did she say to you?"

"Nothing. Kate, it's nothing. I just don't trust her."

"She must have said something."

"No, babe. Don't go there. I just don't like her, and I trust her even less." His smile melted her and was a welcome distraction. "Just watch your back. I'm probably overly sensitive to it…now."

She blushed. She liked that he was overly protective of her. She couldn't wait until she could get close and naked with him again.

A limo pulled up and people began pouring out.

"I have to go," she said quickly. "See you at five?"

"Earlier, if you can," he said.

CHAPTER 29

The idyllic green vineyard vistas and quaint shops didn't feel as welcoming as before. The mood of the area had shifted in Tyler's mind, especially since he'd seen Sheila, and he had to get away from her. There was something dark and brooding, something unhealthy collecting around the winery, and it made him uneasy to think Kate was working there.

Kate phoned him after barely an hour.

"Just had to hear your voice. I know I won't be able to do this for very much longer. Thought I would indulge my fantasies," Kate said.

He was happy to hear from her.

"God I wish I could have stayed here longer, helped you through whatever's gonna fall out. Sorry, babe. You forgive me?"

"Of course I forgive you. Nothing to forgive." He pulled over to speak to her, letting slow tourist traffic pass him by.

The sky was a robin's-egg blue, and the green and yellow rows of grapes had not formed fruit large enough to see. A lone airplane flew overhead. Everything seemed so beautiful and normal.

But the hairs on the back of his neck and on his forearms stood on end. He couldn't shake the feeling something was very wrong and about to get worse.

"Wish we had more time. I'd help you look for another job. I mean, don't get me wrong, I'm grateful you'll be busy and getting a steady paycheck. But there's something about that place I just don't like."

"I feel it too. You're sort of my bellwether, Tyler. Before I met you, I didn't get that vibe at all. But now, I agree, something is wrong. I'm not sure I want to know any more than that."

"Some things, baby, are best not to know." He wondered if Sheila would make good on her threat. "Can you quit and go work for someone else?"

"I could try, but you want me going out interviewing other places when we have so little time together?"

"You're right, baby. Maybe while I'm gone you'd have the time to look into it, although I don't like the idea of you going around by yourself granting interviews."

"Tyler, I'm twenty-eight years old. I've been on my own for more than five years now. Even my parents don't worry about me that much."

"Well, maybe they should."

Tyler showered after his long run, then dressed and drove to the square to find an espresso coffee shop where he could check emails and perhaps write Kate another letter.

He mulled over his conversation with Sheila. He'd seen his share of snakes and couldn't believe he'd fallen for her come-on that night in San Diego. People like that were pure poison, all soft and compliant and friendly in the beginning, but inside they were seething with plans, working their evil ways to achieve for their own selfish ends.

They were just like the leaders who pretended to be friends of the American soldiers, but who would betray the same soldier for a plate of meat that might feed his family for a week. It wasn't the selling information he objected to. Every civilization in history had done that from time to time, according to what he'd studied. It was the faking of friendship which he found so distasteful. He placed a call to Kyle, half hoping he didn't get hold of him. His LPO was babysitting Brandon and wasn't in a talkative mood, which was fine with Tyler.

"You guys getting square, or should I say horizontal?" Kyle asked.

"Yes, I'm getting my regular vitamins, Mom. Stuff's working, too, because I've nearly had to change pants sizes."

The chuckle at the other end was music to his ears. It took a lot to get Kyle to laugh out loud these days. Tyler knew it was because of the upcoming deployment. They were always mentally challenging, but this one was going to be tough, and everyone knew it.

"I remember those days," Kyle finally replied.

"You're not foolin' me, old married man with one in the oven."

"Yeah. Sure would be nice if it was quick."

"Intense and quick, that's what I'll pray for, then," Tyler said.

"Then we'd have to start calling you Armani," Kyle was referring to their Puerto Rican SEAL, Armando Guzman, who had fallen for and married an undercover cop. He was the fancy dresser in the group, except that now he was doing everything he could to get Gina, his wife, knocked up before they left, and had been given the advice to screw often and fast to get the job done.

It wasn't working.

"I'd walk a bit in his pants any day—oh, Kyle, dammit, I didn't mean what that sounded—"

"Shut the fuck up. Now you owe him one. He gets to kiss your lady. Kate is it?"

"He does not fuckin' get to kiss my lady. He can kiss my ass. Don't care who he is."

"*Brandon! Watch your language.*" Kyle said in muffled tones to his toddler son. "Sorry, Ty. Brandon just let fly another f-bomb."

"Sounds like time to look for another preschool?"

"Nah, we're good. Jasmine and Jones's sisters work together at a really great one that has a lot of froglets. They're used to it. Not that I'm sayin' it's right."

"I'm glad. How's Nick doing? Was thinking of stopping by to say hi."

"He's already here. Came yesterday. You guys must have passed each other in the airport."

"So he's staying with."

"We're right as rain. Providing you can walk tomorrow, and you *are* coming back tomorrow, of course?"

"Fuckin' A."

"No tears now, sweetheart."

"No tears. Gonna hurt, but not nearly as much as if I hadn't been able to come up here. Thanks, man, for that."

"I thought that would be the case. So for the good of the Team I let you go. But don't spread it around."

"Roger that. I'll tell everyone I volunteered for a month of babysitting Brandon to get to come."

"Nah, no one'd believe that. But assuming you get your butt down here, we got everyone. Even some new guys who just graduated, lucky stiffs."

"I like T.J. and Frankie. Ollie too, I guess. Just don't know him yet."

"Those two were inseparable until Frankie got engaged."

"Good for him."

Tyler could feel the nervousness percolating between them. They'd come to that part in the conversation where they'd said everything they had to say. Kyle had checked up on him, and he'd passed, or there would be more personal questions coming his way, bam-bam-bam like enemy fire.

"Well, I gotta go. Think I'll go let Brandon tie me up again."

"That's a plan, then. You can let Christy untie you. Naked. Bring her Fifty Shades of Red Hot SEAL."

"Now you're talking about one of your sister's books. All the girls at Christy's office are going to be sorely disappointed to find out you're taken. They've been passing those books around like crazy."

"Bet my sister loves it. Haven't seen her this time to say good-bye. I better go give her a call."

"Yup. You get yourself back here with enough sleep under your belt. Sure as hell you won't be sleeping much on the bird over."

"None of us do."

"That's a fact. Okay, gotta go, Tyler."

"Wait one sec Kyle. How's Timmons?"

Kyle swore into the phone. Tyler heard Kyle address his young son. *"That's right, daddy said a bad word. Bad daddy."* He cleared his throat and then whispered. "Finally got rid of the battle-axe. I think he's filing papers Monday to commemorate our deployment. Moved in with his daughter temporarily, but he's in love, Tyler. You saw it in his face."

"That I did, sir. So that statue is in good hands."

"Like a fuckin' shrine. She polishes that thing off nice and pretty every time he comes in there. He's dying to have those hands work on him. I think it's been years. He's like a teenager. Doreen's gonna clean him out and he fuckin' doesn't care. He's the happiest I've ever seen him."

"That's a nice story."

"Could wind up in one of one of Linda's books."

"Stranger things have happened. Now I'm keeping my mouth shut."

"We all are. Okay, you go have some single fun and then tomorrow you get your head wrapped around this confrontation with Dr. Death. Need you whole, sane, and well-polished."

"Will do, Kyle. Planning on doing a lot of the last part tonight on into the morning."

"Well, try to get a couple of hours of rest too. Signing off."

Kyle hung up. Tyler watched a family with a toddler walking across the square. If he were lucky, that would be his fate someday. And if he wasn't? Well, then some other SEAL would step in and make sure Kate was taken care of. Sure as hell he wasn't quitting. He didn't think she would either.

He left a message for Linda, telling her he'd met a girl he wanted to introduce her to when he got back, and then started his letter to Kate. Didn't take more than two minutes before his eyes got watery.

Well, better here than in front of her, or one of the guys.

CHAPTER 30

Kate,

I'm thinking about you right now, just sitting here in between your world, here in Healdsburg, and the world I get to jump into in a couple of days. I guess you would call this the calm before the storm. I'm not going to let you read this letter until after I leave, so I don't have to see whether I make you cry or not.

I want you to be strong, Kate. Keep the faith. Use the time to think about what I do, and maybe go online and learn more about us. It's all over the internet these days. But there are some good books that might help you learn more of what we are about. Our character.

I plan on writing you every day, but not sure you'll get them that way. I like to write. Settles me. And it will give me more time to think of you, and that's a very good thing.

I still don't know much about you, and yet I do. I'm kind of glad, in a sick kind of way, you'll have to battle the forces of your ex and his family your way. That's your fight, not mine. All I can offer you is protection, and love. Always those two together. I will never let you down. I will always come home to you. I will be there, sweetheart, as soon as I can.

Hope you sell a ton of wine. I guess I should say gallons—no, barrels—of wine! I hope that you throw yourself into your work just like I do. Make a difference. Make it count. It all counts, in the end.

Keep yourself safe. Watch those creeps around you. I especially get a negative vibe from Sheila. You want to stay away from her. Trust me on that. Please keep your distance.

I kinda like the Hellers, at least Sr. seems to have a good head on his shoulders. From what I've heard from you, Randy doesn't measure up to his father, so watch him, Kate. The weak ones can mess things up for everyone else.

So, seriously, don't trust anybody. The only people you can truly trust are other Team families. You're going to form new friendships, Kate. That sometimes means leaving the old ones out in the cold. People sometimes aren't what they seem, so be careful. You're such a trusting person, which is good, but be safe, Kate. Stay connected to the people you can trust.

Here's Linda's number. I've left her a message about you, so if you call, just tell her you're the girl. The one and only one, Kate. You two would get along. And in case I forget, we also have a Team wife in Santa Rosa you should look up, Devon Dunn. He wrote her cell phone number from his phone display. *Her husband, Nick, will be deployed with me and the rest of the Team. She's a realtor there, and a good kid. You two would be good company for each other.*

I'm reminding you to be careful. Keep your eyes open. Trust your gut, but follow your heart.

Love you, babe,

Tyler.

CHAPTER 31

The day seemed drone on endlessly. Kate found herself looking out the large picture windows at the parking lot every few minutes. Several of the tourists looked over their shoulders while she poured their samples, thinking she was talking to someone standing behind them. She made a mental note to stop allowing her distractions to interfere with her job.

She did love the wines Heller produced. They didn't scrimp when it came to selecting the grapes, crushing them in small batches, and they used the finest barrels and fermentation tanks. Later, the blending that Mr. Heller and his winemaker, Sergio, did together was the stuff of genius. The two men had worked together for years at another smaller estate winery before Heller started his own and brought Sergio with him. It was the one part of winemaking that required real talent, and lots of experience making bad wines.

She'd sold several Wine Club memberships today, and had managed to take orders on their scheduled new release of the 2012 Merlot. They'd planned a Merlot and Oysters fest that they hoped would become an annual event for some of their best customers. The entire project had been Kate's idea.

She worked with Sheila from late morning until midafternoon. They kept up the cheerful banter, as they always did. Kate began to relax and re-orient herself to her job and her surroundings. Although she could tell Sheila wanted to say something, to her credit, she kept her mouth shut. But Kate felt the pressure of being under constant scrutiny. She relaxed with the knowledge that soon she'd see Tyler, and all would be well.

An hour before she was to leave, Tyler showed up. She ran to him, inhaling his scent, feeling the reassurance of being held in his arms.

He held her out at arm's length. "You okay?"

She nodded. Trying to brush her fears aside, she put effort into sounding more together than she felt. "Can you help me with some recycling things and trash? Maybe they'll let me off a little early."

"Absolutely. Music to my ears. Just show me."

They completed the room cleanup in record time. Kate looked for Mr. Heller or anyone who would have the authority to let her go early, but no one came into the center. Sheila was in and out. Normally helpful, she was ignoring Tyler completely and remained preoccupied with doing her bottle counting and inventory.

Kate and Tyler dusted and cleaned the product display case, folded some logo tee shirts from cartons of boxes in the storeroom.

Randy entered and consulted with Sheila on her bottle count. They shared a titter. He presented himself to Kate for an introduction to Tyler.

"This him?" Randy asked. It was delivered disrespectfully, but Kate couldn't sense Tyler was feeling anything but casual.

Tyler extended his hand, "Tyler Gray, man. How're you doing?"

"Oh, I've had better weeks," Randy said while they shook. Randy had been full of bravado until he stood close to the SEAL, who towered over him, not only in height, but bulk.

"Well, I'll leave you two, then. Kate, why don't you take off? I'm sure Sheila and I can wrap up."

At first she blinked, since she couldn't think of anything they'd left undone, and then remembered herself. "Thanks, Randy. I appreciate that."

She waved to Sheila who gave her back a big smile in return.

"That was weird," she whispered to Tyler as he opened her door.

He pulled out her seatbelt and fastened it around her, pausing to give her a soft kiss. "That's better. Just remember," he pointed two fingers at her eyes. "Focus on me." He turned the fingers around to point to his eyes. "This is all you have to do."

She watched him walk in front of her car and park his huge frame behind the wheel. She didn't want to miss a second of being with him. Suddenly their time together was becoming very urgent. It was hard not to let her mind drift to the dark side, where the possibility he wouldn't be coming home loomed.

They ate dinner at another small restaurant that carried Heller wines and was gracious enough to seat them immediately. She remembered the time Randy told her his family never had to wait for a table, and almost never paid for a meal, since it was custom to treat wine vendors to dinners on a regular basis.

"I want to meet your folks," he said. "We won't have much time tomorrow. Would they be up for a visit tonight? I know it's short notice, but we haven't got much time left."

Panic swamped her stomach, killing her appetite. With the bottle of wine at dinner, and the lack of sleep the night before, she was getting punchy and more than a little tired.

"Maybe I should just call in sick tomorrow. I'm tired, Tyler."

He wiggled his eyebrows. "Good to know." His smile was crooked.

"Know what?"

"Was beginning to wonder if you were going to wear me out. Not that it's ever happened before."

Any other man would backtrack on that comment. Tyler looked back at her with his honest blue eyes, not apologizing for the fact that he'd had lovers before her. She understood a little bit better how he was able to do what he did every day. He faced things head-on and honestly. That's the way he made decisions. Was his code, his life. And he didn't regret much. That meant there would also be no second chances. She wished she had one tenth of his courage.

"I'll call Mom."

Tyler gave her room to talk to her mother in private by excusing himself to the restroom.

"We're all set. We can go there now," she told him when he got back.

Mrs. and Mrs. Morgan greeted them warmly. Her mother especially seemed to drink in the sight of Tyler and his physique. He was honest and forthright, even telling them about his good intentions about dating their daughter. It was a refreshing change, and something that completely impressed her parents, she could tell.

He leaned over and grabbed Kate's hand. "I wish I could be here over the next few months, but unfortunately we've got a job to do overseas, and terrorists don't make things easy on our personal lives."

How could anyone argue with that one?

"But I promised your daughter I'd write to her every day. And I will."

Of that there was no question. Kate knew that he'd be sending messages or composing letters, just as he'd promised, on a daily basis.

"Like I said, I have only the best intentions when it comes to your daughter." He brought her fingers to his lips and kissed them to emphasize the point.

When they got up to go about two hours later, her parents looked like they were in shock. Her mother accepted a big hug from the SEAL, her hands fluttering over his shoulders and not hugging him back. Tyler then shook her father's hand. "Sir, it was a pleasure."

"Glad we could meet, son."

In the car on the way back to Kate's place, he was quiet. Finally he spoke up. "How'd I do?"

"I don't think they knew what hit them."

"You okay with how fast all this is going?"

Oh, yeah. She was definitely okay with this. In fact, she was more than okay with this. Excitement and passion for life sizzled through her veins again. She was on a path she wanted to be on, holding hands with the man she wanted to share it with.

Dare she have such hopes and dreams?

"Just come home to me, Tyler."

"Roger that, baby. Roger that."

CHAPTER 32

The next morning, Kate decided to not waste a single minute she could with him. Watching him sleep next to her, his arm draped lazily over her naked hip, the other one tucked under his chin like he was a little boy hugging a favorite blanket, she was struck again by how beautiful he was. Even in sleep he was confident. The rise and fall of his chest played a symphony of strings to her heart. She was grateful to have met him. Grateful that he found in her something he could love.

She placed fingers against his closed lips and watched as his big blue eyes opened.

"Good morning, beautiful."

"I could say the same about you, Tyler."

He squinted. "Beautiful? I dunno..." He laughed and pulled her against him. "But you are, my dear." He slowly kissed her on both sides of her neck. She clutched his broad shoulders, letting her palms travel over the movement of muscle and sinew as he pressed her lower torso into his groin so she'd understand he was hard again. "I could get used to this, baby."

"Makes two of us."

Tyler took his time once more, easing her into his slow, relentless rhythm until she found the sweet plateau of her flame, shuddering at the beauty and power of their physical joining. She remembered what she'd texted him,

Is it possible to love someone too much?

And he'd answered, *Not if it's me you're loving.*

Even the slowing down and putting her back on firm ground again was done with such loving skill, her eyes filled.

He knew better than to ask her what it was about. His thumbs brushed away the tears like it was no big thing. He kissed both her eyes as if healing them. "It's going to be okay, baby. You'll see."

"I'm trying, Tyler. I'm really trying. But God, I'm going to m—"

"Shhh. Quiet. I'm still here. I'll always be here," he said as he pressed his palm to her chest over her heart.

Tyler's cell phone chirped, which made him frown. Retrieving it from his pants at the side of the bed he answered.

"Kyle? Something's up?"

Then he said, "Shit. You're kiddin' me." Then, "Oh, man. They don't have flights out every hour. More like twice a day. I'd have to catch a plane from San Francisco."

Kate rolled to her back, the tears streaming down into her hair and leaking onto her pillow. The time of parting had begun. She was so freakin' scared. And heartbroken. She closed her eyes and offered up a little prayer, asking for protection.

Bring. Him. Home. Please. Please.

The thought of never seeing him again was unbearable.

"Roger that. Going to be one helluva cab fare."

"I'll take you," she whispered to his back.

Tyler put his finger up and winked at her.

"Okay then. I'll get there as soon as I can. Some of my gear is at the apartment. Do I even have time for that? Will do. See you in a few."

He hung up the phone. "Now, where were we?"

"You're about to leave."

"Oh, that. Gosh, looking at your beautiful body all naked, and me being naked, and having your scent all over me, I forgot for a second where I was. But yes, baby, now is the time we say goodbye, but only for now. We hook up again real soon."

She turned away from him and burst into tears.

"I can't see that, honey. You know we both have to be strong."

He rolled her over on her back. "A couple of things I need you to know first. Anything happens to me—"

She began to cry again, putting her hands up on her face.

"No, baby. This has to be said. Anything happens to me, my sister will be called because I haven't had time to change any notifications. You would not believe the paperwork we get to fill out all the time. I came here instead."

"Tyler, don't worry about that. Don't talk about that. Not now."

"It has to be said, sweetheart. So Linda will call you. I'll make sure she does while I'm gone." He pulled out the letter he'd written yesterday. "It's all in here, her phone number, and the phone number for Devon Dunn, who's married to one of our own, lives here in Sonoma County."

"Okay."

"Read it after I leave. Not now." He tipped her chin up, kissed her there, and then gave her a chaste kiss on the lips. "Got it?"

"Yes." She searched his warm, tenderhearted eyes. "How do you do this, Tyler? Teach me."

"Honey, I'm going to be honest with you. I never had anyone to come home to before. This is all new for me too. We'll figure it out together. You keep fighting for us, and I'll do all the rest. Just stay strong. Hang around Devon and talk to Linda. Important you talk to people in the community now. Only they understand what you're going through."

She nodded her agreement.

"We sometimes get to Skype. If you don't have it, get it. I'll email you when I can, but it might not be every day. And I'll write, but our letters come all out of order sometimes, so watch for that. Don't feel like I'm not answering you, okay?"

"Sure. So I can maybe see your face sometimes?"

"I'm hoping so. I sure as hell am going to want to see yours. I gotta call a cab."

"Let me take you down to the bus station, at least. They have cabs lined up and waiting there all the time. If you're in a hurry."

"Being in a hurry is an understatement. Normally I'd mind not getting a nice hot shower with you this morning, but I want to be able to wear that shirt you wore Friday night and hope your scent stays on it until I get back."

"And then you give that shirt to me. I'll put it on every night while you're gone so I can remember the scent and feel of you against my skin."

"Good. It will be our little routine. I like routines. They keep us safe, baby."

She gazed up at him, drawing strength from his eyes. She could see perhaps she could do this. With him believing in her, perhaps she did have it in her after all.

"We good, baby? Glad we got the lovin' in early. And it was real nice, too, the best yet."

She inhaled and he smiled, knowing another burst of tears was right there in her eyes.

"See, you're strong. Be strong for me, sweetheart."

"I promise."

"There you go. Your promise is your bond. That goes with me clear across the globe to places you don't even want to know about. You hold onto that love, and we can outdo all the evil that's out there. Remember, love is always stronger. Always."

It wasn't any good. She was going to cry again. He pulled her up and held her so she could cry on his shoulder without him having to watch. She felt the hot tears trickle down and knew some of them landed on his shoulder. His massive fingers dug into the hair at the back of her head, massaging her. He spoke little words of encouragement she couldn't hear through her sobs. He didn't hurry her. When she was done, when her shaking had subsided, he drew her back and wiped her cheeks with his fingers.

"There's my woman. God I'm a lucky man, Kate. The luckiest man alive."

That was an unfortunate choice of words but she inhaled again and willed her eyes to remain dry, and they did.

"See? You can do this." He winked, and then began pulling on his clothes. At first she watched him, then remembered she had to take him to the bus depot.

She grabbed a T-shirt, jeans, and her underwear, and got dressed in thirty seconds. She brushed her hair, put on deodorant and handed the tube to him.

"Humor me. Lavender. Wear it and be proud. Take it. It's the only thing I can give you right now that you don't already have."

He looked at it like it was a thousand dollar bill. "Thank you, sweetheart. I'll use it every day. We need it over there."

The trip to the bus station was way too fast. She'd just begun to wrap her head about the fact that he was leaving when she pulled up to the string of taxis. Tyler got out, hitching his backpack over his right shoulder, his left arm around her waist.

"It's very simple, Kate. I'm a simple guy. You just don't give up. You don't ring the bell. You stay here and you be smart."

"I will."

"If I can call you, the number will be scrambled. So you see any funny numbers, it's me, okay?"

"Okay."

"Love you, honey. I always will."

"Me too. But come back so I can show you proper," she said with as much snark as she could muster.

"I promise. You've not seen anything yet, Kate. We got our whole lives. Just remember that. Have faith in us." He kissed her deeply, sending shock waves down her spine. “Be strong,” he whispered.

“I will. I promise. Love you too.”

The cabby was getting irritated, saying something in a Middle Eastern dialect. She watched as Tyler slipped his huge body into the back seat behind the driver, and waved back to her through the window. The cabbie barreled off in a cloud of exhaust.

CHAPTER 33

Tyler mulled over what Kyle had told him. Part of Team 3 was leaving this morning. That never happened. That meant it was a really critical rescue mission. Some of their own guys were missing, he said.

The sun visor on the taxi driver's passenger side read Mohan Mazur. He was pretty sure that wasn't the driver's real name. Not many of them stayed the same when they immigrated, just like when his ancestors came over, they'd changed the family name to make it more "American" sounding. Gray. He wondered if this was the man's attempt to sound more American. So many in this country were immigrants now, they were becoming the majority.

It was interesting this brown-skinned man from somewhere else originally would be his delivery vehicle. If only he knew what Tyler did at the office every day. Yup. This was part of the America he was pledged to defend, and, if necessary, die for. He thought about Kate. Halfway thought he'd have to peel her off him at the end, and that brought a smile to his face. Bless her warm little body. Man, that sure was a body he wanted to get close to again. Her engine had two speeds: fast and really fast. She loved like it mattered. He liked that about her. She played for keeps. She had big dreams.

If the God of SEALs could only help him stay alive long enough to become part of those dreams, he'd die a happy man. One year, or seventy. He wasn't going to quit. He'd be her protector, her confidant, her partner in every sense of the word, and her lover, until they both were dust. Even if he were toothless and wrinkled, he'd be able to get it up and, if she'd have him, he'd be ready to lock-n-load. Might have to be careful not to break something of hers, though.

Shit, what am I doing? Oh yeah. Getting ready to go get my ass kicked.

He made a mental note of all the things he had to bring, so he could do it in minutes. Coop, Luke, T.J., Frankie, Ollie and Fredo were going to be waiting for him there at his apartment. Armando and Kyle and the rest of their group were already on their way to Djibouti.

He hopped on the first plane to San Diego as military standby. Without checked luggage, he was on his way to the apartment within five minutes of landing.

Fredo's beater and several other vehicles were outside his apartment complex. Libby and Julie were sitting on the lawn, Julie starting to show signs of her new pregnancy. Little Cooper was strutting his stuff in diapers and no T-shirt, very wobbly on his new walking legs. The diapers were held up with the aid of red suspenders, the straps tied together with a shoelace so they wouldn't slip off his bony shoulders. Tufts of near-white curls were all over the toddler's head.

The crowd of SEALs and their wives was having fun watching him stand up, and then twist his body around trying to balance, and then fall on his baby butt. Someone was singing the somewhat-altered song, "Little Loose Coop," and little Will was laughing as he tried to dance to the music.

Tyler stopped to pat Willy on the head, and then raced past everyone with Fredo and T.J. in tow. Luke ran to catch up with them. Frankie stayed on the lawn area with Libby, Julie and Will.

The duty bags were packed. He made a mental note, checking off his list. He'd done this dozens of times before, either on deployment or for trainings. Sometimes they didn't know for sure if it was training or not. But this was definitely a Go mission.

Twenty hours later they landed with the morning sun in their eyes. It had been a hot, bumpy ride and he'd managed to get some rest by listening to Two Steps with his ear buds. And he scribbled a letter to Kate. She'd probably have trouble with the penmanship, but he was hoping she'd be able to at least read his love poem and note. Grabbing his gear, he and everyone else piled out of the plane and immediately were assaulted by the hot, smoky landscape that was Djibouti.

He checked his cell and found a couple of text messages from Kate.

Love you. Hope you landed in San Diego safe.

Damn, in his rush to get all his gear, he'd neglected to text her to let her know that. Her second message came through five hours ago.

Imagine you're cruisin' over the deep blue sea right now. Be safe.

He sent her back a message. *Arrived safe. Miss you. Long trip. Love you, baby.*

They piled into barracks-like buildings made from repurposed portable classrooms. Some were in better repair than others. But they had air conditioning, powered by a huge solar power grid near the remote base. Tyler found the mail drop-off and posted his letter to Kate.

It was about the most desolate place he'd been to, resembling some of the pictures he'd seen of the moon. Made Afghanistan look like Disneyland. Their liaison told them there was a pack of homeless kids everyone was sort of raising, giving them food, and clothes, but warned him about letting them into the barracks. It was a cruel reminder that even a child could become a terrorist. Although the country benefitted in many ways from having a U.S. base there, some had relatives in nearby Yemen, a country actively and openly training terrorist groups.

Kyle gathered them all in the staging room and outlined the mission.

"We leave at oh-twenty-four-hundred and drop into Kandahar to meet up with some friendlies embedded nearby. This is a very small, surgical operation, so no need to mention there won't be any strike force coming to rescue your ass if you get into trouble, since officially we're not here. And we got one shot at extraction. After that, you're on your own. Any of you happen to speak Pashtu?"

The silence was sickening. Heads were shaking, muttered swearing, everyone expressing their quiet grief about the hell they were about to descend into.

"This going to be near where we were last year?" Luke asked.

"About five klicks away. The guy you drilled has a replacement living in his house and even co-opted all his goddamned women." Kyle showed a map of the province and had circled the target area in red marker. They had drone surveillance photographs that showed the complex was isolated from anything large as far as other complexes, but did have a large warehouse attached to the gated grounds.

"We believe this is a weapons treasure trove. But that's not why we're here."

He posted pictures of five military personnel, including two SEALs from Team 8 and a CIA advisor. Several other pictures were of local Afghani family members, including the love interest of their terp, who was now living in the States. Tyler could hardly recognize her, she'd been beaten so savagely.

"Fuckin' assholes," Luke barked. "I worked with Gibbs, one of the frogs. He's a good man."

It was apparent to the room that, while Luke had taken out the first evil warlord, one ten times worse had taken his place.

"He says he wants money, but we have intelligence that says he's going to kill them all. Even the women and kids. They've been implicated in helping the American forces."

More swearing ensued.

"And we think he's moving on, is cleaning up his trail, probably got a high-level buyer for the weapons and doesn't have the manpower to maintain or guard the stash."

"And just where is the intel coming from, since our CIA guy is there?"

"Birds. And we got one pair of eyes on the ground. One very motherfucking careful pair of eyes."

Luke nodded to Tyler. "How the hell did Jackie get back over there?"

"These two," Kyle pointed to the two SEALs, "Got him in. And now they're stuck."

At midnight the Team was flown to Kandahar, where they HALO jumped to area. Fredo had given all of them a small tracking device, and they were rigged with Invisio earpieces and warned not to chatter, due to the size of the group. Fredo wore the radio pack with the antenna wire going up his back and out one arm for maximum reception. As soon as they dropped, a quiet test was made and the equipment was found to be working perfectly. Fredo informed the bird overhead.

Coop worked with a drone, getting ready to send it out for a look when they heard voices nearby. They tucked behind a pile of rocks that might once have been an ancient city wall while Kyle and Armando swung around behind a destroyed Humvee tilted on its side. Tyler knew Armani was locking his sights on them while the seconds ticked by.

They heard the familiar voice of their interpreter speaking to two other older men with AK47s strapped across their backs. Jackie was without body armor or a helmet, and he didn't appear to be carrying a weapon.

Luke picked up a pebble and hit Jackie in the back of the thigh with his slingshot. That was the signal they were nearby.

Jackie became exuberant, beginning to speak in English. "See, you guys need to learn English, know what I'm sayin'?"

The two shrugged, not comprehending. "You have no fucking idea what I'm saying, then?" He spoke in Pashtu and the two broke out laughing. He spoke again in Pashtu and the men stopped walking and paid attention to something Jackie was saying. One of them said in heavily accented dialog, "I'm a bad guy."

Jackie hugged him and then he and the other older man congratulated him wildly. The other armed gunman tapped Jackie on the chest, pointing to his own chest"Okay, my man," Jackie said. He motioned to something, up in the sky and had him repeat something slowly until the man memorized it. "Go tell those American bastards what you think of them. Tell it to the drone," Jackie said as he pushed the man away from him, making a good three feet of clearance between him and the two gunmen. The man dropped his pants, pissed on the ground and said, "Shoot me now."

Which is exactly what happened. Armando's two nearly-silent taps, sounding no louder than pebbles hitting the ground, were so close together Tyler couldn't tell them apart. Both gunmen fell right after Jack Daniels hit the ground.

Luke whispered to Tyler, "Kid's a natural warrior."

Kyle's voice popped in Tyler's earpiece. "Roger that, Luke. Let's dust him off and get to where we need to be before daylight."

Jackie was happy to see Luke. "See, I told you the prophet would watch over you. Now you're all married," Jackie said.

"How'd you fuckin' find out all that?"

"Facebook."

"No way."

"Way, my man. Facebook is the bomb. How you think I found her?" He nodded toward the compound with its lights and barbed wire, more like a prison than a home.

"The SEALs in there too?"

"Everyone who's alive is in there. Someone died yesterday. Brought out a body wrapped in white linen. Our custom."

"Could it be one of the Americans?"

Jackie shook his head. "Small. She was too small. A child, probably in childbirth. You know over 50% of the women die in childbirth."

The unspoken part was whether or not Malalai was still alive. As if sensing their concern, Jackie added, "I think I would have felt it if Malalai had died. My heart would have broken."

Tyler could understand completely.

"Come, we go now," Jackie said.

Jackie's time spent training and doing missions with the SEALs made him a valuable asset. He understood their rhythm, and how things were done. Language was minimal. Things were communicated in the most basic of terms. Jackie knew, just as well as they did, there'd be no hope for them if they were caught out in an open area in the full light of day. It was risky for an Afghani. But for the SEALs, it was certain death.

They ran the few klicks until they reached the edge of the compound. Once again, Luke's slingshot made fast work of two lights on high standards rising from the interior of the complex. Under the shadow of the walls they hovered in a line.

Tyler heard the distinctive clicks of Coop's drone as he set the wings in place. He flipped a switch and the purring of a brushless motor came to life. He found a dark corridor protected from above and began running, stopping just before the cone of another light standard illuminated the ground. Holding the drone and reaching back he threw the plastic missile forward. It leapt to the air and began to soar. Coop tracked its ascent with the monitor, moving the direction of the nose with his thumb on a toggle switch.

The screen lit up deep green, since the drone was equipped with its "night shades" as Cooper liked to call it.

Green leafy patterns began to develop on the monitor. At one point, there were four almost yellowish flames blurring together. Since they were almost in a perfect circle, Tyler thought they might be restrained against a pole of some kind.

"I think you're right," Coop agreed when Tyler said as much. "We got more over here."

Kyle looked over at the monitor. "My bet is the ones who are moving are guards or staff."

"No staff. He uses the women," Jackie disagreed.

Kyle looked squinted at him in the near-zero moon. "Can you get a message to her?"

"Your radio have a hot spot for Wi-Fi?" Jackie asked Fredo.

"Fuckin' no. But we got something better." Fredo pointed to the sky.

"Here's your hot spot," Cooper said to the monitor.

"Yeah, and it's got a signal boost."

Tyler turned back to Jackie, "It will pop up if she searches for it. Does she know how to do that?"

"Of course."

"You get a message to her. If her cell phone goes live, that also sends a signal. So that's two. Two signals is good for a pickup," Kyle said.

Kyle gave Jackie his computer after logging in. "You've got to be kidding me."

Everyone looked at Jackie's lap. He was logging into his Facebook account.

He sent a private message to Malalai. "All we have to do now is wait a little."

"Only a little," said Kyle. "We don't hear from her, we go in anyway," Kyle checked the drone monitor. "By zero three hundred we go. That gives you about forty-five minutes to reach her, Jackie."

"No problem. I think I will be able to get her. She has a little ping sound when she gets a message."

"How'd she get a laptop in there?"

"It isn't hers. The warlord bought it so his new child bride can watch movies. He thought it was just a video player, but the thing had full internet. She likes the Disney movies, Malalai says. He's trying to bribe her to let him have sex with her."

"How old is she?" Tyler asked.

"Eight."

Tyler felt sick. T.J. swore and kicked pebbles. Everyone else was silent. "She know you're in country?" Kyle asked.

Jackie whispered a response. "No. I could not risk that." He continued to watch the monitor. "Okay, she's online. She says he is upstairs sleeping with one of his wives." Jackie skipped over the next line. "There are four men downstairs with big guns. One is positioned outside the leader's door."

"That makes five then?" Kyle asked.

"It appears so." The screen changed and flickered. A bit. Someone swore.

"There's some cloud cover up there and wind. The controls are a bit wobbly," whispered Coop. "No worries."

"She says there are many more sleeping in the big house. They are making bombs and packing weapons into crates. She says she was there yesterday. A group of twenty or so left this morning in a large bus."

"Bus?"

"Municipal bus from town."

"That's going to be a bomb, then," said Kyle.

"They're going to pack it full of explosives. My guess is that's where they're going to put all the hostages," Tyler said.

"And then they'll blow them all away," Jackie said.

Jackie's comment reminded Tyler of how Kenny used to talk to him when they stoned behind the bleachers on the soccer field, "*blow them all away.*" He was struck with how matter-of-fact Jackie was about issues of life and death.

It was a big contrast to his own growing up, the campouts and school dances with pretty girls who matured so darn much faster than his body did, the pickups he tried to make happen, the stolen kisses and make outs at the movies.

But Jackie and all the kids growing up in Afghanistan didn't have a chance at that, and didn't even know what they were missing.

Which he figured was a blessing. And somehow, he wanted to make a difference for them if he could, without losing his own life in the process.

CHAPTER 34

Kate came home quickly to change, resisting the urge to shower, just like she'd promised Tyler. The white winery logo silk shirt and black slacks were the order of the day, because it was Sunday and their best-paying crowd. She put her hair up on top of her head and let a few strands fall down her neck.

Tyler had loved so many places on her body it hurt deliciously to move, and yet she craved even more. Doing anything right now reminded her of him and how he played her body and swept her senses with the skill of a god. She was filled to capacity, her heart expanded with so much joy, and yet so much pain, she wasn't sure she could stand it.

But, God yes, she would. Compared to what he had to do, what she was going to do today—face tourists and try to guide them to purchases they'd love for years—that was simple, even with her ex-fiancé hovering about.

Sheila had been contrite and was behaving more like her old self. They were able to banter back and forth, and some of this made the pain of missing Tyler lessen. Well, not exactly lessen, but distracting her for short periods. Every time she was alone, like when she visited the ladies room, she would take a good look in the mirror and burst into tears.

She had such a strong physical reaction to him she began to feel almost sick. A dull ache in her belly no amount of coffee, water or even chocolate could satisfy. She suspected that if she could have two or three good days of rest, she might begin to feel normal.

Concerned her texting him might make him feel hedged in, she decided to wait for him to contact her. He'd said he would. She didn't doubt for a moment he would. And because she'd promised she'd remain strong, she worked to simply enjoy the physical evidence of his lovemaking last night and ignore the part about having to wait weeks and months to experience it again. If there was such a thing as being addicted to a man, she was, and she didn't care.

In the afternoon, Sheila brought up the subject of Tyler.

"Your guy is quite the looker, Kate," Sheila said between groups of guests.

Kate had to nod. Despite telling herself not to, she blushed.

"I see that glow about you. Never had that with Randy, you know."

"I don't think we were right for each other."

"At first, I didn't believe you. But now I see something settled with you. You're satisfied. Sexually satisfied."

Kate didn't like that comment one bit. But Sheila had a way of digging right to the truth of things, painful as it was.

"It's more than sex, Sheila," she said.

"Of course, Kate," her friend gushed. "How stupid of me. Poor choice of words."

She watched her dip her head down and to the side, sliding out her next comment more carefully than her last one. "Kate, did you and Randy—did you have an active…you know, were you good together?"

Kate had to think about it for a bit. That part of her life seemed so far away now. In less than a week she could hardly remember what it had been like with Randy. And now she didn't want to.

"I honestly don't remember, Sheila. I've kind of moved on."

"That good, huh?"

"Look," Kate said as a new flock of guests entered the tasting room with their tour guide in tow. "Don't get me wrong. I'm really not sure Randy was ever into me. Not the same way—"

The crowd was lined up at the pouring table like blackbirds on a telephone wire. Kate rolled her eyes at Sheila, who returned a giggle, holding her fingers across her lips.

"Sorry," Sheila said.

They each proceeded to entertain the guests. Randy entered the showroom.

"Ladies and gentlemen! We have a very special guest today. The winemaker's son is joining us here, Randy Heller." Sheila's voice glittered with bravado as she extended her fingers toward the ceiling in a flourish, and then pointed to Randy, who beamed at the attention. Immediately he was flocked with a small cluster of tasters. He attempted to make eye contact with Kate several times, but she looked just before they connected.

Randy's smile was plastered on generously. Kate searched herself and could not find anything but compassion for him and his situation. Her guilt was knotting up her insides. She felt she'd let down a good friend and her conscience was bruised.

She'd always known it would be impossible for her to love two men at the same time, but this bothered her. Shouldn't she feel something other than pity, compassion for Randy? Surely there should be something there, some remnant of what they had before.

She could not find it.

Randy took the group on a private tour. Kate pulled up a chair behind the counter and sat down, pulling her cell out and checking for a message. There was none. Sheila watched her carefully.

"What is it, Sheila?"

"Kate, you're way too sensitive. I know you better than anybody. You sure you know what you're doing?"

"Sheila, I don't even know how to answer that statement."

"Just be honest, Kate."

"I am being honest." She was being backed into a corner and she didn't like it.

"Can I just level with you?"

Kate knew this was such a load of crap. It was her signal that she wouldn't like the next thing Sheila was going to say. She held her breath and waited.

"I'm just going to say my piece, and then I'll leave it to you."

Kate nodded. "Okay, shoot."

"It happened a lot during the war, World War II? Guys were being shipped out, and they wanted to get married so they had someone to come home to. But was it love? Was it planned, or was it just an urge, a sort of of socially acceptable form of mass lust-fest, where everyone went crazy for a few months, years even, and marriages were made that never should have happened. Babies born."

"Hold it right there, Sheila. We're not talking marriages and babies."

"Oh, that comes after dinner then? Because the speed at which you two hooked up makes galaxy travel possible."

Anger boiled up in her stomach. She'd been punched in her most vulnerable spot. There was a tiny part of her that doubted what she felt with Tyler was real, just because it had happened so fast.

"Stop it, Sheila."

"What would you say to me if the roles were reversed, Kate?"

"I'd tell you to mind your own business."

"Awfully touchy aren't we?"

"Your comments are insulting, Sheila."

"Insulting or honest?"

Kate untied her apron and threw it on the counter. "This is ridiculous. I don't belong here."

Sheila had a smug smile on her face which Kate longed to smack off with her apron.

Randy appeared out of the corner of her eye. He pulled Sheila aside by her elbow and stood in front of her, as if to shield her from Kate.

"Everyone's saying the same thing, Kate. Sheila is only echoing what we've all been wondering. What did you expect?"

"I don't want to talk about it. It's no one's business. I'm sorry this has been so public. That's why I was surprised your father even wanted to keep me around."

"Kate," he whispered. He was going to take her in his arms!

"Stop it right there, Randy. I don't want this."

"Honey, I forgive you."

Kate could not believe what she was hearing. She held her arms out in front, palms facing him. "Don't do this."

"Don't you see, you *do* belong here? You are part of this winery. You are already part of my family. I *need* you, Kate."

She inhaled and let it out quickly. "I can't do this anymore. I thought I could. I just can't be here." It was feeling like the whole place had conspired against her.

Randy went towards her and Sheila stopped him. "Let her go, Randy. She doesn't deserve you."

They left the tasting room together.

Kate couldn't get a handle on how to feel about that scene. She was numb emotionally. The intensity was gone now, and in its place was a hollow core.

She checked her cell phone again for a text message and—dang, nothing again. She decided she wouldn't check again until he called her, or texted her back. Then she remembered Tyler's letter, the one he'd given her this morning.

Glad she'd had enough brains to put it in her bag, she scrounged for it. Written on plain binder paper, she read over the notes, clutching the edges of the paper until it crackled.

It was all of him she could hold right now. A fluttering, thin piece of paper he'd poured his heart out on. For her.

Several times she had to stop and compose herself. Her eyes ached like they wanted to tear up, but her eyes felt sticky, and she couldn't just let go and bawl like she had this morning. She examined the phone numbers in the letter and decided to call them both.

Linda Gray answered on the first ring.

"You don't know me, but I'm Kate, and I—"

"Tyler told me about you and said you might be calling. Actually, I was getting ready to call you. Good timing."

"How do you do it, I mean what do you do when he goes on these missions?"

A group of tourists poked their head through the door. "Are you still open?"

Kate realized it was after closing time. But she motioned to them to step forward.

"I do it with difficulty. Believe it or not, gets easier."

The tour group had ponied up to the bar.

"Listen, I was just about to close down the tasting room, but now I have some last-minute customers," she smiled at the guests so they didn't feel they had to leave her some privacy on the phone, "so I was wondering if I could call you back later tonight?"

"That works. You hear from him yet?"

"Nope."

"You will. I have a feeling you' the one who will be telling me about his deployment, instead of the other way around. I'm just here writing this evening, so I'll keep the phone with me."

"Thanks."

"You're welcome. It will be nice to have someone more my age to discuss these things with. Looking forward to speaking with you, Kate."

"Likewise."

She took care of the customers and then closed down the tasting room. She decided it had been a good idea to call Linda. She'd stop by the deli and pick up something nice for dinner, take a shower, put on her favorite pajamas, and give Linda a call.

Then she'd dig Linda's book back out and drool over the cover. Funny how she didn't have a photograph of the new man in her life, except on the cover of a romance novel!

On her way to the deli, she called Devon Dunn's cell, but had to leave a message.

Then she called her mom.

"He left this morning, Mom," was how she started her conversation, eager to get it all out.

Her mother sighed. "He'll be okay, but I know that doesn't ease your worry."

"No it doesn't. I'm trying. Really trying." Her eyes stung and then the tears rolled down her cheeks. The golden sun reflected off windshields and storefronts. The cloudless blue sky and the distant vineyards on the hill across the valley were beautiful reminders that she lived in paradise, but it didn't feel like paradise today. She sniffled.

"Ah, sweetie. You need to go to bed early. Have a nice bath and just relax. You have someone you can call? Sheila perhaps?"

God, what an awful thought.

"Sheila and I have…well, we've sort of gone our separate ways. She's angry with me about the whole wedding thing."

"That's funny. I always got the vibe she liked Randy. I'd think she might figure she had a chance now. She didn't before. You knew she liked him, didn't you?"

All that seemed so long ago. Sheila had been someone she met after she started working at the tasting room. She was the bookkeeper, but also helped Kate out with the guests whenever it was needed. It didn't take long before Kate had found her a useful confidant. They'd spent time together often enough that Kate had considered her a good friend. When she first started, she'd thought there was some attraction going on between Sheila and Randy, even though later he denied it vehemently.

"I guess I wasn't paying much attention. Really, it never occurred to me to be concerned."

"That's something everyone likes about you, Kate. Not a jealous bone in your body. Loyal, always seeing the good in everybody. I always thought you were too good for that family, since we're baring our souls here."

"They're good to me."

"I'm sure they were."

"Are. I'm still working there."

"My mistake. Look, Kate, take care of yourself tonight."

"I'm going to. Got a great book I'm going to start."

"Oh? Boy I could use one of those."

"You should read it to Dad."

"That would be something, wouldn't it? Tell me if the book is any good and I'll borrow it from you."

"Will do. Tyler is on the cover."

"Excuse me?"

"His sister is a romance novelist. I spoke to her today for the first time. Sounds really nice. She uses him for her covers."

"I can see how his picture would sell books." After an awkward pause, "Kate, in spite of everything I've said to you before, you looked really happy last night. Your dad and I both thought so. And you sound happy today, even though I know you're missing him. You've found something not very many people get to experience in their lifetimes."

"You found it."

"Yes, I did."

"I'm glad."

"You should be. You wouldn't be here if it weren't so. Okay, I'm signing off to get dinner ready for your dad. Be gentle with yourself. And enjoy that book."

"Thanks. I intend to."

Just as she was hanging up, she got a call from Devon Dunn.

"So glad Tyler has found someone here in Sonoma County. I feel pretty isolated up here sometimes."

"I was hoping you could help walk me through everything."

"Everything?"

"What do you do when he goes overseas?"

"I go on. It gets easier with time. This one, this first one, that's the toughest. I guess they all got there okay and now they're taking off again."

Kate hadn't gotten that memo.

"I haven't heard a thing from him."

"He went over with the other group, with Coop and Fredo, I think."

"I don't know those names. See? These people are all strangers to me."

Devon paused. "Kate, you had dinner yet?"

"No, I was just going to heat up something from the deli."

"Let's go to dinner, then. We'll have a little girl talk, some wine, and I'll tell you everything I know about them. These guys are easy to figure out, but hard to live with sometimes. What they *do* is hard to live with, I should say."

"I'd like that, Devon. I can get us right in for dinner anywhere in Healdsburg. I help manage the tasting room at Heller Vineyards."

"Ah! Very good. I've wanted to eat at the Sisterhood Café on the square for ages. Can you get us in there?"

"Absolutely I can. What time."

"Say six, six thirty? I'm an early riser and I've got a lot to do tomorrow."

"Works for me. How about I meet you there at six thirty, then?"

At home she found her mail scattered all over the floor. She found a letter from Tyler, and despite her need to hurry and get ready, couldn't wait to read his words and hold something he'd held in his hands. He'd written it before he came up from San Diego.

Afterward she tucked it inside the paperback, noting he'd given her his military address on the outside of the envelope, the one thing she hadn't had until now.

Turning on the shower, she began to shampoo her hair, sad that the kisses he'd placed on her body were now washing down the drain.

CHAPTER 35

When Kate stepped out of the shower she saw the text message from Tyler. She realized then that sometimes she'd learn things from others before she'd hear it from him. She now understood what happens with families being separated for long periods of time, and in situations where the communication can suffer.

She tried to message him back, but it was undeliverable. She was going to have to accept that as well. Her mind was going wild wondering what he was dealing with. She hoped he was bored to death in a boxcar somewhere, playing video games, or a little soccer. Someplace safe, and sane. Even though she knew it probably was not the case, she imagined him lying on a bed, sleeping, dreaming of her.

"Love you, Tyler," she whispered. If there was a way to send out a bubble of protection all over him, she would.

Thirty minutes later she was sitting at a table at Sisters, waiting for Devon Dunn. Devon appeared at the doorway like an elegant queen, dressed in a navy blue business suit, her hair shoulder length, and carrying a briefcase. She scanned the room, and when their eyes met, she gave a warm smile and a slight nod. The hostess attempted to stop her from crossing the narrow aisle, but Devon waved her away and then pointed to Kate.

She presented her hand and perfectly manicured red nails. "I'm Devon and you must be Kate."

Kate shook her hand and nodded, "Yes."

"Very nice to meet you," Devon returned. She quickly set her briefcase down on the neighboring chair and removed her jacket, revealing an off-white silk blouse with a large self-tie. With her long neck and dangling pearl earrings, she was breathtakingly beautiful. Kate realized she was still standing after Devon took her seat and looked up at her.

"Something wrong?"

"You're—you're just not what I expected," Kate answered.

"What, you expected a biker chick, someone with only half her teeth and tats going up her neck? My Nick wouldn't like that kind of woman."

Kate shook herself and sat quickly. The woman across the table was fascinating.

"I have wanted to eat here for nearly three years. Never could plan far enough in advance to get a table. And look at this! You got the best table in the house."

"They buy a lot of wine from us at a very good price. Not sure if you know it, but restaurants like this make their money on the wine, desserts and extras."

"Makes sense."

The waiter gushed over Kate, telling her that the chef had prepared a special dinner for them, requesting they not order off the menu, unless Miss Kate's guest had a food allergy.

"If you could make it calorie-free, that would be perfect," Devon answered with a straight face.

The waiter squirmed for a second until he saw her broad smile. "I'm sure whatever is being prepared will be wonderful."

"Oh, thank you. I'll go tell the chef."

Kate ordered a bottle of their 2011 Merlot. "Devon, you want some white as well, or—"

"Oh, I love Merlot. My favorite too."

The woman was confident, striking in every way, including her athletic build. Her creamy complexion, red lips and shiny dark hair were an arresting combination. By candlelight she looked like a goddess.

The wine was uncorked and Kate examined the cork and then did the taste.

"Perfect."

"So, Kate. You must have a million questions," Devon began.

Once again the waiter interrupted to ask if they wanted mineral water or bottled water, and then added, "Are the two of you in a hurry? The chef wants to make his special chocolate bread pudding for you, but it takes a little longer to prepare."

"I'm fine if you are," Kate said.

"I think we'll split the bread pudding," Devon added.

"Perfect." The waiter scurried off to the kitchen.

"So, Kate, I'm all yours. What do you want to know?"

"What should I be asking, Devon? I don't know anything about them except for what I've seen on the news, and of course the movies."

"That's always fun, going to see those movies with Nick. If we go with one of the Team guys, they don't stop talking all during the film, making fun of everything. They try to be quiet, but they just can't."

"Yet Tyler seems so focused, so calm."

"Right." Devon held her glass out to Kate. "To the Sisterhood."

Kate was puzzled. "I've never heard of that."

"It's informal. If we lived in San Diego we'd be doing all sorts of things with the other women. The Team wives really don't hang around women who aren't married to a Team guy, or a SWCC crewman."

"SWCC crew?"

"Special Warfare Combatant Crew. S.W.C.C., we say SWCC Crew. They do the SEAL pickup and deliveries in some pretty dangerous waters and under hostile conditions. Those guys in many ways have a more dangerous job than the SEALs, but don't say that around any of the Team guys."

Kate sipped her wine and stared down at the table. She wasn't sure she could ask the question she wanted to ask, but remembered the courage she had promised Tyler. "Are they ever violent, Devon? I mean, do I ever have to worry about them as far as womanizing, or being physically violent. They have so much training and everything. I was wondering—"

"Well that's actually a very good question. I have to admit the whole swagger and bravado thing initially turned me off. Way too much testosterone for my taste at the time." She smiled in a private thought. "But, in time you learn to deal with it, and then you love them for it."

"For what?"

"For being the guys they are. Very special, Kate. When one of them loves you, they will either be your fiercest protector or your worst nightmare."

"How so?"

"They don't quit."

Kate blushed when she thought about how intensely Tyler loved her, how quickly he moved into position without hesitation, went after what he wanted and grabbed his opportunity without second-guessing himself.

"Ask for forgiveness rather than permission," she whispered into her wine glass before she took another sip.

"You got it." Devon grinned. "You can't talk them down. They don't ever give up. Never. And they love—" Devon teared up. "Once a SEAL has loved you. Well, I don't want to think about it, but I don't think I could be married anymore to someone who did anything else. It is the most intense, wonderful life you could imagine."

Devon looked down and played with her silverware, positioning it evenly with her delicate fingers. "It can also terrify you, if you're not ready for all that intensity. If you don't like hard loving and intense guys who have egos the size of the room lurking under the surface of their calm demeanor, then you do yourself a favor and bow out now. They never relax, but they'll look like it. They're always on duty. And it's hard for them to retire. Leaving the lifestyle and the community is harder than the things they do while in it."

"How do they learn to handle it?" Kate asked.

"They don't. They're born that way. I'm convinced of it, Kate. The training just reveals who has that stuff and who doesn't. They only want the guys who have the stuff."

"I would think it would be very stressful."

"See, this is the hard part, Kate. They are trained for all these things. And yes, sometimes it can get to them. It did nearly take Nick out of the teams. He was lucky. With a little time off after his sister died, he was able to get back up on the horse. If he missed a rotation due to mental issues, he'd have been out."

"You mean rotation as in going overseas."

"Yes. And it's our job to pick up the pieces when they come home. No training for that. They'll depend on you, your strength and your courage. You run the house and the enterprise of the family when they are away. When they come back, they are the kings. You work hard when they're gone, and then you work harder when they're back."

Kate's frown must have been obvious, but Devon let it sink in before they locked eyes again.

"Ask me if it's worth it, Kate."

"Is it?" she asked.

Devon leaned over the plates, grabbed Kate's hand and squeezed it. "With every fiber of my being, yes. You've never worked this hard, but you'll never be so loved."

CHAPTER 36

The plan was carefully laid out, each man focusing on his part. They'd heard the words before, done the same things over and over again. But there was always something, multiple things that could and often did go wrong.

Nothing ever went exactly as planned. That's why there was a Plan B, and a Plan C, and it was each man's job to explore all the other options in case it was left up to him and him alone to execute something he hadn't counted on being in charge of.

They didn't see any sentries on the rooftop, which was good. Tyler thought if the twenty or so men were back at the compound, the leader and his wives would never be more under-guarded. Right now the SEALs outnumbered the warlord, but that also could change at any moment.

Armando and Ollie scaled the wall with ease, using their clothing to get over the barbed wire and broken glass used as a deterrent. They looked for wires or infrared lines that could be tripped and found none. Once they were on top, they would lay cover, if necessary, so the others could gain entry and be semi-protected. They weren't there to kill the leader, but if he took it in the shorts, Tyler and the rest of the guys wouldn't grieve. And Jackie had told them none of the women would either.

They were there to rescue the SEALs and other military men, and the CIA advisor. As far as they knew, the SEALs had not been identified as such, or at least it hadn't come up during negotiations.

But Kyle told them that was because the leader had no intention of letting any of them leave alive, including the women and children this man had terrorized in the many months since he'd taken over the dead warlord's spoils.

"Need to know if all the women will be together in the same room," Kyle said to Jackie.

"Yes. I think here." He pointed to the monitor, where several green shadows moved back and forth in a small space. "He locks them up at night so they don't try to escape."

"Charming," T.J. said with a sneer.

"Will they defend him?" Tyler asked.

Jackie shrugged. "They may pretend, but you tell them harshly to go stand in the corner and shut their eyes and they will do it, even though you are Americans. They are used to taking orders."

"What about the kids? Report says there are about six kids, maybe five now," Luke asked.

"The kids will sit and wait for it to be over. They have learned there is no point to being a hero. You don't have to be a fighter to die, but if you assist the wrong side, you die just as surely, my friend. No, I think they will just sit, and wait for the firefight to be over."

"Ask them if the guard makes regular rounds."

Jackie typed in the request on Kyle's computer and waited. "No, she says. They walk around at random during the night. Whenever they wake up."

"Shit," Kyle said. "So, the women are locked inside the room?"

Jackie waited for the response. "She says yes."

"Tell her we're here and to stay calm no matter what they hear."

Jackie delivered the message. "Okay, boss."

"Get your eyes on, everyone," Kyle said as everyone except Jackie put on their night gear.

"Fredo, go set the charge," Kyle whispered. Fredo left, with Frankie behind for protection. On Fredo's mark everyone turned away from the gate while a timed device destroyed the entire entrance and took half the wall on one side with it. Amid falling rocks and debris, Tyler thought time seemed suspended. He and T.J. waited outside while Kyle, Fredo, and Frankie took cover inside the compound. Two men ran from the residence but were easy targets in the courtyard. Armando had no trouble downing them both in seconds, and before they could fire a shot. Kyle relayed the news to the others. They raced for the front door, which had luckily been left open.

"I got four, five moving targets, Lannie," Coop said into his Invisio.

"Copy."

Tyler thought he saw lights of an approaching vehicle on the horizon, but when he mentioned it to T.J. he couldn't find it again. He whispered his suspicion that someone might be on their way. He was nervous about the roaming guard. Hearing gunfire inside the house, the guys held their breath until they got word from Kyle the other three guards had been neutralized and the leader killed. The whole operation from start to finish had taken less than six minutes.

"Coop, send them word we're in, on our way to see if we got wounded."

"Roger that."

Armando stayed rooftop as lookout while Ollie jumped to the ground and raced toward the door of the warehouse.

"Nothing much moving, Kyle," Cooper said as he watched the drone's monitor. As luck would have it, the door was not locked, and Kyle, Ollie, Fredo and Frankie braced for a firefight, which never materialized.

It was music to their ears when they heard Kyle confirm everyone was accounted for and was healthy and able to move. "Send for the pickup."

Cooper was monitoring the drone and signaled for the extraction team.

"Where's Jackie?" Kyle wanted to know.

"He hasn't come out of the house," Tyler informed him.

"T.J., get inside and check him out. Tell him we're leaving just as soon as that bird gets here."

"Roger that."

"Laying charges here," Fredo barked in his earpiece. "Everyone clear out and stay away. Make sure Jackie tells the ladies."

"I've got him in sight. Big crying orgy here, for fuck's sake," T.J. answered.

Tyler heard Kyle swear. "Get. Him. Out. Now."

"Roger that."

Soon the hostages were at the gate. Water, quick rations, and Mylar blankets were passed out. All of the prisoners were shoeless. Several minutes went by until they heard the helicopter approaching.

"I see one bird," Armando radioed. "Where the hell is the second one?"

Fredo spoke up. "They're saying it took an RPG and it's a big rescue scene. Only one bird coming. Gonna be tight."

Tyler was relieved and relayed the information to the crowd. It was going to be sweet to get home and get back to a base where he could get a shower and some decent sleep.

"T.J., where the hell are you?"

T.J. emerged from the house, practically dragging Jackie behind him. Tyler could see tears streaming down the terp's face. "What gives?" he asked T.J.

"Hard time saying goodbye to the ladies. One in particular. She's pretty bad, Tyler."

Jackie was turning around as they heard the rotors close. Soon dust was swirling everywhere and the sound of the big beautiful Black Hawk vibrated the ground like an earthquake. They could have used the other bird for the women and children.

Tyler looked in the direction of Jackie's line of sight and saw the group of covered women at the entrance to the house. He felt bad for them, since there was no way they could take everyone on the chopper. He knew how Jackie felt.

"Five minutes, set, and it's gonna be big," Fredo barked. The timed charge was to blow up the entire weapons and explosive cache. They needed to be gone by the time that happened.

"I told 'em," Cooper said. "Bringing the bird in."

The drone landed hard a few yards ahead of them as the chopper was setting down. Coop quickly dismantled it, stuffed it back in its pack and ran for the open door of the chopper. One by one everyone boarded the bird, T.J., Jackie and Tyler in the rear close by. Jackie was still watching the group of women, who had now come out into the courtyard.

"Shit, didn't you tell them, Jackie?" Kyle barked.

"I did." Jackie started to go back, but T.J. held onto him. Jackie tried to yell something to the women, but they kept advancing, now breaching the walls of the compound, running for the chopper.

"We can't take them. We gotta go. We'll send another bird and some Marines, but we gotta go now!"

Jackie was screaming at them.

All of a sudden a huge fireball erupted in the complex. Two of the women fell to their knees. It was obvious several were hurt.

"Dammit," Kyle growled. Bits of debris were falling everywhere and the pilot was not pleased. He ordered everyone in and began to elevate. T.J., Jackie and Tyler were not yet aboard.

The pilot began shouting. A large chunk of plaster hit the chin bubble of the Blackhawk. It was obvious they were running out of time. Jackie wasn't going to go with them and no one wanted to leave him behind. Tyler grabbed Jackie.

"Is she worth it, Jackie? You'll die here."

"I don't leave her. I will never leave her."

"Fuck sake," Tyler said. T.J. had made it into the bird.

Sounds of automatic fire from the horizon pierced the night. Tyler chanced a glance at Kyle, and he could see there was no choice. He'd run out of time. T.J. saw the look as well, leaned over, touched Kyle's knee, and jumped back to the ground and rolled.

In thirty seconds, the chopper was gone, taking all on board to safety, but leaving the two SEALs and the terp behind to guard the women.

Tyler's whole life flashed in front of him at that moment. He saw Kate's face, the way she slept, and the way she looked when she was putting on her clothes. He was grateful for what he had. He was still alive. Somehow he'd make it. The fear of death wasn't as strong as the fear of regret, he discovered in that instant. Regret for all the things he didn't get to do.

Just another fuckin' day at the office.

He couldn't afford to dwell on the circumstance. They had to find some protection if they were going to get out of this alive.

CHAPTER 37

Kate returned to her cottage, satisfied that some of her questions about the SEAL community were answered. She decided to write a letter to Tyler, even though she didn't know how long it might take to get to him.

She explained how talking to Devon was a great suggestion, that Devon had developed the courage she hoped she'd have one day. She told him that she was now surer than ever that falling in love with him was the best thing to ever happen to her. Their chance encounter on that fateful flight from San Francisco to Portland had been a miracle in action. And if there was one miracle, there would be many more. She was sure of it.

Stopping, she thought about what he would be doing right now.

Are you dreaming about me? I hope you are. I'm going to go to bed dreaming about you. I've devised this bubble I'm sending for protection. You'll have to tell me if you sense it. It makes me feel like I'm doing something to get you home safe, where you belong. I'm not thinking about the next time we have to be separated, just focusing on getting you home this time. Next time will have to take care of itself.

She finished the letter, folded it and addressed it, copying the info from his envelope stuck inside his sister's book. She examined his picture again, kissing her forefinger and then pressing it against his face on the cover. Though the artist's rendering was wonderful, the experience of seeing him in the flesh was a hundred times more appealing. The image didn't do him justice.

She began reading the novel, and although she liked it, her emotions and her lack of sleep conspired against her. She fell into her pillows and, yes, she dreamed of Tyle.

Kate was not the first one to arrive at work the next morning. She parked right next to Sheila's car. The front door was locked, so she fished out her keys and let herself inside the dark hallway that led to the tasting room. She began turning on lights.

"Sheila?"

"I'm here. Just working," she heard a voice coming from the office down the corridor. Her door was ajar and the light was on. "I've just made some coffee in the kitchen if you need it."

Thank God. Kate had neglected to stop for her usual. She set her purse behind the bar and followed her nose to the kitchen. The smell of fresh coffee in the morning made her day. After pouring a cup, she walked down the tiled path to Sheila's office, and found her standing, delving into a file in the top drawer. The large company checkbook was closed, but centered on Sheila' desk, and the printer was running.

Kate was holding her coffee in her right hand. "You want a refill?" she asked.

"No thanks, I'm finished. Thought I'd go home and shower, get some breakfast and come back. Knock yourself out," she said. Sheila's smile was warm and seemed genuine. "Needed to get caught up on some bill pays."

"Well, I'll go get started on my calls," Kate answered.

"You do that."

"Oh, Sheila, Mr. Heller asked me about some expenses I couldn't identify. Did he talk to you about it?"

"No. Hmmm." Sheila frowned. "Must have figured it out, though. He said nothing to me."

"He was going to ask Randy, I think."

Sheila laughed. "Oh, that will be a waste of time. Randy is clueless when it comes to expenses." Sheila's rolling eyes and shrug didn't dissuade Kate from her conviction that Sheila was worried about something. Perhaps things weren't on a good footing with Randy, as Kate had suspected.

"Well, I hope he figures it out. I didn't want him thinking I was spending too much of the company's money on promo." Kate walked down the hall to her phone station.

She picked up the customer lists and donned her headset. After placing a dozen calls, she remembered she'd left her purse under the bar. She wanted her cell phone beside her in case Tyler managed to get a message through, or answer one of the several she had texted. She removed the headsets and went back toward the tasting room.

Sheila was still there, putting some glasses away from the dishwasher.

"Thought you were going home."

"Oh, I thought I'd just put these away and then take off."

"I could have done it," Kate said.

"You know me. Overachiever." With her back to Kate, drying one wineglass stem that was still wet, she asked, "So when do you expect to hear next from Tyler?"

"I have no idea. He's probably not in range."

"Does he call you?"

"No. Only texting. I should say sexting. That's what I hope he'll do, once I hear from him, at least."

"Okay, I'll leave you to it, then," Sheila said. She walked around the end of the tasting bar as Kate was retrieving her purse.

Kate watched her friend, if she could still be called that, exit the tall glass and metal doors to the parking lot beyond, and drive away in the new Volvo. Her cell phone was on top of her other things in the satchel she brought. Checking the screen, she found it blank. The battery was charged. Now it was nearly twenty hours since Tyler had left. She began to worry. She was sure he would have had time to send at least one message.

She locked the doors and retreated to the call center to get back to work.

Kate's marketing resulted in several cases worth of sales to old customers. She'd focused on those who bought just prior to last year's release, thinking perhaps some pre-Christmas offers would entice them. Heller could provide custom labels for their special clients to use as gifts. She ate lunch at her standup desk and proceeded on to the early afternoon.

Something caught her eye and she was startled when she saw Randy leaning against the doorjamb. She removed her headsets.

"Oh, Randy! Didn't realize you were here."

He slumped down into a chair next to her desk. His shoulders slouched. He held the large black Heller Vineyards checkbook between his palms.

"Kate, I owe you an apology."

She steeled herself for what she knew was going to be a conversation she didn't want to have.

"No, Randy, I'm probably the one who needs to apologize."

"About the engagement? Well, yes, based on what you knew. But there are a few things you didn't know. And now there are a few things I know."

"Excuse me?" It was obvious Randy wasn't coming on to her. With no evidence of his former bravado, Kate's capacity for compassion began to flow. She actually felt sorry for Randy for some reason.

"I've been a fool."

Kate waited.

He looked up, and when their eyes met she saw shame. With his head tilted to the side, his gaze darted over her face and the surrounding room without specifically focusing on anything.

She pulled a chair from the corner and sat across from him, knees almost touching. "What's going on, Randy?"

"I've loved you, but, I—"

She thought he might cry.

"I don't deserve you. I never did. I didn't earn your love and never should have had your trust."

"I don't understand. Just spell it out, please."

"I've been sleeping around."

She sat up straight. The possibility had never occurred to her. At first she was felt the taint of anger, but then she remembered they no longer had a commitment. So this meant he never was committed?

"And?"

"Isn't that enough, Kate?"

She knew there was something more. "What else?"

"One of the ladies I've been, you know—"

"Fucking while you've been my fiancé. Is that what you're trying to say?"

"Yes."

Somehow she knew the next part almost before he said it.

"One of them is Sheila."

Figures.

Kate stood up. Instinctively she checked her cell phone. She so wanted to be transported from this little room to anywhere closer to Tyler. She thought perhaps she might be able to feel him just by putting her fingers on the blank screen. But there wasn't anything there and she didn't feel anything.

"I'm not sure that's any of my business any longer," Kate whispered, looking down at the lists. Tears were filling her eyes. Not from Randy's reveal, but because nothing around her was as she had left it when she went to Portland that week-plus ago. Nothing made any sense. The only thing that made sense was that she needed to find Tyler. Whatever she had to bear, if he was here beside her, she could bear it. She had to admit, his admonitions about staying away from "those people" had been spot on. She had no business being here. Being part of any of this.

"So, I guess I should say I'm surprised, but I'm not. It's sad, but I think I picked up a little of that just yesterday." She turned to look down on his bowed head. "You could have gone on without telling me. So why now?"

"Because I think she deceived even me."

"I can't say I'm surprised at that, either. I think she'd go after Tyler, if—"

"She already has."

"Well, I'm sure she has. Lucky for me—"

"She told me they were lovers."

"That's ridiculous."

"He has a tattoo on his chest of a compass? Frog prints from his elbow to his wrist?"

"Anyone could have seen those."

"Really? When did you guys come by here when he wasn't wearing a shirt, Kate?"

Her stomach was fluttering. She felt herself getting sick, chilled by the horrible, sinking feeling her whole world was gone, and her happy cocoon had suddenly evaporated. Her body wobbled from side to side.

Randy stood, throwing out his arms to steady her.

Kate stepped back and scowled. "Don't touch me. Haven't you done enough already?"

"But Kate—"

"Shut up. Shut up. Just fuckin' shut up."

Was the man she'd fallen in love with so hard and so fast a man she now could no longer trust? Did he do to her what Randy had never done—take her heart and shredded it? She shook her head. No. It was. Not. Possible.

"Okay, I get where you're coming from. I'd be pissed too—" Randy started.

"Pissed? You think I'm pissed? I wish I'd never met any of you. *Any* of you. He might be a bastard, but at least Tyler was right about one thing, I can't trust any of you. This is a hell on earth, being here with you people."

Randy was still standing, but stronger. "It's about to get worse, Kate."

"Really?" Rage was boiling in her veins.

"She's nearly bankrupted us. She's taken our money. I think my family's winery is about to go under, unless we can get the money back quickly."

Kate wasn't tracking properly. What was this about money? She was still focusing on the sex. Who said anything about money?

Randy held up the black checkbook with the gold H crest on the cover. "From the looks of it, I'd say she's taken nearly one hundred thousand dollars this week alone. I'm seeing other things that don't make sense. Advances to an RPG media services? Crestman Catering? Any of these companies sound familiar to you?"

"No."

"When Dad came to me last night and asked, I couldn't believe it. I told him I was sure you didn't have anything to do with them, and you handled all the catering here. He said he'd already talked to you. That only leaves one other person."

"Sheila," Kate murmured. Could Tyler somehow be involved?

She glanced at her phone. She wanted to fire off a message, but realized she'd been waiting for a text that was never going to come. Was he even overseas?

"You've got to call the police, Randy. You've got to get on top of this right away. Sheila was here this morning, working in the office." She pointed to his checkbook. "She might have done something else this morning."

"Already checked. Already called the bank. I doubt we'll see her again. She wrote another check this morning and cashed it at the bank in person. Our last thirty thousand dollars. Your paycheck and that of everyone here at the winery is going to bounce sky high."

Kate dropped into the chair behind her.

Randy leaned over, putting his hands on the armrests. "You have to face the fact that perhaps Tyler is waiting for her now."

"No. I don't believe that."

"Did you think she was capable of this? And how do you explain her knowing where his body ink is located? I take it that information is accurate?"

"Yes, but—"

"There is only one explanation. He's in on it."

"No he's not. He can't be."

Well, then, look at this." He held up the checkbook. Yesterday there had been a check written to Tyler Gray in the amount of ten thousand dollars. "It was deposited to a joint account, a new one. And Sheila's name is on it as well."

CHAPTER 38

Lights from the approaching bus mingled with the rosy glow of a new day, except for Tyler it felt like the same fucking nightmare of a day he'd been having the last twenty-four hours.

They herded the women back to the compound and inside the house, where they closed the door but didn't barricade it so it would be easy to break in, as if only a house full of women and children lived here. They wanted the surprise to be on their side, and if they were lucky, the soldiers wouldn't suspect any male defenders to be present.

He sent everyone upstairs, for safety, away from any possible firefight below. He knew if the intruders didn't get in the front door, they'd for sure set fire to the place and pick them off the roof like birds on a telephone wire. They had a better shot at getting at least a couple of them who might not expect the women to be armed.

If they were lucky, they wouldn't be spotted as American Special Forces, since there would be a long, painful death or incarceration in their futures if that were the case.

And their current plan might also give the rescue forces time to put together a plan to come extract them. If he could send a message with Malalia's iPad. Without the drone's Wi-Fi, they'd have to get somewhere that had it. With the firestorm heading for them, it might not be a bad idea if they could survive the next few minutes.

Jackie took the women to the bedroom and told them to stay down while Tyler and T.J. checked what they had between them in terms of firepower. T.J. had thrown his bag to the ground when he got off the chopper, so both of them had enough clips and extra surprises to make a fun morning out of it. Beyond that, it was going to be a real crapshoot. The walls of the house were thick, but depending on the caliber of the weaponry, they might still penetrate the stone and plaster mud hovel.

Lady luck was smiling on them. The buses' brakes squealed loudly, and from the shadows of the upper story T.J. and Tyler saw there were only four local militia types.

"You suppose the leader had a pistol?" T.J. said.

"He did, and I have it," Jackie held up a Browning Hi-Power and two clips. "Under his pillow." Jackie also held up a laptop. "I think your American forces will like having the information in this laptop he left behind."

"We gotta fuckin' get outa here first. But, hell, yes. Good job, Jackie," Tyler whispered. They readied themselves.

The door downstairs was kicked open easily, giving the false clue they'd hoped for. The men shouted as if expecting to be obeyed. Jackie crouched outside the closed door of the women's bedroom while Tyler took point and T.J. backed him up. The windows were wide open on the front, but the sides were shuttered. They were careful to count all four voices coming from downstairs so they didn't have to plan a two-pronged defense.

The SEALs hid until they heard heavy footsteps on the lower landing. The language of the militiamen got louder and more demanding. Counting to three, T.J. and Tyler nodded to each other and burst from their cover, catching the men off guard, pummeling them with rounds, felling them before they could get a shot off.

Tyler and T.J. sat back against the wall and breathed easier. They could hear the women sniffling, which got louder when Jackie opened the door and reassured them all would be well.

"So far so good. Now what the hell do we do?" T.J. barked.

"Pray." Tyler meant it, but T.J. swore. "I'm going to go check the leader's room for anything else we can use. Lot of those guys are plenty handy with knives and swords. Anything that's quiet might be useful. Intel as well."

"Should take a DNA sample," Tyler said.

T.J. shook his head. "Cell phone picture and an ear or a finger. You choose. But you're carrying it."

Tyler grinned back at him. "God I love my job."

"Gotta be fuckin' nutz," T.J. was saying as he climbed the third story.

Tyler kept his H&K close while he took the few steps to the first landing where the men lay in a bloody pile. They had knives, some papers he'd ask Jackie about, and a couple of them had an odd assortment of Russian-made pistols he'd never seen before. No one wore armor, so they never had a chance.

He was crouched over the third combatant when he heard the repeat of a round and then felt the sting in his upper thigh, which sent him sprawling on his back, his weapon clattering down the stairs. Right away he felt his warm life's blood ooze down his pants leg and out through the seams, over his shoes and socks, and he allowed himself to register that it was a pleasant feeling of warmth, like home, like something he missed.

Jackie returned fire, killing the other combatant.

"Tyler, you okay?" Jackie said as he knelt at his side.

"No, fuckin' Jackie, I'm not fuckin' okay," Tyler returned harshly, more to let them know he was still tough and still expected to make it out alive.

T.J. had been up on the roof and reached Tyler's side in a rush. "Fuck me, Tyler. You're not going to be able to walk on this leg." He removed a braided strap from his pack and tied a tourniquet around Tyler's upper thigh, as high as he could without taking his manhood with it. He cinched it as hard as he could, hard enough that Tyler groaned.

"You fuckin' pussy. You die on me and I'll shoot you full of rounds myself," T.J. spat.

"Who said anything about dying? How about walking? Or am I gonna trace like my sister's vampire heroes?" Tyler joked. It made him feel better, being lighthearted about something he had no control over. There were only two possible outcomes. They lived or they died. And probably together.

"Don't fuckin' mess with me, Ty. There's a dust cloud on the horizon, and unless you called Welcome Wagon, we're about to be given the *We Fucking Hate Americans* treatment and a basket full of bullets."

"Where the fuck did this guy come from?" Tyler asked.

Jackie pointed at the dead Afghani's jacket. "Municipal. He's a municipal bus driver."

"Jackie, you know how to drive a fuckin' bus?" Tyler asked.

"Sure."

"Really?" T.J. asked.

"No."

"Then I drive," T.J. said. "Give me something to cover up and I'll be the bus driver. We gotta get out of here in, like, a minute or we won't live to tell the tale."

They loaded the women first, and then T.J. and Jackie carried Tyler into the bus, placing him in the back where he could fire from the rear window as well as the sides. He couldn't walk, but he could defend those who could. And then the rest of it would just have to happen the way it happened. He tried not to think about it. But he was feeling weaker by the moment. The tourniquet was only going to keep him alive for a few minutes...maybe an hour if they were lucky...unless he got medical attention.

"You good?" T.J. asked.

"Shut the fuck up and do your fuckin' job, you douchebag."

"Good. Glad to see you're still fighting. Okay," T.J. raised his voice and looked around, "hang on everyone. I'm driving like I used to in Texas running from the cops. Also did me some racing in my teens."

As T.J. started the bus, one of the women brought Tyler a water bottle. He broke the seal, gulped half of it down, and eyed the label, and recognized it had been bottled in Sonoma

County, "At The Source." He chuckled and hoped it was a good omen, not a bad one, since he didn't plan on being anywhere close to that other Source any time soon if he could help it.

"Hey T.J.," Tyler shouted. "I didn't know you were from Texas, man."

"I'm not."

"So why were you running from the cops?"

"Cause that's where I set off a little device. Payback's a bitch."

"Remind me not to get on the wrong side of even *one* of your ass hairs."

"Good advice." T.J. chortled. "So Jackie, am I going in the right direction? There are tire tracks all over the place, and I can't tell where the hell the road is."

"Yes, you are headed the right way, so go straight. Should be no houses, no small farms nearby. You'll come to a little outpost, which hopefully will be manned by someone I can speak with."

About five minutes later two four door Toyotas, military trucks, zoomed past them, headed for the complex they'd just come from. Tyler had a bad feeling about them, and, sure as shit, one of the two vehicles turned around and started following them.

"How many, Tyler?"

He looked over the back of the seat. The jeep was gaining and would overtake them quickly. "I count three."

"Three against three. I like those odds," T.J. said.

"Jackie, time for you to take over," came the command from Tyler. "T.J. lay down a smoke bomb, make it look like the bus's disabled."

"I like your thinking, Ty. C'mere, Jackie." T.J. yelled.

"Okay, boss."

"I'm only going to tell you once," T.J. eyeballed Jackie, looking fierce. "Don't slow down. I can't teach you how to shift the gears. No time for that. So don't stall the fuckin thing, okay?"

"Sure. But—"

Tyler watched as T.J. pulled the Afghani youth onto his lap. "We're not dating, so don't get any ideas." It made Tyler chuckle to himself. If he was going to die, he was going to die laughing.

"You push down here when I take my foot off, okay?"

"Yes, boss."

The bus jerked a bit as T.J. removed his hulking frame from the seat and Jackie's skinny frame took over. He was searching the rear view mirror and side mirrors.

T.J. ran back to him. "There," he said pointing straight ahead. "That's the only place you look. Only place that matters."

"Roger that," Jackie said.

T.J. got a smoke flair out of his pack and busted open a window. Using a Velcro strap, he lashed it to the window frame up at the top, between the opened windows behind him, and pulled the clip. Some of the thick grey smoke filled the bus, but most of it trailed out behind them. Tyler watched the vehicle swerve to the right and left to avoid the irritating chemical emitted by the can, and was relieved to see it slowed them down a bit.

"How far are we from the outpost, Jackie?" Tyler bellowed.

"I can see it now. A click."

"These ladies all healthy? Can they make it?" Jackie spoke Pashtu to the women who started chattering like a flock birds.

"You're not seriously thinking of staying behind and letting them walk? I say we crash whatever's up there, Tyler."

"If we're lucky, we'll have a military vehicle, not a Municipal bus."

"And if we're not lucky?"

"I dunno. What difference will it make, anyway? We'll be dead."

"You heard what I said, you're not gonna fuckin' die on me, Tyler."

"Yea, but I didn't promise you I wouldn't die in a firefight. I didn't promise that. Someone's got to escort these women and Jackie to someplace safer. And I guess that someone would be you." Tyler gave him a grin. "It's all good, T.J. What we signed up for, remember?"

There was something peaceful about not having a lot of choices. It made the choices easier to make, Tyler thought.

Tyler checked his weapon and made sure everything was clipped in place. T.J. started to go for his bag to arm up, but Tyler grabbed his arm.

"Give this to Kate."

"You fuckin' give it to her yourself."

"I mean it, T.J. Give this fuckin' letter to Kate." He handed the bloodstained envelope to his Team buddy. "You take care of her, and don't let her buy any dolls or you'll wind up like Timmons."

"No fuckin' way." T.J. grabbed Tyler by the shirt and pulled him up off the seat, which hurt like a sonofabitch. "You're gonna make it out, Tyler." He dropped him unceremoniously back on the bench seat, stuffing the letter back in Tyler's pocket and smoothing the Velcro closed.

Tyler could feel sensation in his leg diminishing by the minute. He was sorry the letter was stained with his blood. It would scare her a little. Hell, it would scare the living daylights out of her.

CHAPTER 39

The military transport pulled up alongside the bus, with two of the occupants brandishing rifles. The driver pulled close to the bus, as if he planned to ram it.

Jackie played his part well, flailing his arms and shouting something in Pashtu, which triggered wailing from the women. Then he added in English, "I'm going to have to stop. Please tell me what to do."

"You're doing fuckin' great, Jackie. Slow down but don't stop," Tyler said. "Ready, T.J.?"

"Fuckin' A."

Jackie shouted something in Pashtu and two of the women began to scream in unison, along with several of the children. Tyler knew T.J. would be swearing at the top of his lungs on a normal day. But this was no normal day. He was crouched behind one of the seats, a little mirror hanging from a wire so he could monitor the outside.

Tyler remained stuck in the rear of the bus, in the shadows, slumped down nearly flat on his back, legs stretched out in front of him, barely able to see above the window ledges while the bus began to slow down. The smoke bomb was done, but dust from the red soil was everywhere, filling the small compartment and making everyone cough. He pulled his desert scarf up over his mouth and then wrapped it around his head.

The hysterical crying was loud enough for the militia to overhear and they began to confer amongst themselves.

"Help me. I have to stop. Help me," Jackie barked.

The bus grumbled slowly and ground gears, then hiccupped and bucked to a quick stop, jerking forward and back as the springs gave up the ghost. Tyler could hear T.J.'s "Oh, shit," muffled by another headscarf.

The combatants carefully climbed out and searched the open windows, surveying the women and children who kept up their moaning and crying. The women cowered from the windows, switching to the other side of the bus when the militants came up to them. Finally they clustered in huddles towards the center of the aisle, which was just fine with Tyler, because they made good cover.

None of the men were curious about the back seat.

The two heavily armed men shouted at Jackie, demanding he get out of the bus, and he did so, holding his hands above his head. As one man stepped up into the passenger level, the other was right behind him. T.J. quickly jumped up and popped them before they even registered he was there, making the women scream even louder.

The two on the outside were getting ready to spray the bus with rounds when Tyler leveled his H&K and surgically fired off rounds through one open window without hitting the military vehicle's sides.

Tyler checked the surroundings and didn't see indications anyone was approaching, even from the rear. There was no question the sounds of battle would carry along the dusty ground devoid of plant or hill. But with the way of the desert and echoes, no one would be able to pinpoint exactly where the sounds had come from.

T.J. barked an order to Jackie, "Get your butt in here and shut them up. I can't listen to this anymore."

Jackie did as commanded, hopping over the seats, avoiding the dead bodies until he came to the group of women. He consoled Malalai, who sunk her forehead to his chest and sobbed in earnest. A couple of the young boys were peeking curiously out from the windows to see the carnage first hand. The crying and sobbing stopped.

Tyler managed to locate his cell phone's shape by pressing through fabric of one Velcro pocket, making a note to check it for the battery he knew to be dead, like it had been a half hour ago.

The air was heating up without the forward motion of the bus. Tyler knew they would fry if they didn't get underway in a hurry.

"T.J. we gotta get moving."

"Roger that. What do you want to do with these guys?" he pointed to the two men slumped in the aisle of the bus, and jerked his chin toward the two outside as well.

"I think we have to take them along. Can we prop two of them up front behind the driver's seat?"

In quick time, Jackie and T.J. had two armed militia strapped together and supported by the seat with Velcro strips and duct tape, one against the wall of the bus. With their heads slumped to the side, they looked like they could be sleeping.

The other two they carried to the rear of the bus, stripping them of weapons. T.J. held up a cell phone.

"Jackpot," he said.

"You got any reception?"

"I got two bars."

"Enough," Tyler said and extended his hand. He called the number he'd been given for the SOP command center and gave his name and rank. "I know we're about five klicks from the complex at Operation Pickle Jar—Jackie, what town are we headed to?"

"Walakan. Near Walakan."

"Near the town of Walakan. We got one special operator seriously wounded, that would be me, and one healthy. We got a terp and five Pashtu women and six children on a bus. The thing is painted bright red and green. Just like Christmas. It would sure be nice if Santa Claus could come and get us right now."

T.J. shot two of the tires flat on the Jeep and pocketed the keys. He fired up the bus as Tyler was signing off.

"I think I got through, but you best keep haulin' ass outta here," Tyler said. "Jackie, you see anything up front that looks familiar?

"Nothing yet."

Soon abandoned vehicles and dead farm animals were found strewn over the countryside, indicating an army had been through. A thatched and mud hut was smoldering. They passed corrals, and live chickens that acted just like the chickens at home, Tyler thought, picking at the ground for bits of seed or something else to eat.

Nearly a half hour later, they came to a small outpost with a checkpoint that was abandoned. Tyler was feeling feverish, and the swelling in his leg hurt. It had been over an hour since he'd been shot, and he knew he was running out of time. He knew once he started to cool off, he would be in critical condition. Until then, the swelling and pain and heat were a good sign, the best he could have. He tried to get his phone, and nearly dropped it. His fingers were so puffed up from the infection he knew was raging inside him, they were stiff. He managed to get a glimpse of a message Kate had left, but the screen went black and he couldn't recall it.

"Shit." He put the phone inside his T-shirt. For some reason, he wanted to have the text message Kate had sent him right against his heart. Maybe some fuckin' Corpsman would find it and charge it for him. They'd know who to call, whom to notify, if—

He didn't want to think about if. It was *when* now. All the time he had was in the present or forward.

He heard his bag hit the floor of the bus as it rumbled down the red clay of Mars. He'd always remember this area as being Mars. A far outpost he never wanted to return to. But he would, if they asked him. He just didn't want to die here.

Glancing down to the bag, he saw the lavender deodorant Kate had given him. Painfully, he reached for it, flipping off the top, which flew to the seat in front of him and landed on the floor. He sniffed the lavender fragrance, and it reminded him of Kate's sheets. Kate's bubble bath, her shower gel. Reminded him of her soft skin and how bad he wanted to see her. He pushed the deodorant under his T-shirt next to the phone. As much of Kate as possible was going with him, no matter where he was going. Her text. Her scent. Along with some fuckin' bad guy's DNA.

He heard the crackling of the letter T.J. had refused to take.

He extended the combatant's phone to T.J., along with the letter. "You fuckin' better take these. Make the call. I'm going to pass out, here."

T.J. grabbed it.

And just then Tyler did pass out.

CHAPTER 40

The search for Sheila was unsuccessful. Her home was vacated. Her car was missing, and there was no evidence of her at any of the places she normally frequented. She had simply vanished. The police put a trace on her and, since she was presumed to have fled the state, and considering the size of the theft—some four hundred thousand dollars' worth of theft—the FBI was brought in.

The winery was shut down and workers were asked to furlough. The bank the Heller family had been with for three decades, since they still had considerable personal assets, covered their checks.

Though it was quietly investigated, on the third day a news crew got wind of the scandal, and a front page article appeared in the local paper. This drew a call from Devon.

"So sorry, Kate. Why didn't you call me?" Devon asked.

"I wasn't sure how it would turn out. You know, they've implicated Tyler in all this. They didn't want to make it public." Kate admitted to Devon what she hadn't wanted to admit to herself.

"Tyler? No way!"

"I know, but I saw the check…well, one check, anyway. Saw it myself. Made out to Tyler Gray and cashed, the bank said."

"That's a lie."

"Is he even a SEAL?"

"Of course he's a SEAL. Why would you think otherwise? You think something like that would get by me? Nick hanging around a poser?"

"He had a thing with this lady, the bookkeeper. Her real name I guess is Joan something."

"Impossible. Just not possible. How do you know this?"

"She described his tats. Only way she would know about them is if she saw him without his shirt. I didn't take him there shirtless, Devon. I guess I could give him the benefit of the doubt, but somehow I did get the impression he knew her from his past. *Hopefully* his past. But I don't know anymore."

"I'm supposed to hear from Nick tonight. You'll probably get the same Skype call. Be ready for it."

"Not sure I'm ready for a Skype with Tyler or anyone."

"You should have called me, Kate. Why didn't you?"

"I just didn't think it was possible at first, but I was asked not to mention the investigation to anyone, and the police still think he's involved."

"Kate. You've got to trust me. Tyler had no possible way of being involved in this at all. It would never happen, Kate.

Never. These guys don't do this. It is so completely unlike anything they're about. These guys rescue people, they don't prey on them."

Kate was getting another call, and she recognized from the number of Tyler's sister.

Oh great, maybe she's involved too.

She decided to take the call, so wrapped up her conversation with Devon.

"Kate, this is Linda Gray."

"Yes, Linda."

"I'm afraid I have some bad news." Kate's heart stopped. Could anything worse be happening? "Kate? Are you there?"

"Is he really overseas? Is he really a SEAL on a mission? That what you're gonna tell me?"

"I'm not sure I understand you. Of course he's a SEAL. And yes, he *was* on a mission."

The *was* grabbed a prominent part of her attention. Past tense, *was*, as in *is no more.* She began to shake. Tears streamed down her cheeks. Did she want to hear the words? Could she bear to hear those words? After what she'd suspected of Tyler?

"I'm afraid they've reported him missing, along with another SEAL. Kate, it isn't looking good. They usually don't call unless they want you to get used to the idea he might not come back. They have word he was injured, and critically, it appears. But he's not in friendly hands as of yet, so they don't know his condition, but fear the worst. I'm sorry, Kate." And then Linda began to sob.

"Oh, Linda, what are we going to do? I just feel like my whole world has come crashing down over my ears, and you must feel the same way." Kate's harsh breathing matched

Linda's. She did share Linda's sorrow, despite all the confusing emotions swirling around. "I'm afraid I'm not going to be very good for you right now, and I'm truly sorry."

"At least he got to do what he wanted to do. Of that I'm sure," Linda said with a quaver.

Kate didn't want to ask about anything to do with Tyler, not wanting to add to Linda's pain. She was confused. And then Linda offered something else she wasn't expecting.

"I got a beautiful letter from him this morning, Kate. Odd that it would come today, of all days. Of course, there never is a good time to hear about the fate of someone—" Her voice broke to a whisper.

"It's okay, Linda. Go ahead and cry."

"I feel like I need to tell you this. He wrote this beautiful letter, and all it was about was you. He told me he'd never met anyone like you, that the thought of coming home to you was what he was taking with him over there. He sounded so happy. So sure he was on the right path, doing the right thing. And you were so much a part of his life, Kate. I just thank you from the bottom of my heart. You made my brother's last days here the best of his entire life. I'm going to mail you a copy of this letter. I think you should have it."

Could this really be happening? The range of emotions battering Kate was making her seasick. After Linda hung up, Kate turned and ran to the bathroom to throw up.

The mailman delivered mail through her door slot like he always did. The late morning sunlight still shone through the glass French door of her cottage. Somewhere someone was mowing a lawn with an electric mower. Birds twittered in the nest under her eaves.

There were three letters from Tyler. He'd promised that he'd write every day, back when the rosy glow of their new love was the only thing she knew. When she knew his promise was his bond. These letters were evidence he hadn't disappeared, after all. He had been on the mission overseas.

Did she dare open them? What if he was going to tell her he didn't love her? Maybe his Sheila had been like her Randy. Maybe she'd trespassed into a territory she had no business being in?

She looked at the postmarks, but the dates were smudged. She opened all three of them. Tyler had, thankfully, dated each one. She smoothed over the paper on the one he'd apparently written before he left the country. It was a good place to start, she thought.

Dear Kate,

I am in San Francisco, waiting for my plane, and I already miss you so much. This will have to be a short letter. But I wanted to keep my promise. I said I'd write you every day, and, since today will be a long travel day for me, I'm guessing this will be my last opportunity.

When I think about coming home to you, all kinds of things happen to my body, of course. But, more importantly, what I love about you is what this does to my soul. You are the life partner I've been searching for, just never knew it. Yours was the face I wanted to see out there in my corner. Your love was what I was missing, even though I was happy, even though my carefree life was perfect. I was still missing you before I even knew I could miss someone so much, or love someone so completely.

Now that we've had such a brief time together, I'm hoping you feel the same way and that together we can figure this thing out. But if there is a God in Heaven, I hope he'll let me have years and years to explore you, get to know you, love you the way I know I can.

Your love,

Tyler

Kate no longer feared Tyler was part of this sick conspiracy on the Heller family. Her new fear gripped her as she sank into her pillow and wept. She knew she would never get over loving him.

Tyler. Somehow you have to come home to me. Please come home to me. You promised.

CHAPTER 41

Tyler woke up in a hospital room, but had no clue how he got there. He was relieved to hear people in the hallway and the little nurse who woke him up to take vitals spoke English.

English!

He'd never been so happy to hear English spoken in his life. Then he wondered about T.J. and Jackie. And the women and children. He didn't have to wait long.

"There he is, the fuckin' Lawrence of Arabia!" T.J.s banter was music to his ears.

Tyler tried to move and the pain in his hip nearly made him pass out. "How long have I been here?"

"Got here day before yesterday. Was touch and go for a bit. They did a first-class triage in Djibouti, but had to reset your shattered femur and remove the shit that was embedded there after you got stateside, not that your sorry ass knew the difference. You're gonna walk with a limp."

"No fuckin' way."

"Yes, my man," Jackie walked into the hospital room. "The ladies are gonna like all this wounded warrior shit. You'll get all the handmade pillowcases, and invites to houses in Virginia and Florida. Oh yes, I think you will be very popular," Jackie said with a smile.

"Where the hell am I?" Tyler asked.

"Reed. Where the hell did you think you were?"

"Last I knew, I was passed out in the back of a fuckin' bus heading towards the Mars rover."

"Oh, so glad you never got to see how we got you out, my man," Jackie quipped.

"What?" Tyler looked between T.J. and Jackie.

"Dressed you up as a woman, a very tall woman, mind you. In labor. Messy bloody labor. Your dress was soiled and you were passed out."

"No way. You put me in a burqa?"

"I got photographs to prove it," T.J. said. "When they were cutting off your clothes, they found some interesting things tucked into your T-shirt. Very interesting," T.J. winked.

Tyler shook his head. He could hardly remember. Oh, yeah, he'd put the DNA in there, and the lavender deodorant, and his cell. "My cell. Where's my cell? Maybe there's—"

"There is, and it's plugged into the wall over here getting charged up. All in good time." T.J. stood. "I'm supposed to check in with Kyle and the rest of them now that you woke up. Before I go, wanna see what you look like in a dress?"

"Who needs to see that?" Tyler spat.

"Weep, my man. This is payback for all the dumb shit you pulled on me over the past few weeks. I'm putting this on the team bulletin board unless I get your complete undying cooperation."

"T.J. You're a fuckin' asshole." Tyler hit his forehead with the palm of his right hand, except it nearly toppled a drip. "Ow. You said you learned to drive a bus while being chased by cops in Texas. Tell me that story."

"Much later, Ty. Now you rest. Then you call your person, there." He pointed to the cell phone on the stainless steel stand. "But you can have this back, if you want." T.J. lobbed the lavender deodorant stick in Tyler's lap. The top of the stick was crusted with dried blood and caked red clay. Putting it up to his nose, he discovered it still smelled glorious. Just like Kate.

"Jackie, what about Malalai and the others?"

"Safe for now. Djibouti, working on some translation for our forces, and some housecleaning. Seems as though helping you and T.J. get out of there was something good to put on their resumes."

"They must have family looking for them."

"Not any more, my man," Jackie said solemnly. "Afraid everyone else is gone, or, you know."

"Sorry to hear it. I'm glad Malalia's safe."

"Thanks. Owe you. All you guys."

T.J. and Jackie left to inform Kyle and the rest of the Team who had stayed behind. They'd elected to stay on the East Coast until Tyler was out of danger.

Tyler buzzed for a nurse to bring him his cell and she refused until he started swearing, trying to be as soft as he could. The young man next to him in the room must have just come out of surgery, because he was out cold and never said a word.

"I know my fuckin' rights and I demand to have that phone, right now."

She passed it to him, withdrawing it at the last minute. "You get one call, and then I'm putting it away until someone else tells me you can have it. One." She held up one forefinger to emphasize the point.

Tyler punched the divot in the plastic front and swept his fingers across it to unlock the screen. A message was waiting, like he'd seen before. It was a text from Kate's phone.

Hope you're well. I've moved on and changed my plans. Please don't try to contact me as I won't pick up your calls. I've met someone else. Kate.

Tyler's head hit the pillow with such force it nearly flipped the bed. He was going to throw his phone when he decided a well-placed "piss off" would do him a world of good. He'd wait and think of something really good to say. To have come this far, to have thought she was there waiting for him, that she felt the same way, only to find out he didn't mean to her what she'd meant to him, was beyond tragic. It was epic.

He read the message again. Same message. No other messages but the ones he'd read already, professing how much she missed him.

He hurled the phone and heard it hit the wall behind the ceiling-mounted TV with a splintering crash, sending bits of plastic parts all over the doorway and out into the hall.

Immediately the nurse popped her head in the room with an orderly at her side. "We have to restrain you, Special Operator Gray? You destroying U.S. Government property?"

"Fuck the U.S. Government." His big forearm was over his eyes so they wouldn't see his tears.

Tyler rejected the chaplain. He threw his lunch back at the sweet young volunteer who brought the green tray. But when Kyle and Cooper and the rest of the team showed up, he allowed them entrance.

"You've been behaving badly, Tyler. One would think you'd be more fuckin' grateful those Marines pulled you out."

"I'm grateful to be alive, Lannie. Don't push it."

"You're a pussy," Nick said.

"You watch it. I'm so hopped up on stuff I'd kick your sorry ass and strangle you with this shit," he rattled the tubing stuck into his arm and the wires attached to his chest. "In fact—"

Kyle and Cooper both jumped on Tyler, stopping him from pulling out all his tubes and electronic monitoring leads. He struggled a bit against them, but he was no match for both of them, with the state of his emaciation from the desert.

"We read your fuckin' message earlier, and no way did that come from Kate," Nick said. "We were going to tell you that now."

"Well, if I had it here, I'd show it to you. Said Kate right on the fuckin' screen."

"And I'm telling you no way. Devon had dinner with her three nights ago. She was on board, champing at the bit to jump into your life big time. Tyler, wise up, man. Even you don't work that fast." Nick looked at him as if he had sprouted a purple horn between his eyes.

"So how do you explain—"?

Cooper jumped in, "Someone else sent the message Tyler. Someone who wanted you to get it. Got any enemies out there near her?"

Tyler remembered Sheila. "This girl that worked with her. We knew her, man. Remember that blonde we couldn't get rid of?"

"That hot pants frog hog? Shit, she even jumped Fredo's bones."

"Well, that's because he thought she was a professional," Kyle added.

"She's probably the one who stole all the money from where Kate works, too. Devon told me all about it."

"Shit, guys. I gotta get out there," Tyler said and started again to unhook himself, which set things buzzing. If the Team had let him, he'd have walked right out with them.

"Let the police handle it."

"No, you don't understand, this lady's really bad news. I've got all my faculties now. We're wasting time. I gotta go. You know if they don't strap me down, I'll escape and go do it by myself somehow. Help me. Help me get outta here."

Within the hour Kyle had acquired a full release for Tyler by making nice with the pretty Navy doctor who'd been eyeing T.J. They pitched in for a night she'd never forget. Soon after, he was wheeled to the transport plane for a straight flight to San Francisco from D.C.

CHAPTER 42

Kate woke up to the late afternoon sun shedding a golden glow through the mature, leafy trees of the large home next door. The colors became more golden as it dropped farther and farther down to the horizon. It remained warm, but a breeze kicked in.

As the light turquoise sky turned darker, she saw a single light in the mansion next door, and figured her landlords had come back from Europe. But as it got increasingly dark, the single light remained, but more lights were not turned on, nor did she hear any movement. And the kitchen, where the couple spent most of their early evenings, remained dark.

She figured it must have been a motion sensor, and then wondered if perhaps a neighbor's cat had strayed into an opened window. She had a key to be used for emergencies, and the alarm code had been posted on her refrigerator. Since the sticky note was gone, she figured it had gotten old and dropped to the floor somewhere between the cabinets and refrigerator. But she remembered it anyway.

She decided to re-read Tyler's last letter before she went next door.

The hills are beautiful here, although it gets cold at night. Back in the mountainous regions there are upper valleys filled with green fields and wildflowers. Kind of reminds me of Germany, if you can believe that.

I think about walking with you there, although I'd never take you here. Normal life, or what we'd call normal life, ceased to exist years ago. These are a people who say they want their freedom, but have no concept yet of what that entails. I find them to be honorable and kind, but completely foreign. They are as afraid of us as we are of them.

The kids are our future here. If there is a future. It would be nice to be part of that someday. Right now it's further away than how distant your bedroom is to my bunker. God willing, we'll see each other long before they'll ever get to experience the freedoms we have. Can you imagine growing up where your elders, your parents, particularly your father, decided whom you could marry and when? Well, on the other hand, perhaps your father would be okay about that one. I'd like to think he'd let me take your hand.

So, when I get back, we have to talk. You have to tell me if you want this life. All I can offer you is a lot of sleepless nights when I'll be in harm's way. Is it something you can handle? When you need someone to talk to, namely me? When perhaps we've had an argument the day I ship out, like what happens sometimes here, and then we can't make up for six months? Is that fair to a woman to ask that of you?

So, you tell me now. Are you ready for this? Because you know me, once I start, I finish. I don't quit. I never quit. And I work fast. Why wait for tomorrow when we can have it all today? I know you agree with this.

I might have gotten the wrong impression, but somehow I don't think so. I think you are the most beautiful woman I've ever met. I know where your heart is. I want to stand by you, protect you. Being with you makes me a better man, in all respects.

I can only hope you share in my feelings. Is it foolish to think I can have this? We can have a life together? Is it something I'll regret, something that brought us close together and then no farther? Or is it something we can have while we grow old together? I'd share you with a family if that is your wish, but I'll take you all by yourself if you say that's what you want. I'll take you any way I can.

Tomorrow we go out into the field, so this may be the last post for a while. But I brought my little book and a pen, and I'll still write something every day, and post it to you when I can.

Don't worry. Keep me alive in your thoughts and prayers. But mostly, be strong. If for some reason I don't return, find someone else who shares my passion for the Teams. It would help you. That's how we do it here. And if it's too much, I understand. But if I'm not there to share your life, then you find someone else strong, another warrior to protect and love you the way I would.

Good night, Kate. Rest well. And I'll see you later in this life, or in the next. Either way, we'll say hello again, and it will be just as if the years and the distance never separated us.

Your love,

Tyler.

Her cheeks were drenched with tears. The top of her T-shirt was wet. Her sorrow was private, and quiet. So painful, this knowing she was separated from him. But if by some miracle he came back to her, she'd make sure she didn't waste a day, an hour, or a minute. However difficult it was to love someone so completely and have to be without them for long periods of time, if she had to, she would. She knew she could do it.

Be strong, Kate, he'd said to her in that first letter he wrote after they'd become lovers.

"I will, Tyler. I'll wait my whole lifetime if I have to. But, God," she began to sob again, "don't make me wait that long."

It was time to go next door and check on the light. At the last minute she decided to put her cell in her bra, since she didn't have a pocket and she didn't want to take a purse. If by some miracle Tyler was alive and did call, the vibration of the phone would press against her heart, just like he had.

Taking her fluorescent lantern, she walked along the stone path to the back door of the big house.

To her surprise, the back door was locked, but the alarm wasn't set. She turned on the pantry closet lights, and then the under counter lights in the massive granite-counter-topped kitchen. She'd been to many parties in the home, and a television film crew had made two documentaries of the get-togethers her landlords had lavishly created for special guest events. The laughter and clinking of glasses of expensive wine were a long distance away from tonight's venture into the kitchen. It was eerily quiet. Fear snaked up her spine.

"Alicia, Barry? Are you guys home?" she called out. The echo fell on warm brown pecan flooring, still drapes and unoccupied upholstered couches. "Hello. Is there anyone home?"

Again, not a sound.

Breezes outside whipped branches of the sycamore trees against the side of the house. Their leaves and branches slapped against the windowpanes in the dining room, and then were silent.

She moved to the base of the expansive carved stairway with the double-sided flared landing at the bottom. "Anyone here?" she called again.

Convinced she was alone, she remembered the light seemed to be coming from a room up on the second floor, emanating from a small window, like a bathroom or closet. Perhaps a window left open had attracted some animal, a bird perhaps. But nothing stirred as she climbed the stairwell. The wood was so tightly laid down there was barely a creak as she stepped, one by one, up to the first landing, then rounded the turn and proceeded up to the top, where the second floor bedroom hall stretched out on front of her.

The light would be on her left, she thought, so she turned. Flipping on the hall light, she held her lantern out anyway as she passed by several closed doors to the room she thought might contain the light. Indeed, under the crack in the door there was a faint line of light.

The bedroom door opened with a creak, which scared the bejabbers out of her. The room was cold, and a breeze came from the window over the bed, which was slightly ajar. She placed her lantern on the bed, reaching over to shut the window and saw movement on her left. The bathroom light behind illuminated a shadow of a figure. A shadow of a woman.

Kate held up the lantern and saw her face.

"Sheila?"

"Close enough, Kate."

"Or should I call you Joan?" She tried not to sound fearful, but her hands were shaking, her knees were knocking, and the lamp was wobbling so obviously, Sheila would have to be blind not to notice.

"Ah, you shouldn't believe everything you read in the papers, Kate."

"What are you doing here?"

"Right. As you know, I sort of needed a place to lay low for a while. You told me yourself they were in Europe. Thought I'd borrow the place so I could be alone, sort out my thoughts in private."

Something Tyler had told her stuck in her head. *Don't trust her, Kate. Be careful. People aren't always what they seem. Especially don't trust Sheila.*

He'd been right. Sheila had a composed expression plastered over a feral demeanor. Her eyes darted from side to side. Her hair was disheveled. And as she stepped forward into the center of the room towards the bed and the light, Kate saw she'd dyed it black.

Sheila noticed her taking stock of her new hair color. "I don't owe you an explanation, but perhaps this will be easier if I give you one anyway. First, let me assuage your concerns that Tyler will be coming to rescue you. You may not know it, but you've broken up with him. You've found someone else."

"What?"

"Turns out you make decisions quickly. As soon as you fall for someone, you fall out of love with them just as fast. Tyler has been told this. Trust me, he won't be coming back."

"What have you done?"

"It works out rather nicely, really, you coming here." Sheila held up a handgun. "I'm not wanting to hurt you. Murder is not my thing. I need some time to get away. You shouldn't have come snooping over, but now that you have, if you cooperate, I won't hurt you. I just need time to get away."

"You ruined the Hellers."

"You know they have insurance that covers it? Embezzlement is an easy claim to file for. I'll have to watch over my shoulder for a few months, looking for insurance investigators, but after a few, I'll be free to roam, as they say. This isn't my first party, Kate."

"So you lived in San Diego. You knew Tyler there."

"Oh, I knew Tyler, all right. He was one of my favorites. Boy I latched myself on to him and didn't want to let go. We had ourselves one hell of a night. The best ever. I doubt you've opened him up the way I did. I know what he's made of. He's all devil and hellfire, not the sweet romantic you think. He's got some demons, and I'm one who can handle demons. I actually prefer them."

Kate was nervous again.

"I didn't want to leave him, but in the end, I needed to move on. What a surprise to see him. What a complete surprise and a complete delight. Of course, it sped up my plans, as well as gave me some great ideas. You'll see. If you cooperate, that is."

"So what's the plan, then? You said no one would be coming to rescue me."

Then she felt the vibration of her phone tucked inside her bra. In some twisted bit of fate, she had apparently flipped the switch to vibrate from ringer when she'd stashed it. Sheila didn't seem to notice.

When it buzzed a second time Kate turned, speaking loud enough to block any noise from the cell's vibration.

"I'm not sure you'll get away with this. But if it's time you need, I can give you that."

"I know that." She waved the gun at Kate. "You don't have a choice."

Kate held up her hands, palms out. "Sheila I don't want to give you any trouble. I'll cooperate."

She remembered Tyler telling her stalling was the smartest tactic. Stall until someone else did something that would distract the person. Look around for a way to improvise. And she did, but there wasn't anything useful within reach except the lantern.

"Come. We're going to the wine cellar." She gestured for Kate to walk in front of her.

Kate wanted to read her cell message so bad, but she dared not. Once they reached the ground level near the dining room, a small arched door led down a narrow stairway to the cellar. Kate was impressed Sheila had found it.

"They have quite an impressive collection, Kate. They have some wines that are nearly two hundred years old that could be very drinkable."

Kate wasn't interested in the banter. On one of the turns, she took the chance and reached for her cell. The screen lit with a message from Tyler.

Coming for you, baby. Tyler.

It wasn't from Tyler's phone but someone else's with a local Sonoma County area code. Then there was a message below it.

Tyler. Just landed in SFO. On our way up there. Be smart. Be careful.

Kate quickly slipped the phone back in her bra. Sheila had been talking about the wines she'd tried. "Really remarkable collection. I was looking forward to another week or two of sampling. Had I known they had so much here they would never miss, I'd have been over helping myself sooner."

Kate was at the bottom and turned to face her captor.

"Okay, this is where we hit the end of the road. Part ways, Kate. I want to thank you for all you've tried to do, and in exchange, perhaps you can understand my side of things. This was never personal. Someday I'll settle down, fall in love and become legitimate. I want you to know Randy is really a very bad fuck. He's not the type I could stay with my whole life. Tyler, on the other hand, now he's a winner."

Kate waited. "So what's the plan, Sheila? You don't want Randy. You can't have Tyler—or he doesn't want you is more accurate, I guess."

"Careful, careful, Kate. I'm a little peeved about that one."

Kate took a deep breath. She was drawing strength from the fact that perhaps, just perhaps, in less than an hour Tyler would be here. And he was apparently very much alive. Alive and healthy enough to come to her rescue. If she could just stall a bit more. Drag their conversation out a little longer, engage Sheila more, perhaps there was a chance they could stop Sheila from taking off, from perhaps causing Kate harm.

"So were you after the money, all along, Sheila?"

"Better to marry a rich man than a poor man, Kate. Didn't your mama ever tell you?"

"But you've embezzled. Surely you didn't think Randy would stand by and let that happen?"

"Ah. I see what you're asking. No, it was always about the money. So, when he fell for you, I was left with only one option, and I took it. You're the reason I took the money. Your fault, really."

The phone in Kate's chest began to vibrate again. How Kate wished she could be allowed to read it.

"So, we're going to play a little game, Kate. Remember olly, olly, oxen free from when you played hide and seek as a kid?"

"Of course."

"You give me time to get away?"

"Yes, I'll do that."

"I'm going to guarantee you do. Give me your wrists."

Kate tried to see what Sheila had in her hands. It was a clear plastic zip tie.

"Come on, put your palms together and hug this." She walked to an old clay pipe about four inches across. As Kate placed her palms together, Sheila tucked the gun under her arm briefly until she got the zip tie around Kate's wrists and cinched it, cutting into Kate's flesh.

With her back up to the massive wine rack and her arms secured around the pipe, Kate had nowhere to go and no possibility of getting away.

"My more devious self says I should get rid of you for good, because somehow I don't think you want any part of my life or my wicked schemes. Just stay away, okay? I call olly, olly, oxen free. Count to one hundred, and I'll be gone. Gone from your life forever," she whispered in Kate's ear.

The buzzing started again and this time Sheila heard it and viciously dug the phone out of her bra.

"Oh, my God, Kate. Gotta go." She tossed the cell phone against the wall and ran up the cellar stairs. At the top of the stairs Kate heard the click of the massive lock.

Sheila's footsteps echoed throughout the cellar. Kate was halfway relieved to finally be alone until she began to smell smoke. Then she realized. Sheila had set fire to the house.

She'd remembered a conversation she'd had with Tyler about improvising. What was it he said? He could get out of any restraints. They'd practiced it. He'd even said something about zip ties. There was a way to get out of them. There were always ways to get out.

She moved her palms up and down the pipe, feeling for something that protruded to use as a temporary saw. A plastic pipe had been affixed to the ceramic one, and tied with a metal band with a nut and screw holding the band in place. The edge of the screw was sharp. Kate rubbed the zip tie back and forth over the screw edge to see if it would cut into the plastic, and while it didn't break the tie, rubbed off some of the ribbing that held the tie in place, and after several attempts, the tie fell loose and she was able to get free.

Running up the stairs she worked the door handle, which had become warm from the fire that probably was raging on the other side. Smoke began to fill the cellar. She knew she didn't have much time.

Glancing up toward the ceiling, she saw the fire humidity and heat sensor. Her landlords would have the information going to their cells or laptops, wherever they were. Perhaps they would alert authorities. It was easily eight to ten feet in the air and could not be reached from the floor.

She gathered up two wine liters. Aiming for the sensor, she threw them at the ceiling. The first one missed by a foot. The second one hit the sensor but appeared not to damage it.

She needed a more substantial bottle. She scanned the racks and saw some dusty champagne bottles. She lifted two and found them so heavy she wasn't sure she could heave them far enough. Climbing back up on the table, she hoisted them at the wall, but the glass fell easily two feet short. Delicious bubbly sprayed all over the bottles below.

Her arm was getting tired. She heard a car leave the driveway, and realized Sheila had probably commandeered her SUV.

Kate decided to try one last time. Without climbing up on the rickety table, she underhanded a vintage bottle of champagne straight at the sensor, and this time the case cracked and she went weak with relief when she heard the a bell start ringing.

Now all she had to do was wait, and pray someone would come before she was overcome by smoke or fire. Would they find her here in the cellar?

She heard other vehicles outside, and began to scream. "Help! Please help me. I'm in the cellar!"

Finding a metal wrench, she began banging on the clay pipe, yelling at the top of her lungs. She heard footsteps and coughing. Someone tried the door.

"Yes! Yes! I'm in here. Please help me!" she yelled.

She ran up the stairs, banging on the oak door and fell forward and onto the floor as the door was suddenly opened and a cloud of smoke engulfed her. A shirt was placed over her head and powerful arms led her outside to the yard. He stumbled, unsteady on his feet and she fell with him onto the lush green lawn.

Under the stars of the night sky, coughing her lungs out, she saw Tyler's bare chest and realized the shirt she wore on her head had all the wonderful smells she'd missed. A pair of crutches lay sprawled to the side. She noted his upper leg was in a dark brace, held with white inch-wide straps. She fell into his arms as he lay back against the cool green grass. He held her close, while she sobbed for the sheer joy of feeling her chest press against his, while he powerfully took command of her world.

She felt protected and safe for the first time since he'd left five days ago. It didn't matter what else happened, she was safe.

CHAPTER 43

Tyler was sure he'd damaged his leg, but didn't care. The pain in his upper thigh wasn't anything like the joy he felt at having found her. Nick and Devon had been right. There was no way this woman was ever going to let him go, and he was not going to let her go until he had to.

The fire turned out to be only superficial and was put out quickly. Investigators questioned them.

"Anything else you want to tell us, like where this Sheila or Joan or whatever her name is, where she's headed?"

Kate laughed. Tyler was getting looked over by the paramedic who was poking and prodding him, and causing him a bit of pain. "I know she's headed to greener pastures. Somewhere where she'll be surrounded by stupid rich guys."

The investigator shared her chuckle. "Unfortunately, that could be just about anywhere."

"It could, except for one thing."

"And what's that Miss Morgan?"

"I can tell you how to find exactly where she is, and where she goes after that."

Tyler turned his head. "What? How?"

Kate shook her head. "At the time, I thought it was a stupid idea. The guy who sold me the car she took said I'd be glad I bought it someday, and you know, he was right. For once the salesman was right."

"About what?" Tyler asked.

"No. It couldn't be that easy!" the investigator exclaimed.

The flashing red lights and white spotlights played circus acts across Tyler's face. "Someone tell me what's happening?"

"She bought one of those car locator things," the investigator said. "I'll be God damned. Wish I didn't have to share this with the FBI, but they'll want to pick her up. Hate it when I make it that easy for them, after all the bullshit they give us."

Kate didn't care. "The best thousand bucks I ever spent."

Within seconds, cooperation between the insurance company and the police yielded the car, with a very surprised Sheila talking on her cell phone to one of her girlfriends.

Kate was relieved this chapter with Sheila was over. This would give them important time to work out the details of their new lives together.

Two weeks later, Gretchen flew down for their engagement party. Tyler's parents came down as well. Kate's nieces were all over Tyler, who still had to be careful about his leg, though he was off crutches. They'd all gone on long walks in the wine country, since Tyler had some time off and the girls loved having him around as a father figure. Kate's mom and Tyler's mom got acquainted and enjoyed each other's company. Linda Gray talked about the spicy love affairs she was cooking up in her books, avidly listening to Tyler talk about his SEAL buddies, which were fodder for her stories.

The two of them worked a little over at Nick and Devon's winery. Tyler told her about the nursery sale and Sophie, Nick's sister, who had always had the dream of living in paradise. Just seemed right to be working on the legacy she had started, with her new friends. Part of Kate understood what Sophie saw in the little valley floor, surrounded by vineyards. Maybe, with her knowledge of the wine business, she could add some of her own magic to the mix.

After the engagement dinner, held by candlelight in the modest living room of her parents' home, Kate's mother asked for the floor. All the guests, including Tyler's parents and Linda, had left, and the girls were put to bed. Gretchen was staying over, so only Tyler, Kate, Gretchen and Kate's parents were left.

In a very solemn mood, Mrs. Moore brought out a cardboard shoebox and placed it on her knees. She looked at her husband, who pulled his chair up alongside her, placing his arm around her shoulder. He kissed her on the cheek, then removed his arm and waited for her to speak.

"I'm afraid I have a confession to make to all of you," Kate's mom began. "Something that's been brewing for over thirty-four years."

Gretchen and Kate shared a look. Kate didn't have a clue what her mother might say next.

"Tyler, when Kate told me her story, about meeting you on the plane, it affected me so deeply. And Joe and I have talked about it, and we need to tell you our story. And this affects you, Gretchen, as well."

"Me?"

"I met a young Marine who was coming home at Christmas to visit his parents before his final deployment over in the Middle East. We met and talked. Talked about a lot of things. I had a boyfriend at the time, but I was afraid to tell him. This handsome," she looked at her husband, "young man in uniform was really the first fighting man I'd ever met. I was immediately struck with his sense of honor. His duty to country."

Kate's mom cried quiet tears. Her husband took her hand. "You're doing great Louise. We're all here."

"We wrote to each other after we parted. I have to say that we fell in love over those letters." She placed her palm on the box. "These letters."

Gretchen was watching her parents, first studying her mother and then her dad. Her spine had straightened.

"We agreed to meet, and he flew out one weekend, and we stayed together in San Francisco. It was a very painful parting. I don't have to tell you how difficult it was for me. But he wrote to me every day."

Kate's mother looked down at the box.

"The letter I wrote telling him I was pregnant never reached him. It was returned with several other things he'd asked to have sent to me in the event of his death."

Kate looked up at her sister and saw Gretchen crying softly as realized the young Marine had probably been her father.

"I loved him, Gretchen. He'd never been raised in a family, didn't even know where they were, or it might have been different. When I met your father some weeks later, and we began to date, he came to love the baby growing inside me, Gretchen. You were that baby. And we decided that the best way to honor that young Marine was to give you the family he never had. These are his letters, all of them. I want you to have them, honey. They belong to you."

CHAPTER 44

It was touching to watch Gretchen go upstairs, after hugging her parents close, wiping the tears from her mother's face, kissing her cheeks, and then taking the private box of loving words up to her room. Tyler loved these people as much as he loved his own family.

He was filled with gratitude toward the young Marine who had come into Kate's mom's life, into her heart, and departed this world, making the ultimate sacrifice and leaving behind some little piece of magic, the magic that was Gretchen.

He knew this was something that could happen to him and Kate. And he realized right then that Kate's mom had made the right choice. She went on with her life. She created as perfect a world as she could, gave her baby a father, a good man, who would always love Gretchen as his own child.

It was part of what made his relationship so special with Kate. They had fragile hours, fragile times that could be brought to an abrupt end so easily. And he wanted to do his job. He wanted to be the guy everyone depended on. And yes, even with the potential of sacrifice, he still wanted to do it.

Kate had been pensive. "I think it affects me as much as I know it affects Gretchen," Kate said to him while she sat by the open window of the Inn where they were staying. The night breeze had brushed clean her beautiful face, ruffling her hair, making it dance while she sat and watched the lights flickering on the trees outside. The downtown area was always brightly lit, like Christmas, she'd told him. One year they decided to leave all those decorations up year-round.

They had put a deposit down on a house not too far from Nick and Devon's winery. Kate wanted to work with Nick on the winery project, along with Cooper's father-in-law and several others of the SEAL Team 3 investors who were part owners. The little cottage was barely larger than the one Kate used to live in when they'd first met. But anything with Kate was just right. The size of his life was just right. The size of his job was just right. The size of his love would be growing forever.

"My time," he said as he drew her up to her feet. "Remember?" he said as he showed her two fingers and then pointed them at his own eyes. "Eyes focused on me."

"Yes, Tyler. My eyes always will be focused on you."

He rubbed his thumb across her lower lip and then pressed his against her mouth. "We are the lucky ones, Kate. We have today. So many people don't even find a today like this."

She hugged him. He could feel dampness on his arm. He stroked the back of her head, fingers lazily kneading through her hair.

"No more tears, okay?" he said as he pulled back and lifted her chin. "Love me like that first time in Portland. That first night, when we found ourselves under the umbrella in the rain. Remember that night?"

"I do." She smiled and showed him with her hands.

"I can see you do. We'll have lots of nights like these. Our stories will go on for decades. Old and toothless. I told the guys that once. They thought I was nuts."

Tyler would remember the beautiful sex that night. He wasn't going to tell her he'd always remember her face in the moonlight as she cried out for him, as her thighs hugged his hips and he felt her shudder beneath him. How it would be the last thing he would think about if his time ever came. How she made him feel. How she brought joy, and that ache of hoping to God he didn't have to ever live without her.

All her soft places were stronger and harder than his. All her sighs held worlds of possibility. He wanted to experience every crevice of her body, every thought of her mind. Everything from the way she folded her clothes to the way she dug in the garden. He'd read books to her. He'd rub her feet and change diapers if that were granted. He'd rub her back when she was tired and he'd tell her she was the most beautiful woman in the world when she was past her prime. He never wanted her to feel anything but loved.

She was what he'd always wanted. She was, after all, his heart, and always would be.

The End

OTHER BOOKS IN THE SEAL BROTHERHOOD SERIES:

BOOK 1

PREQUEL TO BOOK 1

BOOK 2

BOOK 3

PURCHASE ON

amazon.COM

AVAILABLE ON AUDIBLE

BOOK 4

CRUISIN' FOR A SEAL

SHARON HAMILTON

NEW YORK TIMES BESTSELLING AUTHOR

AVAILABLE ON AUDIBLE

BOOK 5

AVAILABLE ON AUDIBLE

BOOK 6

AVAILABLE JULY 2014

Connect with Author Sharon Hamilton!

sharonhamiltonauthor.blogspot.com

www sharonhamiltonauthor.com

facebook.com/AuthorSharonHamilton

@sharonlhamilton

http://sharonhamiltonauthor.com/contact.html#newsletter

ANTHOLOGIES:

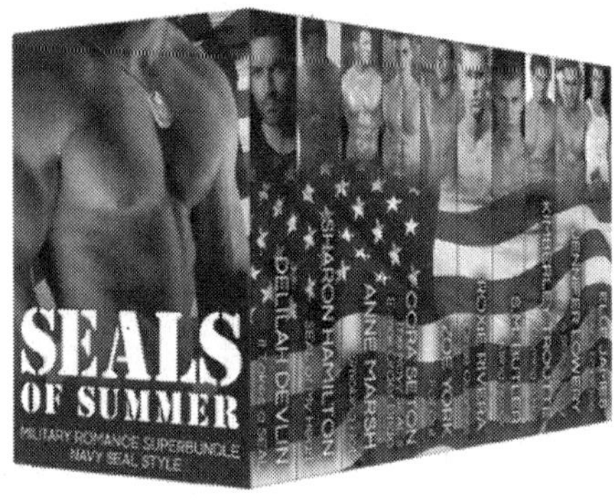

SEALs of Summer

SEALed With A Kiss

PURCHASE ON

amazon.com

OTHER BOOKS BY SHARON HAMILTON:

The Guardians Series

(Guardian Angels, Dark Angels)

BOOK 1

BOOK 2

The Golden Vampires of Tuscany Series:

BOOK 2

BOOK 1

Made in the USA
San Bernardino, CA
13 May 2015